PRAISE FOR HILARY DARTT

"Author Hilary Dartt's debut novel – The Dating Intervention – contains every essential element that a fantastic, page-turner type book should contain: a deep sense of character, a near-tangible sense of place, and a captivating plot that moves quickly and fluidly throughout."

RACHELLE SPARKS

"I didn't want it to end! Hilary Dartt is a real talent!"

AMAZON REVIEWER

"Dartt's writing style is distinct, witty, fun, and heart-felt. She creates characters that feel like real people … Love it!"

BLOGGING & WRITING BLOG

ALSO BY HILARY DARTT

The Seedling Homestead Series

The Composition of Order

The Architecture of Vision

The Intervention Series

The Dating Intervention

The Marriage Intervention

The Motherhood Intervention

The Garden Club Series

Jasmine's Pact

Studying Sequoia

Just Holly

THE STRUCTURE OF PERFECTION

HILARY DARTT

ISBN: 978-1-950335-08-4

PROLOGUE

DURING HANNAH BRADLEY'S CHILDHOOD, magic was the status quo. Growing up on Seedling Homestead was perfect. It was like living in some kind of Heaven. Before her sisters, Sarah and Margaret came, it was just Mama and Hannah. They did everything together: they walked the fence line checking for breaks, they mopped the floors while singing old show tunes, and they strolled along the creek listening for the sounds of bullfrogs and birds, identifying the meadowlarks and tree swallows by their calls.

The light always seemed to sparkle. And even when it wasn't sunny, the world was filled with a kind of wonder: rain drops making tiny ripples on the creek's surface, the snow creating a soft silence while Hannah and Mama snuggled under a blanket in front of the fire.

Of course, being a child, she took this idyllic life for granted.

Then one day, when Hannah was just learning to read, she sounded out the words on the sign that hung between the pillars on either side of the driveway:

"Seed … ling. Seedling. Home… What's that say, Mama?"

"It says homestead. Seedling Homestead."

"What's that mean?" Hannah wanted to know.

Mama took a deep breath, and she didn't answer right away. When she finally started to speak, Hannah noticed she seemed to be choosing her words carefully, as she often did when she tried to explain a big idea.

"Well, do you know what a seedling is?"

Of course Hannah did. She'd been planting seeds and transplanting seedlings for as long as she could remember. She nodded. "It's a baby plant."

"Right," Mama said. "And a homestead is a place where you make a home."

"Okay," Hannah said, drawing the word out.

"When I moved here," Mama said, "I was sad. I was looking for a place to make a home. I felt like a baby plant. Like I was starting over. Do you remember what a plant needs to grow?"

Hannah thought for a minute. "Sunlight?"

"Yes," Mama Katherine said. "And there's plenty of that here in Wyoming. What else?"

"Water?"

"Yes, and what else?"

"Soil."

"Right," Mama said. "Sunlight, water, and soil. I imagined myself as a tiny tree, and I found all of those things I needed here, at Seedling Homestead."

"But you were already a grown-up."

"I was," Mama said. "But I needed to start over."

"Why?"

"Well, that's a conversation for a different day."

"Why were you sad?"

"That's a conversation for a different day, too."

Hannah shrugged. She was used to Mama saving stories for a different day.

Some time later, when Hannah was about seven, she was playing near the creek, throwing sticks in the water and watching them float along. Mama came up and sat down on the creek bank.

"Hannah," she said, "How do you like our life here?"

A big feeling—something like happiness, only bigger—swelled up inside Hannah's body. It that made her want to squeal and run up and down along the water's edge. That's what she did, while shouting, "I love it!"

"Do you think another little girl would love it as much as you do?"

Hannah was so stunned by this question that she stopped running and sat right down on the wet ground at her mother's feet. She was perceptive. She knew this question was an important one. She knew it meant that maybe there was an actual little girl somewhere, one who would be part of this life, too. Also, she could tell Mama wanted her to say that yes, another little girl would love it here at Seedling Homestead.

So she nodded, and she could feel that her nod was a little slower than usual. She wondered if Mama noticed.

"I need to talk to you about something."

Hannah nodded again. Slowly. Then she stood up.

"Remember a while ago, when you asked me what Seedling Homestead means? And I told you that it was a place for new beginnings."

"Uh huh," Hannah said.

She'd picked up a stick—one she knew would float quickly along in the creek, bobbing only a little—and now she scraped shapes into the mud with it: a stick-figure girl and a dog.

"Well, I've come to know of some little girls—little girls like you—who could use some new beginnings."

"They're like baby trees?"

"Yes," Mama said, and Hannah could tell this pleased her. "They're like baby trees. What would you think about having a couple of girls come to live here? We could plant them and give them water and sunlight and we could help them grow. You and me, together."

"But ... they're humans, though, right?" Hannah said. "We won't really plant them."

"It's a metaphor," Mama said.

Hannah tested the word out and found that it felt funny in her mouth.

"Anyway. We would give these girls a home. We would feed them and love them and help them grow up. They would be your sisters."

"Where are their mothers?"

"Ah," Mama said.

Hannah hoped she wouldn't say this was a conversation for another day, and she didn't.

"For whatever reason," Mama said, "their mothers can't take care of them. So they need new families."

"But why?"

Hannah found this concept scary. If other girls' mothers couldn't take care of them, did that mean it was possible that there might come a day when Mama couldn't take care of her?

"Let's sit," Mama said, and she sat right down on the bank of the creek, as wet as it was. Hannah joined her, and Mama wrapped an arm around her shoulder and gave it a squeeze.

"I can see your wheels turning," she said, "and you don't have to worry about a thing. I will always be here to take care of you. But what do you say? Do you think we could take care of a couple of girls?"

Leaning up against the side of her mother's body, tucked in like this, Hannah thought they could do anything. "Yes," she said. "I think so."

Mama nodded. "Good. I have a feeling you're going to love having sisters."

"When are they coming?" Hannah said, and Mama chuckled a little. "I'm not sure. We just have to wait for the right ones."

This made sense. Hannah had seen cartoons where a stork delivered a blanket-wrapped baby to someone's doorstep and things always seemed to work out.

"Mama?"

"Yes, love?"

"Did you always know I would have sisters?"

Something changed in the way Mama was sitting. She didn't move, but Hannah could feel a shift.

She simply said, "No, I didn't."

"Did you always know there were little girls who needed nurturing, like a baby tree?"

Mama made a little sound, like a gasp, and Hannah wondered if she'd said something wrong.

"I knew," she said. "But I didn't think about being the one to do the nurturing until recently."

"What made you think about it?"

Standing up, Mama grunted a little, and smoothed her long skirt before answering. "I'm not even sure. I just got to thinking about ways I could help out, you know? And I thought it'd do you good to have somebody to run around this place with. Besides me."

"Oh," Hannah said. "When you named this place Seedling Homestead, why did you need a place to grow?"

She still asked the question every now and then, when she sensed Mama was in a talking mood. But she always got the same answer:

"That's a conversation for another day," Mama said.

Sarah, the first new seedling, arrived a couple of months later. Mama had warned Hannah that when her new sisters came to live with them, there wouldn't be much advance notice. Sure enough, one morning at breakfast the phone rang. Mama jumped. People rarely called them, especially not at this hour, when the sun was just peeking over the horizon and the sky was still a light gray.

Mama did a lot of listening and nodding and humming while the caller did a lot of talking. By the way Mama dried her hands, again and again, on the dish towel that hung from her apron, Hannah knew this was a serious call. And when she hung up, Mama confirmed it: "Well, Hannah, this is it. A social worker is bringing us a little girl. Sarah."

Hannah had about a million questions: she wanted to know how old Sarah was, where her parents were, why she was coming here, whether she'd stay forever or just for a short time. She wanted to know what Sarah liked to eat, what she liked to play, and whether she would be talkative or playful or serious.

"Don't pester her with all those questions as soon as she walks in the door," Mama scolded. "Give her time. You'll find out the answers soon enough."

It seemed like days later when the strange, boxy-looking car rolled into the driveway, its tires crunching on the gravel. Mama went out to greet Sarah and the social worker, and Hannah, suddenly shy, stayed inside and watched through the window next to the front door.

The social worker was as strange and boxy-looking as the car was. She wore a weird coat, long, like Hannah imagined a spy would wear, and her hands were wide enough to use as paddles for a boat. She was probably an excellent swimmer, Hannah thought, before the social worker used one of those flat hands to open the back door of the car.

When Sarah first climbed out of the back seat, clutching a plastic bag, Hannah was surprised. She'd been expecting a little girl like her, one with the slightly chubby, sunburned cheeks of a child who played outside, with bright eyes and a smile at the ready … one who was as excited to be here as Hannah was to have her.

But Sarah looked terrified. And, Hannah thought, sickly.

Her eyes were much too round, and they had dark smudges underneath. Her skin had obviously never seen the sun. It was pale and dingy. And boy, was she skinny! Her teeth and knuckles and elbows stood out, and her knees were so knobby Hannah thought she might need braces on them, like the little boy at the library. Even in a ponytail, her blond hair looked greasy. One stringy piece had come loose and was hanging in front of Sarah's ear.

The social worker laid a hand on Sarah's head and said something. Sarah nodded, and then Mama offered her a hand. Together, the two of them walked toward the house. Hannah thought the social worker looked like she might cry as she watched them. Then she got into the car and backed down the driveway.

The front door opened, and when Sarah saw Hannah, she scooted even closer to Mama, hiding. Hannah offered what she hoped was a welcoming smile, but Sarah didn't return it. Mama had told Hannah about the possibility that her new sisters would take some time to warm up, and Hannah was determined to make that time as short as possible.

"Want me to show you your room?" Hannah said.

Sarah nodded, and Hannah held out a hand, just as she'd seen Mama do. Sarah took it. As they walked toward the back of the house, Hannah pressed her lips together to keep from pestering Sarah with all those questions.

"Your bedroom's right next to mine," she said, pushing the door open.

After some conversation, Mama and Hannah had decided to leave the room almost plain so that whoever joined their family would be able to make it her own. Now, standing here with Sarah, looking at the plain white walls, the light blue bedspread, and the white curtains, Hannah thought that might have been a mistake.

"We left it plain so you could decorate it," she hurried to say. "You can do whatever you want. Mama said you can paint the walls black if you want."

This was enough to produce a tiny giggle from Sarah.

"Go on," Hannah said. "Bring your stuff in."

Sarah walked slowly into the room, looking around as if it were a cavernous castle or something. She walked over to the bookcase and set down her bag. She began pulling things out—a few paperbacks, some clothes, and a little box decorated with sea shells. Hannah had never seen sea shells in real life, but she recognized them from books.

"Go ahead," she said. "Put your stuff on the shelf. You can put your clothes in the dresser."

Sarah nodded. Then she proceeded to line everything up neatly, even organizing the few items of clothing by color.

"You're very organized," Hannah said, Mama having told her that giving people compliments was a great way to start a conversation.

Sarah nodded again, and Hannah wondered if she knew how to speak.

"Are you hungry?"

A nod.

"Do you eat pancakes?"

A shrug.

"Have you ever had pancakes?"

Sarah shook her head.

"What do you eat for breakfast, then?"

Another shrug.

"Come on. I'll make you some pancakes."

Maybe Sarah had never had pancakes, but she sure knew how to eat them. She devoured eight—two with syrup, three with powdered sugar, and three with peanut butter and syrup. Then she went back into her bedroom, laid down on the bed, and slept for three hours.

Meanwhile, Hannah told Mama how strangely Sarah had set up her bedroom.

"From what I understand, Hannah, Sarah comes from a very chaotic household where things are confusing, and she doesn't know what to expect. When people come from chaos, they often seek order … they can be very … well, *organized* is one way to put it."

That made sense, Hannah thought. She hoped Sarah would loosen up a bit, though, and she said as much.

"Just give her time," Mama said.

After a few months at Seedling Homestead, Sarah *had* loosened up— a lot. She still organized her things (shirts by color, books alphabetically by title, toys by shape). But she was no longer silent and drawn. She laughed, a lot, and she loved to run through the fields, chasing Hannah or being chased, hollering happily as the sun turned her cheeks a rosy color. One day at lunch, when the newly-loosened-up Sarah had finished her own applesauce and was trying to sneak Hannah's, Mama got another phone call.

This one seemed different: Mama's initial hums were followed by silence, and then she looked so, so sad. When she hung up, Hannah asked what was the matter, and Mama just shook her head.

A different social worker, a tall, slender, pretty one in a maroon old-lady car, brought Margaret to the house. Margaret, with her wild, curly black hair and bright green eyes, seemed different than Sarah had when she first arrived. She was subdued, but she moved with surprising confidence, eyes alert and cat-like. Still, Hannah didn't miss the look of fear on Margaret's face when she accidentally picked a green tomato after Mama told her to pick a red one.

Mama wasn't mad, though; she offered to cook it up, and even while Margaret devoured it, she sat on the edge of her chair, like she was ready to run at any second. Hannah made Margaret a peanut butter and jelly, and Margaret accepted it like she'd never been offered a homemade meal before. She scarfed it down, at the same rate as she'd eaten the green tomato, and Hannah wondered if she'd ever been offered *any* meal before.

Margaret adapted much more quickly than Sarah had. Within a couple of hours, she was exploring the property, getting wet and muddy at the creek and swinging from the tree branches like she didn't have a fear in the world. Later on, Mama told Hannah that Margaret was used to fending for herself, and that she was *adaptable*.

This was a word Hannah didn't quite understand, and it wasn't until the girls were teenagers that she could really apply it to Margaret's situation. But in those early days, Hannah marveled at how easily Margaret seemed to fit in, how quickly she made friends, and how eager she was to immerse herself in the chores and goings on at Seedling Homestead.

Just like that, they were four.

The Bradley girls became fast friends, playing and fighting like real sisters. Although each of them had her own room, they'd wind up in a single bed every night, limbs flung over one another, heads on the same pillow.

Sometimes, when Hannah described a dream she'd had, Sarah and Margaret claimed they'd had it, too. They'd elaborate on her stories, add in details. Hannah didn't recognize them at all, but the longer she let her sisters believe they were cosmically connected, the more she started to believe it, herself.

Sometimes Hannah would wake in the middle of the night to hear Margaret moaning, clutching the sheet so hard Hannah couldn't pry it out of her grip. Sarah would twist this way and that, turning her head from side to side as if she was trying to get away from something—or someone. Hannah would stay awake, rubbing her sisters' backs until they settled back down. They both claimed they didn't remember their nightmares, but Hannah couldn't forget. The sounds they made haunted her daytime hours.

One day, Mama kicked the girls out of the house to get some fresh air and their wiggles out.

"Go on down to the creek and catch some crawdads," she said. "Fill this bucket and we'll boil 'em up for dinner."

Hannah got the bucket, Sarah pulled out some hot dogs for bait, and Margaret hopped and skipped between them, chattering away about how yummy the crawdads would be. They walked on down to the creek, and together, made what Hannah thought was a terrible trap: the hot dogs wouldn't stay put, the bucket kept tilting, and Margaret repeatedly insisted on pulling it up every few minutes to check and see whether any crawdads had found their way in.

Being the oldest and the wisest, Hannah suspected Mama had known this would happen. She had likely counted on this project taking the girls hours. She had washing to do, and she wanted to mop the floor. Having the girls underfoot would make everything take longer, and she hated footprints on her clean linoleum. So she humored Margaret, pulling up the bucket every thirty seconds, adding more hot dog chunks each time.

Amazingly, by the time an hour passed, they'd collected dozens of crawdads, which moved around the bottom of the bucket in slow motion, opening and closing their shiny claws. Mama seemed a little shocked when they lugged the bucket back, water slopping over the sides, crawdads clambering to escape. But, true to her word, she filled a pot with clean water and set it on the stove. When she put the bucket next to it, though, Margaret's face twisted into a horrified expression.

"You mean, we're going to throw them into a pot of water and boil them? While they're still *alive*?"

The timbre of her voice made the hair rise on Hannah's arms, and chills run up the back of her neck, over her scalp.

"That's how you cook 'em," Mama said. Hannah thought she seemed oblivious to the horror Margaret was experiencing. "That's why it's called a crawdad boil. Throw in some potatoes, corn on the cob, sausage. We'll throw it all on the table and eat it with our hands. Dip the bites in melted butter."

"No!" Margaret was crying now, tears streaming down her face. "You can't boil them! I won't let you!"

She started to pull the bucket off the counter, but she was too little to hold it. The water—and the crawdads—spilled all over the clean kitchen floor in a rush. Margaret started making a strange keening sound, almost howling, and Hannah felt compelled to try to gather up the crawdads, which were slippery and had huge, dangerous claws.

The girls scrambled around the kitchen, collecting crawdads and throwing them back into the bucket as fast as they could.

"Don't let them die," Margaret wailed, on repeat.

Hannah felt simultaneously sad for Margaret and annoyed with her for causing such a ruckus. Still, she was dutiful in saving as many of the little creatures as she could.

Then, in an ironic turn of events, one of the crawdads Margaret was trying to save latched onto her thumb. She froze in the middle of the kitchen, staring at it in horror, before shaking her hand to dislodge it.

When Hannah saw Margaret's thumb turning purple, she ran to her.

"Hold still," she said, her voice more irritable than she meant for it to be. "Stop shaking it."

Margaret obeyed, her mouth still open, nothing more than a tiny hiss of air leaking out as Hannah pried the crawdad off her skin and dropped it on the floor before it could pinch her, too. It scuttled away. In the near-silence, Sarah and Mama continued tossing crawdads into the bucket, each one making a *plunk!* sound in the remaining water.

"Where do you think chicken comes from?" Hannah said then.

From across the kitchen, Mama gave her a look, eyebrows down, and a tiny shake of her head.

"What do you mean?" Margaret said.

"Never mind," Hannah said.

"Tell me!"

As if on cue, a chicken squawked in the yard.

"Let's just get these crawdads picked up, Margaret," Mama said, giving Hannah another dark look.

"Yeah, let's," Hannah said.

Margaret carried the bucket back down to the creek, the water sloshing out with every step. She came back sniffling, vowing never to fish for crawdads, ever again. Ever.

And that night, when she crawled into Hannah's bed just after they heard Mama go to bed, herself, she whispered, "What were you gonna say about chicken?"

"Just forget it," Hannah said. "Go to sleep."

"What was it?"

Sarah came in next, sliding in on Hannah's other side. "She was gonna say the chicken we eat comes from chickens who were alive once. Just like the crawdads."

Hannah elbowed Sarah, and Sarah said, "What? She's gonna find out eventually. We can't have her going to school thinking chicken comes from the chicken factory, wrapped in plastic."

When Hannah didn't argue, Sarah went on: "They were alive, just like the chickens in our yard. And they grow up on chicken farms. And then the farmers kill them and somebody plucks their feathers, cuts them up, puts them in packages, and sends them off to the grocery store."

Silence.

Actually, it wasn't silent. Hannah could hear the crickets chirping and the bullfrogs singing outside. She could hear Margaret holding her breath, tiny grunting sounds escaping from her throat.

"Is it true?" she said, finally.

Hannah nodded. She knew Margaret could hear her head moving on the pillowcase.

"Are you nodding," Margaret said, "or shaking your head?"

"She's nodding," Sarah said. "Because it's true. So I don't know why you were so wound up about eating those crawdads."

Margaret sighed. "I won't be eating chicken anymore," she said. "Ever."

The next morning at breakfast, she held up a slice of bacon, making eye contact first with Sarah, and then with Hannah, who gave a little nod and whispered, "Pigs."

Margaret gasped and put the bacon back on the serving platter.

Of course, Mama noticed and immediately gleaned what had taken place. Later that day, when Margaret was planting flowers at the base of the aspen tree in the front yard, Mama cornered Hannah in the laundry room. At first, Hannah thought she was going to get a lecture about telling Margaret where chicken came from. She'd already planned her defense, based on what Sarah had said: Margaret would have to find out sometime. She couldn't be the only kid in school who thought chicken nuggets grew on trees.

But that wasn't Mama's angle at all.

Instead, she said, "Hannah, you have to understand something. Margaret's relationship with death is … well, it's different from yours. If you're going to educate her about the facts, you're going to have to tread a little more lightly."

"She asked, Mama. What was I supposed to say?"

Mama rubbed her eyebrows with her fingertips, a gesture Hannah knew meant she wasn't sure how to answer.

"I don't know, Hannah. I'm just saying, tread lightly. When it comes to your sisters, I need your help. You're the only one who hasn't experienced significant trauma. The other two require delicate handling."

Here, she grabbed a pair of pantyhose that Hannah had just hung to dry. "Like my nylons."

Hannah understood, and she said as much. Margaret's vegetarian phase lasted only for a few months, until Mama made her favorite meatballs one night and she couldn't—or didn't—resist eating them.

And soon, Hannah realized that Mama must have experienced significant trauma, too. It was one of the reasons she'd wanted to adopt children who needed homes. And, of course, it was the reason she'd named her new home the Seedling Homestead. At age ten, Hannah didn't know what kind of trauma Mama (or her sisters, for that matter) had experienced … but she knew they all needed to start over. Hannah was the only one who didn't. She'd grown up trauma-free, which made her feel lonely and lucky all at the same time. But most of all, it gave her life meaning: she was a caretaker. She was the one who had the most solid foundation, the one who had the highest capacity for navigating all of life's twists and turns.

But just because she had the most solid foundation didn't mean that foundation couldn't crack.

CHAPTER ONE

HANNAH BRADLEY's realization that her life was far from perfect began the summer she turned forty.

For the past twenty-some-odd years—since Sarah got married and moved away, and Margaret went off to college before becoming a jet-setting architect—Hannah and Mama had lived together on the Seedling Homestead in an arrangement she'd always considered more than satisfactory.

Yes, Mama was getting older. Yes, Hannah felt the strain of working full-time as a teacher at Walker Elementary, caring for Mama, and taking care of the property. And yes, every once in a while, when her sisters brought it up, Hannah wondered if there was *more*. But overall, life was good. She would even venture so far as to say it was perfect.

Of course, things went wrong: the truck broke down, she squabbled with her sisters about why they didn't visit more often, Mama drove her crazy with little quirks (and she was sure Mama'd say the same about her). But things were pretty darn good.

Then, this summer, four major developments took place.

Most recently, the fourth development: Sarah made a discovery that upended absolutely everything Hannah thought she knew—about herself, about her Mama, and about her life. But Hannah was trying not to think about that. Instead, she focused on the first three.

First, Sarah and her husband Donny, who were on the brink of divorce, brought their daughter Amelia back to Wyoming to visit before taking her to college.

Second, Margaret found out she was losing her vision, and consequently decided to move back home. She fell in love with a local, Ethan, and he proposed (she accepted).

Third, Donny and Sarah repaired their marriage, and decided to stay in Wyoming. Donny suggested that they split Seedling Homestead, adding two new lots for two new houses—one for him and Sarah, the other for Ethan and Margaret. Margaret, an architect, drew up the designs—her final project, a special farewell to her vision.

Now, a new normal was taking shape at Seedling Homestead: all three Bradley sisters would be under one piece of sky again, living on what they were affectionately calling a commune. They'd share the bounty from the garden, the eggs from the chickens, and, hopefully, the work required to run the place.

Then, they (well, Donny, if Hannah was being specific) hired a builder. Which brought Hannah to another element of this new normal: Tanner Lucas, builder extraordinaire, who had been a thorn in Hannah's side since college. And now, not only was he on the property almost every day, but also, her mother was smitten with him.

She told herself she wasn't hiding as she leaned against the trunk of the big maple, watching him lead Mama around the framed-in skeletons of her sisters' new houses. She'd just come outside to make sure spaghetti was okay for dinner, and she found herself observing Tanner (okay, *spying on him* would be a more accurate phrase, but no one had to know).

Tanner said something charming to Mama, and Mama guffawed and slapped her thigh in response. Hannah rolled her eyes. Donny had vetted Tanner before hiring him, and all of his references gave him glowing reviews. Hannah was almost positive one of the female homeowners had said something about the way he looked in his jeans. Or maybe it was something about his dimples.

Tanner had become one of the gang, really, helping himself to coffee in the mornings, and staying for dinner about as often as Mama's old rooster pecked the feathers off a hen's back (which happened several times a week).

Even before Sarah's discovery, Hannah couldn't figure out how she felt about any of this. Living on this commune with her sisters would be nice. They got along well. Having them here this summer had been more than fine. It had been *fun*.

It was just so *different*.

She'd always loved her life at Seedling Homestead. But, truth be told, her sisters always had a way of getting her to question whether she was truly happy, or just content. They often talked about Hannah's future husband, even though there definitely wasn't one on the horizon. They often "encouraged" her to do something—anything—other than work and take care of Mama.

"You need a hobby, Hannah," they said, or, "Wouldn't it be fun to take a vacation?"

As if there was time.

When they talked about these things, she feigned disinterest or irritation. But the truth was that the conversations opened up new, strange desires in Hannah. Things in her brain got all tangled up as she questioned whether there was more to life than what she was living. Even stranger were the thoughts she had about Tanner. Not romantic thoughts, to be sure. Just … *observational* thoughts.

Somewhere between college and adulthood, he did seem to have mellowed out; he no longer debated every word everyone said. He also seemed to have aged well, which Hannah would never mention out loud to anyone. She watched him now, noticed the little lines at the corners of his eyes as he smiled at Mama, the way his hair curled over his collar.

Something about his presence made her uncomfortable, too. Maybe it was the fact that he (and she gritted her teeth as she admitted it to herself) looked even better now than he had in college. Maybe it was because she kept finding herself observing him, her interest growing slightly stronger each day.

"Hannah," Mama Katherine hollered. Hannah jumped, startled out of her observations on the rich, cowboy-like quality of Tanner's voice, which carried over to where she was standing (not hiding).

She stepped out from behind the tree trunk, positive she looked guilty. Would it do any good to pretend she'd been examining the leaves? Here she was, contemplating every single detail of the completely uninteresting and unexpectedly handsome man who was, at this moment, talking to her mother not fifteen feet away in what Hannah thought would be Sarah's kitchen.

"Yeah?" She sounded meek and mouse-like, even to her own ears. She and Mama still weren't on speaking terms, not really.

"Come on over here," Mama said. "Tanner and I need your advice."

Hannah trudged over to where they stood, and even though she could feel Tanner watching her, she carefully avoided eye contact, instead looking at her mother's rain-boot-clad feet.

"I told your mother she doesn't need rain boots," Tanner said.

Hannah knew his comment wasn't really about the rain boots at all. He was letting her know he was aware of her refusal to look at him. Now, she turned toward him, staring straight into his eyes. She immediately wished she hadn't. They really were the most interesting color—a layered hazel that was more green than brown.

He grinned as if he could read her mind, and she felt herself smiling in response. Completely involuntarily.

"It isn't supposed to rain for two more days," they said at the same time.

Hannah flinched. Tanner grinned again. Hannah cleared her throat. "So what did you need my advice about?"

"Window placement," Tanner said.

"I thought Margaret's designs for the houses included window placement," Hannah said.

"They did," Tanner said. "But now that we're about to start framing them in, I've noticed that a tiny adjustment to the angle of this wall will give Sarah and Donny a great view—of that mountain range there, and of the maple trees, there."

"Hmm," Hannah said.

It really was thoughtful of Tanner to notice the view.

"It's a great idea," Hannah said. "You should adjust the angle of the wall."

"Okay, good," Tanner said. "Two votes in favor. I didn't want to make an executive decision."

Hannah nodded, still pretending Mama wasn't there, and found herself wondering why Tanner had gone into building. He'd majored in education in college, same as her.

Mama Katherine beamed. "You're so thoughtful," she said to Tanner. Now he flashed that grin at her, and Hannah could have sworn she swooned.

Not for the first time, Hannah counted down the number of days remaining before the new school year started and she could escape, at least for most of every day. Three. Three more days until she could find refuge in Room Five at Walker Elementary School.

"I'm going to make dinner," she said. "Spaghetti okay?"

"Sounds great," Tanner said.

Hannah had to bite her tongue—literally—to keep from saying he wasn't invited.

"Just kidding," he said. "I've got to get over to Lyla's house. She wants me to have a look at a spot in her roof. Thinks it's leaky and wants it repaired before the rain comes in. Said she'd feed me dinner if I took a look. I told her it'd better be steak. Anyway, thanks for your vote, Hannah."

With a tip of his hat and a, "Ladies," he walked away.

Then Mama spoke to her, the first casual words she'd managed in days: "You sure are smitten with that man," she said, well before Tanner was out of earshot (she spoke so loudly he could have heard it from anywhere in the Walker city limits).

"*You* are," Hannah said.

She knew it was juvenile, but she didn't care. As she walked back to the house, her steps as fast as possible, she heard Mama Katherine cackle. And just underneath the sound of that bawdy laugh, she thought she heard Tanner Lucas's quiet chuckle. Hannah's face burned. She went inside and let the kitchen door slam behind her.

———

THE NEXT AFTERNOON, Hannah decided the wisest course of action was to make herself scarce while Tanner and his crew wrapped things up. She told herself it wasn't because she was avoiding her family, even though she knew, deep down, that was part of it. She just couldn't face them right now. Hollering for Mama's old, creaky-legged dog, John Wayne, she made her way through the meadow. Within a few strides, he'd caught up. She gave him a quick scratch behind the ears, and he looked up at her, smiling.

When thoughts about Mama's betrayal—contained in the big discovery Sarah had made earlier in the summer—threatened to creep in, Hannah focused on the concrete: the end-of-summer warmth on her skin, the bright yellow of the few leaves that had turned, the way those leaves smelled. Fall. The thought of it ran a little thrill through Hannah. She looked forward to the change of seasons, which was so palpable here in Wyoming. She loved nothing more than to come home from school on a cool day, put on a comfy sweater and slippers, and drink tea while grading papers and watching the yellow-and-brown leaves flutter to the ground.

This year, along with the change of seasons would come a change in family dynamics. Margaret was set to marry Ethan James, computer programmer and likely the only eligible bachelor in the tiny mud puddle that was Walker, Wyoming, in just a few weeks. And a few weeks after that, the two of them, and Sarah and Donny, would would have completely moved in to their new houses. Then what?

Hannah had always found her role as the steadfast caretaker a comfortable one. As she and her sisters grew up, it seemed natural that she made sure everyone packed their school lunches, ate their proper servings of fruits and vegetables, and had enough clean underwear to get through each week.

Looking back on it now, Hannah was positive Mama was supervising all along, and just letting Hannah's caretaking (also known as bossy) personality flourish. When Sarah married Donny and moved out, and Margaret went off to college, Hannah had no one to mother—except Mama. She'd continued to care for her ever since. Branching out, living a different life, wasn't ever a consideration.

Until now, Hannah thought as she watched a couple of birds bicker on the branch of a tree. John Wayne charged the trunk, giving a few half-hearted barks, and the birds flew off, chastising him in squawks.

This past summer, when Sarah and Margaret descended on the Seedling Homestead and decided to stay, Hannah had found herself in a kind of panic: would her role change now that her sisters were here to share the duties? If she wasn't the one running this place, then what was she? *Who* was she?

And not that she was interested in Tanner Lucas—not at all—but he represented something for which she'd never had space in her life: romance. If Sarah and Margaret helped around the farm, and helped care for Mama, then she would have more space in her life. What would she do with it?

She'd recently gotten just a taste of the answer to that question, which was that she didn't know. With Sarah, Donny, and Margaret here —and happy to help with chores and dinner—she'd found herself, on more than one occasion, with time to spare.

She recognized it was there, but she often squandered it away, sitting at the kitchen table until a cup of coffee went cold between her hands, or standing at the wide back window, looking out over the property until she realized her eyes had glazed over, or sitting on the porch with a glass of wine or a beer, and more time.

Sometimes, she spent so long debating with herself about whether to do something—take John Wayne for a walk, go to the farmer's market to browse, dust the window blinds—that she ran out of time to actually do it.

John Wayne had fallen behind, and now, he streaked past her, to the creek's edge, coming to a full stop as his front paws splashed into the water. He made an abrupt right turn and ran along the bank. Sometimes, Hannah realized as she watched him trot along, she wasted far too much time on the unnecessary.

One morning when Sarah and Donny volunteered to help Mama with the weeding, she wiped down the kitchen counter four times before Amelia came in and pointed out that her arm must be getting tired.

Another afternoon when Margaret helped Mama repair a broken spot in the chicken coop, Hannah made three dozen cupcakes. She didn't even know who'd eat them all (actually, come to think of it, she'd put her money on Margaret), but she had been unable to think of anything else to do.

John Wayne dashed back to her, a stick in his mouth. She laughed when he dropped it at her feet. The truth was, she missed this—she loved taking the dog for walks, but she rarely did any more because she didn't want to leave Mama alone now, even for a short time.

As if reminding her he was there, John Wayne whacked Hannah on the leg with the stick. She took it from him, tossed it as far upstream as she could. He charged after it, sending up little chunks of mud that hit her shins when he ran off.

In the midst of another round of fetch, Hannah thought maybe she should take this opportunity to remind herself of all the things she'd liked doing before Mama started requiring more help. How many times had she wished for someone else to help Mama with dinner, like Margaret was doing right now? And when she'd wished for that, what had she imagined doing with that time?

John Wayne was back, offering her the stick again. She threw it, and kept walking.

She could go to school and work ahead on lesson plans or redecorate her classroom, which she hadn't done in ages. Years, actually. She could take Mama into Jackson Hole and go to the mall. She could redecorate her bedroom. With Margaret's help.

Truth be told, although Hannah had been telling herself for years that she craved free time, now that she had it, she looked forward to the start of the new school year more than ever before—because it would give her structure and get her back into her routine. Back to normal.

Only, "normal" wasn't quite that any more, Hannah thought then, her mind bringing her back to the topic she tried so hard to avoid thinking about. Hannah had *thought* the change in family dynamics was all she had to worry about. But then, just a few days ago, Sarah had dropped a bombshell that proved her wrong.

John Wayne came up behind her as the leaves on the trees shimmered. Hannah couldn't tell whether her tears were from hurt or anger or sadness. She decided it didn't matter. She turned back toward the house, and just as she had done a million times since the bomb exploded, she went over the sequence of events that had transpired during the past couple of weeks.

When Sarah, Donny, and Amelia first arrived in Wyoming, Donny had just announced he wanted a divorce. After they dropped Amelia off at college, he said, they'd sell their house in Arizona. They were set to spend a few awkward weeks in Wyoming, first. One day, Hannah and Sarah went to the farmer's market, and Sarah, still in shock, bought an old metal recipe box. She liked the colors and thought it would make a nice decoration in the kitchen wherever she ended up, post-divorce. Although Sarah and Donny had since worked things out, and the topic of divorce had been shelved, Sarah's whimsical purchase had a lasting impact.

The recipe box ended up being much more than a trinket: tucked inside, Sarah found an old diary, written forty years before by someone named Hazel Rickshaw Carlisle.

Hazel detailed the tragic love story between her and her husband, Philip. Their arranged marriage started off on rocky ground. Neither of them much wanted to marry the other, but they agreed to wed because doing so meant a merger and the survival of their family orchards. Hazel was afraid getting married would mean an end to her copywriting career, but Philip encouraged and supported her. They ended up falling in love. Sarah, a romantic, loved the story so much she felt compelled to share it with her sisters.

When Hannah first read this part of the journal, she pictured the two of them dancing under a canopy of apple trees, the sky purple and twinkling with stars.

Hazel and Philip's first son was born a couple of years into their marriage, and, because Hazel preferred her career to motherhood, she always felt like a horrible mother.

Then, their son died in an accident on the orchard.

Hazel blamed herself: he'd woken from his nap, climbed out of his crib. His nanny, who was preparing dinner, didn't hear him. He wandered outside, where one of the workers ran over him with a tractor. Hazel believed that if she'd been home, mother's instinct would have warned her that her tiny son was in mortal danger.

But she was at work.

She and Philip couldn't overcome the tragedy. They couldn't speak to each other or even look at one another. Hazel believed the only thing to do was to start over. So, seeking a clean slate, she moved away from the California orchard she shared with Philip—and she didn't even tell him where she was going.

Sarah told her sisters that when she read this part of the story, a realization began to dawn. Something that had been niggling at her brain since she read the first page. The way Hazel Rickshaw Carlisle wrote, she sounded awfully familiar.

Thinking about it now gave Hannah goosebumps, even though it was too early to feel that fall chill in the air.

That's when Sarah knew. But she hadn't told Hannah, at least, not right away. Still, Hannah could tell something was going on.

She realized it one day a few weeks ago. Wanting to give Margaret an opportunity to see some of the country's best sights before she completely lost her vision, Hannah came up with the idea of taking Margaret on a road trip in Sarah and Donny's RV. Knowing she had to get Sarah's buy-in before presenting the idea to Margaret, Hannah tracked her down. She found Sarah hiding in the RV, where she'd spent much of the summer. She was reading the journal, so engrossed in the current entry that she didn't even seem to notice Hannah had climbed the stairs.

"I need to talk to you," Hannah said, and Sarah looked up, obviously startled.

"Geez," Hannah said. "You look like I just caught you with your hand in the cookie jar."

She smiled, hoping to keep the mood light so Sarah would be more receptive to her road trip idea. Still, Sarah didn't speak. Which was strange.

"Good reading?" Hannah said.

She came up the steps and looked over Sarah's shoulder. Sarah closed the journal.

"I need to talk to you, too," Sarah said. She licked her lips, which was one of her tells—she was nervous.

"Wow," Hannah said. "You look serious." She gestured to the journal. "What's happening now? Intrigue? Romance? Steamy sex?"

"You could say that," Sarah said.

Hannah should have heard alarm bells, then. Buzzers. She should have seen flashing warning lights. But she was too focused on her mission.

So she said, "Huh. Okay, well, I need to talk to you."

"So you said," Sarah said. She laid the journal on the dining table and put her hands in her lap. "All ears."

Hannah took a deep breath and launched into her explanation about why they should take Margaret on a road trip. In the end, it didn't take too much convincing (of course, Sarah thought Margaret should focus on the practicalities of losing her vision: how she'd work, whether she needed mobility training, whether she'd want to move), and in retrospect, Hannah realized she should have been able to tell something else was going on.

It wasn't until later that Hannah found out ... and her world changed completely.

———

ALTHOUGH HANNAH HAD CONCEIVED of the road trip for Margaret's sake, she found it was healing for her, as well. She rarely got off the Seedling Homestead and out of Walker, and it was even less often that she ventured out of Wyoming. Seeing all the sights—Zion, Bryce Canyon, Moab, Arches National Park—reminded her that there was a world outside of the little snow globe in which she lived. Maybe it even gave her an itch to explore it. Margaret seemed to have a good time, too, even if it was in part due to the constant supply of Bloody Marys Hannah kept flowing from the blender she'd packed in the RV.

And they enjoyed a new kind of camaraderie, thanks to the vulgar conversations Margaret had with Ethan via text message. Because

Margaret couldn't read Ethan's texts, she played them out loud on her phone—which meant everyone in the RV participated. This provided almost unlimited opportunities for hilarity.

The first text from Ethan said, "I really enjoyed dinner the other night. Next time, we should try dessert."

Margaret gasped. Hannah gasped. Sarah said, "Wow," and Mama Katherine gave a whoop.

"Well, I can tell this app is going to be fun," Hannah said.

"What are you gonna say back?" Sarah said.

"I'm going to say, 'It's none of your beeswax, Sarah,'" Margaret said. "Just don't listen when I do voice-to-text, because I'm going to tell Ethan just how much I love his dessert idea."

Then, they were all laughing—until Margaret's phone made another notification sound.

Into the silence, the phone said, "What do you like for dessert?"

"You know," Sarah said, her voice high-pitched, "you should probably change that thing's voice to one that sounds more manly, if you're going to start sexting. Especially if you're going to start sexting when we're all together."

This had Hannah practically shrieking. Margaret, lips twitching, told her phone to activate voice-to-text. Then she said, "I like cucumbers."

This stumped the other passengers in the RV, and they fell silent.

"He sent me a picture of a cucumber," Margaret said. "The other day."

"Then you should add something like, 'Covered in chocolate,'" Hannah said.

"No!" Sarah said. "Something like, 'But only when they're in my mouth.'"

"Well, I never," Mama said. "I am truly scandalized. I had no idea I was raising a bunch of harlots."

"It's not me," Margaret said. "I'm still a proper lady."

Then she activated voice-to-text and replied to Ethan: "I'm willing to try anything once."

A few seconds later, his reply came in, the feminine voice of the application breaking through the road noise: "Well. This should be interesting. I'll get a menu together."

For the seven days they spent in the RV, Hannah felt like everything was just right. In a way, she wished she could make some kind of time capsule, put the four of them inside of it, and keep living this way forever.

But real life beckoned, as it always did, and when they returned home, Sarah and Donny took Amelia off to college and Margaret became immersed in her own transition from sighted to blind. One day when everyone else was gone, Mama came into the kitchen while Hannah was washing dishes. The truth was, they weren't even *dirty* dishes. They were rarely-used items like the bundt pan and the giant blue casserole dish with the big chip on one corner from the time Margaret dropped a measuring spoon on it. Hannah, short on things to do since her sisters had taken care of most of the chores and Tanner Lucas was out on the property, taking measurements, decided a good cleaning was in order.

"We haven't used those in ages," Mama said when she saw what Hannah was scrubbing. "What are you washing them for?"

"I don't know," Hannah said. "It's just been a while. I looked into the cupboard and saw that they were dusty. I think this one even had a moth in it."

"Hannah," Mama said.

"Mama," Hannah said. "You'd've washed them too, if—"

"I need to talk to you."

Hannah's awareness perked up. Was Mama about to announce that she was sick? Dying? Maybe she had cancer or some other incurable disease. There had been an E.coli breakout a while back.

"Okay," Hannah said slowly. She dried her hands on the dish towel. Leaving the dishes in the soapy water, she gestured to the dining room table. They sat, and Mama said, "I'd like to tell you a story."

When she started talking, Hannah recognized the story as the one Sarah had been reading in the journal. She figured Sarah had shared the story with Mama, and even though she wondered why Mama was telling it, she didn't interrupt.

Finally, she got to the part where Hazel's son died. Mama sounded a bit like she might cry, Hannah thought. Hannah hadn't yet heard this part of the story, and she was surprised at the strength of her own reaction: her stomach churned and her eyes burned. She didn't even know Hazel, or Philip, or the baby. But maybe it was because Mama seemed emotional about it. Hannah looked at the top of the table and used her thumbnail to scrape off some dried food from the night before while Mama talked about how Hazel could no longer look her husband in the eye, as guilty as she felt. If it were possible, her voice started to sound even thicker.

"So," Mama said, sighing and clearing her throat, "Hazel moved away. She moved to a place with a big sky. Somewhere about as far as she could get from the orchards and Philip and her little boy's grave. Do you know where she moved?"

When Hannah looked up at Mama, she noticed a strange intensity in her eyes.

Now, Hannah cleared her throat. "No. Where did she move?"

"Wyoming," Mama said. "To start over. She moved to Wyoming, where there's an endless sky and the freshest air. And that's when she learned she was pregnant. She hadn't known. She'd had an inkling, maybe, but she hadn't known for sure. And when the doctor confirmed it, she realized there was no other choice but to keep this new baby a secret."

Hannah's heart picked up its pace, creating a thrumming in her ears. That night when Margaret had crawled into bed asking about chickens was the first time Hannah noticed that silence is rarely actually silent. In this moment, as she stared at Mama and Mama stared back at her, everything was still. But it wasn't silent.

There was the rushing, beating sound in her ears. The cuckoo clock ticked, and the little motor inside whirred. Outside, a chicken clucked once, and then again, and the ice maker in the freezer released a load of cubes, which clattered down into the tray.

"You're—are you saying what I think you're saying?" Hannah said.

Mama continued to look at her, as if she was waiting for Hannah to come to her own conclusion. "It was the only choice," she said.

"Was it?"

Again, a moment passed where neither of them spoke. More sounds: someone using a saw, a truck rumbling by on the road.

"At the time, it felt like it," Mama said.

She'd always known. Well, not *always*, but since the spring when she was five and she saw a pair of horses copulating at the farm down the street. She and Mama had taken one of their long weekend walks, down the driveway and out along the main road, which bordered farm and ranch properties for miles.

"What are they doing? Is that one horse trying to ride the other one?"

Hannah remembered the scene with such clarity. Her voice bordered on a giggle, as funny as she thought it was that one horse might be attempting to climb onto its friend's back. Mama hadn't bothered coming up with a clever explanation. She'd opted for the truth. Hannah had always admired her for her truth-telling. Until now, that is.

"They're reproducing," Mama said to five-year-old Hannah, who, of course, asked for an explanation. "Any time two mammals—a mommy and a daddy—want to have a baby, they do that." Here, she inclined her head toward the horses. The one that had been underneath the other one had run away now, shaking its head. Its mane shook, too.

"Humans are mammals, right?" Hannah said.

"Mmhmm," Mama said.

She took Hannah's hand and they started walking again. The sun was just a little too hot that day, and Hannah squinted, eyes watering, as she looked up at Mama.

"So, when you wanted to have *me*, did you reproduce with a daddy human to make me?"

Mama's stride faltered, just the tiniest bit, and she made a funny noise in her throat. Hannah thought it sounded a little like when she accidentally stepped on Mr. Mouser's tail. Mr. Mouser, the daddy barn cat, didn't like having his tail stepped on.

"I did," Mama said. "That's how all mammals reproduce, or make babies. But that's a story for another time. When you're older."

After that conversation, Hannah took more notice of, and a greater interest in, the makeup of families. Up until this point, when she and Mama went into town—to the library or the store—they typically saw pairs of mothers and children, or mothers with a handful of kids in tow. Hannah had never thought anything of it, because it was her normal. It was all she had exposure to.

When she started kindergarten that fall, she noticed that most of her classmates had mothers *and* fathers who came to the meet-the-teacher event and dropped them off on the first day. On the playground at recess, she heard people talk about both parents: "My daddy works at the grocery store, in produce," or, "My dad said the Broncos are going to win the Super Bowl this year, but my mom, she's a Packers fan."

From the way these kids talked, their parents lived in the same house, argued over chores, and washed each other's clothes (someone's dad had accidentally turned all the whites pink when he threw a red towel into the load). As they all got older, they identified the fatherless children, but only as a matter of categorization. Hannah wasn't the only one whose mom was the sole parent: Terence Stuart lived alone with his mom and sister, and Jamie Hill's mom was raising her two daughters alone. Some kids migrated back and forth between their parents' houses.

And really, there were only a handful of instances in which it seemed to matter that Hannah didn't have a dad.

On career day, some parents came in to talk about their jobs. The grocery store dad from produce, of course, and Timmy Barrett's dad, who was a commercial airline pilot. Someone else's father was a rancher. A handful of mothers showed up: a seamstress, a nurse, and a teacher. It seemed like everyone's parents had jobs. But Hannah's mom didn't work, at least, not besides her chores on the farm. And, of course, Hannah didn't even *have* a dad. A few kids asked Hannah if she even knew who her dad was, but the teacher quickly shushed them.

Hannah could talk to Mama about almost anything. But over time, she understood that this topic, and the conversation that should accompany it, were off-limits. Every time it came up, Mama shut it down.

The last time Hannah approached it was when she was a pre-teen, in seventh grade. Some of the girls in her homeroom planned to attend a father-daughter dance their church was offering. During recess one day, they talked about it in high-pitched voices, describing the dresses their mothers had bought them and the corsages their fathers had chosen. Hannah went home that afternoon and told Mama about the dance. They were in the kitchen, and Mama was making meatloaf. As Hannah spoke, it seemed like Mama knew what was coming. She kneaded the meat mixture harder and harder, her shoulders moving up and down, up and down. After Hannah told her about the dresses and the corsages and the decorations, she paused. Mama kept kneading, and the meat made squishing sounds.

"Where's *my* dad, Mama? Why don't I have someone to take me to a father-daughter dance?"

Finally, Mama stopped kneading. Her body, which until then had been stiffly erect, drooped slightly. When she lifted her head, she didn't look at Hannah. She looked out the kitchen window, and Hannah imagined she was watching the windmill turn.

"Hannah," she said. "I just can't talk about it, okay? You probably won't ever have someone to take you to a father-daughter dance. And you know what? When you grow up and become an adult, you'll realize it was never that big of a deal to begin with. And these girls in your homeroom class, who think it's a big deal now, they'll fall into one of two categories: the first, people for whom the father-daughter dance is the highlight of their sad lives, and the second, people filled with anger and resentment and bitter disappointment because they grow up and realize their fathers aren't who they thought they were."

Hannah felt her eyes go round. The two categories idea stumped Hannah. Mama *never* talked like this. She rarely said anything mean-spirited about anyone. It seemed like Mama suddenly realized her words had become a runaway train, because she softened her tone when she went on: "But you, my dear, will be in a third category."

This was about the time Hannah had started to develop a mind of her own, and she thought—but didn't say—*a category full of fatherless children whose mothers never told them the truth.*

"Hannah, you'll be among the girls who grow up strong and independent and able to think for yourselves. You won't need a man to make you happy or take care of you, because you'll know how to do those things on your own."

This answer wasn't satisfactory to Hannah. She wanted to know why he didn't care enough to be part of her life, even if he and Mama had gotten divorced.

"Now, I know this answer isn't satisfactory to you," Mama said, and Hannah wondered if her mother could read her mind. "And I'm sorry for that, but it's not going to change. I just can't talk about it. It would be really helpful to me if you didn't bring it up again."

Hannah, who prided herself on being a dutiful daughter and, above all, a helpful person, nodded. She walked out of the kitchen, her limbs numb. And she honored Mama's request: she never brought it up again, no matter how many times she wanted to. She had so many questions, questions that increased in quantity and complexity: did Mama even know who Hannah's father was? Did Hannah's father know about her? Where was he? Was he alive? Did she have any siblings, half-siblings with different mothers?

But now, here they were, Hannah more than forty years old, the topic back onstage. In the spotlight. As she replayed all those moments from her childhood, emotions began to swirl through her blood. She pictured them as colors, blooming in her veins: red for anger, blue for sadness, black for betrayal. She waited for her mother to speak.

"You know," Hannah said. "I always knew I had a father. And your reaction whenever I brought up the topic made it clear the conversation was off-limits. I assumed you didn't want to talk about it because you didn't know who he was, or because you knew who he was but you'd sworn to keep his identity a secret. In one of my fantasies, he was the President. Or a millionaire CEO or something. But this? You kept my father's identity a secret from me because it made you *sad*?"

The tone of her voice was ugly.

"I couldn't talk about it," Mama said.

Again, a flash of anger. Hannah gritted her teeth. "You've said that. But of course you could. You could have told me his name, where he lives, whether he even knew about me. You could have told me the story of how you met and why you moved here. You chose not to. Not being able to do something is very different from choosing not to do something."

Mama, her elbows on the table, dropped her head into her hands.

"You're right," she said. But then she didn't say anything else.

Hannah felt like she might explode. How was this even possible, that they were sitting right here, face-to-face, and her mother still refused to elaborate on this story, *her* story?

She thought again about all those questions she had. She didn't know which one to ask first. Just trying to prioritize them made Hannah even angrier. But even as she clenched her teeth and balled her fists so tightly her fingernails dug into her palms, she noticed how frail Mama looked. The skin on her forearms was so thin, now, and the wrinkles around her eyes had deepened. The bones on her shoulders protruded, and, although she'd always seemed larger than life, now she looked like she'd shrunk.

What did Hannah really want to know? Which was the most important question?

"Does he know about me?"

Mama shook her head.

"He doesn't even know I exist?"

Again, a shake of the head.

"But, *why*, Mama? Why didn't you tell him? Don't you think he had a right to know? To make the choice about whether to be a part of my life? Don't you think I had a right for him to know? Or, *have* the right? For my own father to know of my existence?"

"Hannah—"

Hannah could only imagine what Mama planned to say. That she didn't know what else to do, that she didn't have a choice, that she thought she was doing what was best? It didn't matter. Hannah could think of what else to do. She could think of a better choice. And she could think of a situation far better than this.

For the first time ever, she hated her mother.

"Don't bother trying to explain," she said. "It doesn't even matter. You deprived me of my father. Who, by your own account in that journal, was a perfectly decent man. I can understand that you were going through a painful time. I can understand you thinking leaving was the only option. But what I can't understand, Mama, is that you never told me. You never came clean. You put your thoughts and feelings and explanations and secrets into a journal, and then left that journal out for someone else to find. But you never told me. And because of that, I missed out."

Hannah knew what she was implying. She was implying that her childhood had somehow been lacking. And while it had been magical, and she knew how lucky she was—especially when she lined her own story up next to Sarah's and Margaret's—she believed a father was part of some equation in which the elements came together to create a deep happiness and sense of belonging. And she knew he wasn't there.

Mama had done her best. And she'd done a good job. But she had also betrayed Hannah. Not only Hannah, but Philip Carlisle, too. And Hannah didn't know if she could forgive her for that.

CHAPTER TWO

WHY IN TARNATION Margaret had asked Hannah to help plan her wedding should go down as one of the biggest family mysteries of all time. Hannah had never had a serious boyfriend, much less planned a wedding. And she never spent much time out and about—she moved between work and home and the farmer's market, rarely paying attention to things like the hottest colors of the year or the most amazing bridal gown styles of the decade.

She felt a bit like a fish out of water as she shared her opinion on all things wedding related. Especially because until a month ago, Margaret had been absolutely immersed in the latest fashions and fads as she traveled around the country as a superstar architect, designing buildings for libraries and coffee shops and hotels in all the swankiest, trendiest cities.

And although she swore she wanted a quaint country wedding when she married Ethan James right here at the Seedling Homestead in a few short weeks, Hannah suspected that would equate to a down-home-luxe event that cost tens of thousands of dollars. Which was like chump change to Margaret.

The four of them—Hannah, her sisters, and Mama Katherine—sat around the living room, thumbing through wedding magazines and sipping wine.

"I don't know why you want my help with this," Hannah said. "I don't know anything about weddings or marriage or complementary colors."

"Or men," Margaret said, before slapping a hand over her mouth. "I didn't mean it."

"Yes, you did," Hannah said. "And it's okay. You're right. I don't know anything about men."

"But you'd like to," Sarah said. "You'd like to know more about Tanner Lucas."

"Would not," Hannah said, although an obnoxious voice in the back of her head reminded her that just a few hours before, she'd been wondering why Tanner Lucas became a builder and where he got his ideas. Oh, and noticing the layered colors in his eyes.

"Would too," Sarah said.

"Ladies, ladies," Margaret said. "I need your help, Hannah, because, as I can't believe I have to remind you, I can't see. I need your eyes. And even if you don't know about weddings, marriage, or men, you do know about flowers."

Hannah shrugged, then remembered Margaret couldn't see her shrugging. She made a humming noise that she hoped conveyed a combination of assent and annoyance.

Margaret going blind was some kind of cruel cosmic joke. Renowned across the country for her vision as an architect, she'd recently learned she had retinitis pigmentosa, a condition that affected the photoreceptor cells in her eyes—causing vision loss. Although she had good days and bad, it was only a matter of time before her vision was limited. It'd be like she was looking through holes the size of pinheads.

"So, Hannah," Sarah said.

Hannah groaned.

"Why haven't you ever had a serious boyfriend?"

"I'm sure Hannah doesn't want to—"

"It's okay, Mama," Hannah said, half of her wondering why Mama had taken so long to intercede and the other half feeling like they'd all been tiptoeing around this conversation for weeks and might as well get it out of the way.

"I guess I've always felt like my life was pretty close to perfect," Hannah said. "Just as it was. Is. I mean, I love living here, on Seedling Homestead. I love being with Mama, tending to the garden, watching John Wayne chase the chickens, teaching my students. I don't need anything more."

"But haven't you ever—" Margaret said.

"In Walker?" Hannah said. "Please. There are no fish in this pond. Walker is more like a mud puddle. And I'm not a jet-setter like you."

"I found Ethan right here in Walker," Margaret said.

"Probably the only good … help me out here, Sarah," Hannah said, and Sarah finished, "the only good mosquito eater in this mud puddle?"

"Something like that," Hannah said.

Mama cleared her throat, a sound so obviously ridden with meaning Hannah had to laugh.

"Tanner Lucas is not a sexy mosquito eater, Mama. Just because you have the hots for him …"

Mama swatted her knee and sipped her wine. "Who's to say I was referring to Tanner Lucas, hmm? I think it's interesting you brought him up. But now that you have …"

Come to think of it, Mama had never had a boyfriend, either. She'd recently taken up some sort of relationship with their neighbor, Farmer Eddie, but Hannah wasn't quite sure what to make of it.

Although, there was the not-so-little matter of the huge bombshell Sarah had dropped earlier this summer, which did help to explain why Mama had kept to herself all these years.

"I want pink flowers," Margaret said. "Something you'd find on a farm. Peonies, maybe?"

"Pink?" Hannah said. "I thought you'd be going for red or something. Red seems way more cosmopolitan."

"I don't want cosmopolitan for my wedding," Margaret said.

"She wants sweet," Sarah said. "Ethan is sweet, their romance is sweet. Pink is sweet."

She held up the magazine, turned it around so Hannah could see the bouquet she'd found: all pinks and whites and light greens. Hannah shrugged and tried to be inconspicuous as she unfolded the pages she'd dogeared in her magazine—the ones filled with photos of sleek centerpieces and slicked-back hair styles.

"How will you wear your hair?" Hannah said.

"I don't know," Margaret said. "Do you think you could make me a crown? Out of flowers?"

"A *flower* crown?" Hannah said, and Mama Katherine swatted her on the knee again.

"What? This is just so different from what I expected."

"What did you expect?" Margaret wanted to know.

Hannah shrugged again, then remembered and said, "I don't even know. Maybe, like—a jeweled tiara."

"It's all about the *feelings*, Hannah," Sarah said. "Their love is flowers. Delicate and beautiful. Not hard, glittery jewels."

"Right," Hannah said.

She resolved to keep her mouth shut and find some pink flowers, make a beautiful crown, and then return to normal life—because normal life was fine, just as it was.

"Ooh, Margaret!" Sarah said. "I found *the* dress for you. We'll just have to take a trip down to Jackson Hole. It'll look so good on you! With a flower crown. Look, Hannah!"

Sarah held the magazine out so Hannah could look at it. The dress was beautiful: it was fitted and lacy and looked like something out of *The Great Gatsby*. It would show off Margaret's curves exquisitely. It would be stunning. And Hannah would never have picked it out—not in a million years.

Nope, she was not cut out for this.

"Love it," Hannah said. "It's perfect."

The rest of the evening transpired in much the same way: Sarah pointing out items Margaret would like; centerpieces and silverware and plates (plates!) and Margaret giving her full rein to order whatever she thought was best. Mama Katherine oohed and ahhed over Sarah's choices, made clucking noises over the prices, and beamed over how beautiful the ceremony would be.

And Hannah remained quiet.

She went back to her bedroom that night feeling a little left out, but also more resigned than ever to maintain her comfortable normal. She pulled on her pajamas—a plain white t-shirt, and realized she wasn't being totally honest with herself. "Normal" had shifted recently, and not for the better. As Mama Katherine got older, and required more help, normal was becoming a bit lonely.

Mama Katherine's fainting spell was an excellent example. Sarah's daughter, Amelia, was set to graduate from high school in Arizona, and as the date approached, Mama Katherine said she didn't feel up to traveling.

"You can still fly out, if you want to," she told Hannah. "I'll stay here and hold down the fort."

And Hannah wanted to. She wanted to see her only niece graduate from high school. She imagined Amelia, her curly hair in the breeze, her dimples flashing as she walked across the stage at graduation. It was a rite of passage and Amelia's aunt should be there.

But Hannah couldn't do it. She couldn't leave Mama Katherine alone and travel to the other side of the country. When she thought about how she'd feel if something happened to Mama while she was gone, she experienced a strange, preemptive, and suffocating guilt.

So she called Sarah and Amelia and apologized. And although she could tell Sarah was disappointed, she also heard relief in her sister's voice; at least someone would be with Mama. Then she called Margaret, half-hoping her middle sister would offer to stay with Mama so Hannah could go to Arizona. After all, Hannah rarely went anywhere, and Margaret was constantly traveling the country.

But Margaret seemed strangely distracted and didn't make the offer. Hannah resigned herself to staying home, missing the graduation, and thinking of Amelia all day.

And that's how the day had started. At first, Hannah and Mama went about their daily chores, mucking out the chicken coop and weeding the garden and sharing stories of Amelia growing up: the time she'd caught a frog in the creek and stored it in the barbecue, planning to show Sarah when she got back from the farmer's market, not realizing it would overheat in there ("I've never seen such a sad little girl," Mama said, laughing), the way she used to insist on collecting eggs half-dozen times a day when she visited, how she always wanted to bake oatmeal raisin cookies—which no one else liked.

It was an absolutely pleasant morning full of reminiscing and happy memories. Then, somewhere between the weeding and the watering, Mama froze. Hannah, who was on her knees between the corn and the tomatoes, noticed the change in her posture—from relaxed to absolutely still—and said, "Mama?"

Mama's head swiveled toward Hannah and she said, "I'm feeling a bit funny."

Then she collapsed.

It happened in slow motion: her knees buckled and hit the ground. Her hips landed next. Then her torso. Finally, her head hit with a padded *thud*.

Silence.

Before any coherent thoughts formed, words started running through Hannah's mind: *stroke, heart attack, death*.

One word in particular kept coming back up: *alone*.

Hannah had never felt so alone. No one was there to help her. She couldn't ask someone to call an ambulance, or to stay with Mama while she ran inside to get a phone.

No one was there to share in that sheer terror.

She scrambled over to where Mama lay, and checked her pulse and breathing. Good, she wasn't dead.

She got to her feet and ran inside. Frantic, she searched for her cell phone. She couldn't find it. Couldn't remember where she'd left it. Fortunately, Mama insisted on keeping a land line. Hannah dashed into the kitchen to pick it up (while berating herself for letting precious seconds tick by while she looked for her mobile).

She gave the dispatcher her name and phone number and address. The dispatcher asked if Mama was conscious—to which Hannah answered no—and whether she was breathing.

"She was when I left her," Hannah said.

Panic set in. What if she wasn't breathing now? There was no one there to give her CPR.

She hung up, then rushed back into the yard. Mama lay in the same position, still breathing. Hannah's heart was beating so fast and hard, she thought she might have a heart attack.

The ambulance finally arrived, and the paramedics loaded Mama onto the stretcher. By some small miracle, Hannah found her phone just before she climbed in alongside the stretcher—she'd left it on the table next to the shed.

She texted her sisters to let them know what happened, but realized when she checked the time that they were probably on their way to Amelia's graduation at that very moment. She hoped they wouldn't get the text until afterward—it was certain to cast a shadow on what should be a special day for Amelia.

Meanwhile, here Hannah was, in the back of the ambulance with their unconscious mother and no one else to lean on. She closed her eyes, wishing she had someone—anyone—with whom to share this ... the sense of responsibility, the intense fear, the sheer weight of the situation.

CHAPTER THREE

FINALLY, the first day of the new school year dawned. It was a welcome relief for Hannah, who'd spent the final few days of summer break avoiding her mother. Not talking to Mama was strange. Almost eerie. Hannah had gone from being petrified that Katherine would die and leave her alone, to pretending she wasn't there, tiptoeing around the house.

Although she'd set her alarm for 5:30 a.m. to give herself time to feed the chickens and water the yard before getting dressed for the day, she woke up fifteen minutes before that and couldn't doze off again. So she pulled on an old pair of overalls and went into the kitchen to find the coffee already brewed.

"That's weird," she said to the empty kitchen. Still, she poured herself a cup and sneaked outside with it, only to bump right into Tanner Lucas. He, too, was carrying a full mug, and the impact sent the liquid in both cups sloshing. Despite the collision, she couldn't help but notice how good he smelled, like soap and the forest.

"What are you doing here?" Hannah said, using her free hand to brush at the front of her overalls where the coffee had spilled. "I mean, good morning. Sorry, you surprised me and I'm not properly caffeinated. I should have said, 'You're early this morning.'"

At first, he didn't answer. He just smiled at her in a way that made her think he could divine the strange feeling she was experiencing between her legs. She wished she could turn herself inside out and hide in the shell of her skin.

"Well, in case you didn't realize it, Miz Bradley, I work here."

"Oh, I realized it."

"Did I leave you enough coffee?" He inclined his head toward her mug. "Your mama put it on for me."

"She's up?"

"Naw," he said, sounding so much like a cowboy she had no choice but to check out the way his jeans fit. "She set the timer last night. Does it every Sunday. I'm usually a little earlier than I expect on Mondays. Can't sleep, anticipating the week."

Here, they looked at each other for a moment. It was some kind of acknowledgement, Hannah thought, that neither of them had been able to sleep, and maybe that meant something. Or, it didn't.

"First day of school, isn't it?" Tanner said. "My sister was dreading this morning."

Tanner's sister, Lyla, had a small gaggle of children, if Hannah recalled.

"I know it's hard on parents," Hannah said. "The transition from summer to the school year. But I love it. The smell of fresh notebooks, the kids in their first-day outfits, the promise of a great year."

Tanner nodded. "My projects are just like that. There's first-day-of-school promise: fresh dirt being turned over for the foundation. Waiting to see who my problem child is going to be. There's always a problem child, right?"

"True." How did he know this?

He probably dated (scratch that: slept with) all the teachers in town. It wasn't like Walker, Wyoming, population five hundred and forty-three, offered a deep dating pool of eligible women. There were teachers, grocery store cashiers, and retail workers.

"I'm going to get a refill on this coffee," Tanner said. "Then I'm going to do a quick walk-around on the houses. Want to join me?"

Strangely, Hannah did want to join him. Which is exactly why she said, "Love to, but I've got to get ready. First day, right?"

She did a quick about-face and headed for the house. Then she heard his footsteps behind her and did a mental forehead slap. She'd been trying to escape him and here she was, setting herself up to spend more time with him.

"I can get you that refill and bring it out to you," she said, thinking it was more of a way to cut their contact short than to actually do him a favor.

"It's no problem," he said. "I've been grabbing it, myself."

Great. So he and Mama had some kind of weird agreement. Probably because Mama had a crush on him. Hannah rolled her eyes.

"Suit yourself," she said.

They got to the house and she reached for the door handle, but Tanner beat her to it. He opened it and gestured for her to go ahead. Charmed, she did. But because she was charmed, she walked quickly to her bedroom, while listening carefully to the sounds of Tanner getting his coffee. Yes, he was pleasant now, but she knew an argumentative, self-righteous young man resided beneath the sweet exterior. She still got prickly when she thought about that debate they'd had in college, about video game violence. She'd never been so mad in her life, not before or since. And he'd sat there, smug and calm, watching her get all riled up as they argued. Her face felt hot as she picked out her clothes for the day.

Fortunately, Tanner was outside when Hannah finished getting ready. She ate her breakfast alone, and sneaked out the front door before anyone else was up. Hopefully Mama would feed the chickens.

An hour before students were due to start walking through the door, Hannah surveyed her classroom. In all her spare time this summer, she'd changed themes, ditching the baby animals and choosing instead brightly-colored superhero characters and coordinating comic-book style decorations that shouted things like, "Bam!" and "Pow!"

The posters carried messages about being—what else?—super.

At this point, everything was in its place, which was exactly how Hannah liked it. The bookshelves, lined up against one wall, held reams of paper and baskets of supplies along with all the books she'd collected over the years. In the reading corner, pillows in primary colors sat on a fluffy white rug.

The desks were grouped into tables, and she'd numbered each group, planning to have the kids earn points for good behavior, competition-style.

Fifty minutes until the first bell, Hannah thought, which was just enough time to hand out the welcome packets she'd made and tape down all the name tags. She picked up the stack of packets and started walking around the room, laying each packet at precisely the same spot on each desk.

Every time her mind wandered to Mama and her betrayal, Hannah snapped it back to the present. There was work to be done here, she reminded herself, and she didn't need to be distracted.

She was just thinking she couldn't wait for students to get here when the first one walked into her room. Out of reflex, she checked the clock: it was still forty minutes before parents were allowed to leave their children on campus.

"I'm early," the girl said.

Hannah cleared her throat, thinking that she'd have to find a nice way to let this kid's parents know they couldn't leave their daughter this early. She didn't remember seeing this girl at Meet the Teacher Night. She would have remembered: the poor thing had stringy hair the color of dirty dishwater, and she stood slightly hunched, defensive, as if she were anticipating a good, hard punch in the shoulder.

She also had the brightest blue eyes Hannah had ever seen, with the darkest circles under them. And the strangest outfit: yellow fleece shorts that were almost certainly not dress-code appropriate, and a long-sleeved black shirt. One sleeve was covered in what Hannah assumed was white cat fur.

"It's okay," she said, realizing she'd probably taken way too long examining this girl. "I'm Ms. Bradley. I don't remember meeting you the other night. Are you sure you're in the right place?"

"I'm pretty sure," she said. "I checked the class list on the office window. Sadie Lineman."

Ah. She was right. Hannah remembered seeing that last name on the roster. Though Sadie looked more like an injured bird than she did like a lineman.

"Welcome, Sadie," she said. "You're a little early, so—"

"Yeah," Sadie said. "Sorry about that. 'S just that no one else was up this morning. I wasn't sure how long it would take me to walk here, and since there wasn't anyone to ask, I just got ready and left the house. But now I know. So I won't be this early again. Unless you need help?"

She nodded toward the stack of packets in the crook of Hannah's arm. Hannah's mind flashed on an image of packets on desks, placed haphazardly. She cringed, and hated herself for it.

"Have you had breakfast?"

"Nope. I think my uncle ate the rest of the cereal last night."

"You could go down to the cafeteria and get something," Hannah said.

"Can't," Sadie said. "My aunt and uncle haven't signed me up for the food program, and I haven't got any money."

She nodded, now, as if to confirm she was speaking the truth. Her eyes darted around the room: to the white board, the book shelves, Hannah's desk.

"Would you like a granola bar?" Hannah said. "I have one in my purse. I don't want you to start the day off hungry."

"Sure," Sadie said. Her eyes landed on her own hands, which were folded together. "Thanks."

She scarfed it down in about three seconds, which wasn't enough time for Hannah to finish laying out the welcome packets. It was, however, enough time for her to come up with a different job for Sadie to do.

"Would you like to choose four books for each table?"

"Um, sure," Sadie said. "Like, any books?"

"Yeah," Hannah said. "I mean, try to get a variety. Some books seem like girl books, and some seem like boy books. So maybe just put one of each, and then a couple of generic books, in each basket."

Sadie nodded, her bony shoulders moving up and down in a shrug. The movement was awkward, Hannah thought. Had this kid been raised by a pack of dinosaurs?

"Thanks," Hannah said. "I appreciate it."

They worked in silence for a few minutes, and Hannah felt relieved that she'd have at least one kind and helpful child in her class.

"How many kids are there?" Sadie wanted to know.

"In our class?"

"Yeah."

"Twenty-six, I think," Hannah said. "Although there are always a few new ones who show up on the first day. So we may grow by a couple."

"Hmm," Sadie said.

"Is it your first year here?" Hannah said. "I don't think I've seen you before."

Again, she'd have remembered, she thought. There was something striking about Sadie.

"Yeah," Sadie said. "I'm living with my aunt and uncle here in Walker, for now." Hannah didn't want to ask what had happened to Sadie's parents, but she didn't have to. "My parents are in prison. My aunt and uncle didn't want to keep me, but I've got no other family.

They agreed because they get money every month. I'm hoping it's just temporary."

"I'm sorry," Hannah said, uncertain of the appropriate response.

"It's okay," Sadie said. "They feed me."

Only, Hannah thought, they didn't, because Sadie hadn't had breakfast. And food certainly wasn't the only thing a child needed. She needed longer shorts, for one. And a comb.

"What else can I do?" she asked. "Got any pencils to sharpen, or anything?"

Hannah hadn't planned on sharpening pencils just yet, but she handed Sadie an unopened box and Sadie went to work. Maybe she could be Hannah's designated helper. There was always one student who was reliable and loved to do little jobs.

Everything changed when the classroom filled up. Sadie became quieter and more withdrawn, and sat at her desk with her hands clasped together and her shoulders hunched. One of the other girls assigned to her table introduced herself, and Sadie made about a millisecond's worth of eye contact before resuming her strange posture.

The morning went smoothly, and Hannah was grateful to have school to focus on. She threw herself into the ice breaker activities she'd planned, only thrown slightly off-kilter when Sadie refused to participate, crossing her arms and looking at the floor. Normally, Hannah would coax reluctant, shy students into participating, but Sadie seemed to have a hard edge, one Hannah wasn't sure she should push. So she skipped over her and carried on, pleased when the kids lined up neatly to head down to morning recess.

Well, all of them except Sadie, who straggled behind when the line wound out and around the side of the building.

"It's recess," Hannah said. "Don't you want to go play?"

"Nah," Sadie said. "Isn't there something I can do in here?"

Hannah looked around. There wasn't, not really.

"I'm sorry," Hannah said. "You've already helped me so much. Why don't you go on out to the playground and get some energy out? It's a beautiful day."

"I don't want to," Sadie mumbled. "Can I just stay in here? You won't even notice me."

"I mean," Hannah said. "I guess you can. I just thought you'd want to go outside. Fresh air and all that."

"I don't," Sadie said.

She looked like she might cry. Hannah felt a surge of empathy so strong her own throat closed. "Why not?" she said to Sadie. While she waited for an answer, she busied herself straightening her desk, which was already pretty tidy.

"I don't really like kids, Ms. Bradley," she said. "Or, I should say, kids don't really like me."

Hannah didn't look up. She knew eye contact could kill a conversation before it even got started.

"You seem pretty likable to me."

"Do I?"

"Yeah. Look how helpful you've been already this morning, just since you've been here."

"Yeah," Sadie said. "Good point. Which is why you should let me stay inside instead of going out to recess."

This was interesting.

"Okay," Hannah said. "At least for today. But you've got to sit down and read a book, okay?"

Sadie nodded, and sure enough, Hannah didn't hear from her again until the rest of the class came back. She'd had troubled students before, kids with mysterious backgrounds who took some time to emerge from their shells. Maybe she'd make Sadie her project this year. Step one, she thought: find a student to mentor her.

Tuesday and Wednesday, Sadie asked to stay inside at recess. She wore the same outfit to school that she'd worn on Monday, and Hannah wondered if she had any other clothes. She'd have to ask the school nurse if she had any in Sadie's size.

Meanwhile, Hannah observed her class with a mentor in mind, and by the time the final bell rang on Wednesday, she had a candidate and a plan.

Thursday morning, she called the candidate—a girl whose older brother she'd taught several years ago—up to her desk.

"Lily," she said. "I need your help."

Lily's big brown eyes widened a little, and she nodded. "Okay, Ms. Bradley. What can I do?"

She already loved this kid.

"I am going to ask you a big favor, Lily. And it's because I've seen how kind and friendly you are, here in the classroom. There's a student in our class who is struggling to make friends. Do you think you could introduce her around, kind of take you under your wing? Make her feel comfortable?"

Now, Lily's eyes flicked over to the desk where Sadie sat.

"Um," she said.

"I know," Hannah said. "I'm asking a lot. But she's new here, and she's having a hard time meeting people. I think she's just really shy, you know?"

Lily nodded, slowly. "Okay."

"Okay?"

"What do you want me to do?"

Hannah released a sigh. "Thank you so much. Could you just invite her to spend recess with you and your friends, to start?"

Now Lily glanced to the other side of the classroom, where her best friend, Reagan sat. Reagan was one of Tanner Lucas's nieces, blessed with the Lucas charm. She'd have been another good candidate for Sadie's mentor, but Hannah worried that in addition to the Lucas charm, Reagan might have Tanner's tendency to come on too strong. Lily must have decided Reagan would approve of (or at least tolerate) this arrangement, because she finally said, "I guess so."

"I can't tell you how much I appreciate it," Hannah said. "I think Sadie just needs a little extra kindness."

Lily, looking a bit reluctant and a bit resolved, nodded and turned away.

"Lily?" Hannah said before she'd started walking. "Thank you."

"You're welcome."

It wasn't a flawless plan; Sadie refused to go out to morning recess or lunch recess that day. But with some gentle sweet-talking, Lily and her friends persuaded her to join them Friday at lunch. She followed them out of the classroom, giving Hannah one last sad, wistful look before crossing the threshold and moving out into the sunshine.

Relieved and hopeful, Hannah pulled out her own lunch—a chicken salad sandwich and a diet cola—and ate alone.

CHAPTER FOUR

FOR THE FIRST time ever in her teaching career, Hannah dreaded Friday night. She'd managed to spend almost all of her waking hours at work this week, but now she had no excuse but to go home and face her family.

Still angry at Mama, and also humiliated at the prospect of facing her sisters, she didn't want to talk to any of them. She wished she could just lock herself in the bedroom and stay there. But she'd promised Margaret that tonight she'd start cooking samples for the wedding: appetizers, main dish options, and dessert.

So there she was in the kitchen, making meatballs, her hands submerged in a mixture of beef and Italian sausage and spices, when Tanner Lucas walked in.

"What're you making?"

"Meatballs." As soon as she said the word, "balls," her face grew hot. She felt like her pre-teen self again.

"That's a pretty fancy dinner for a Friday night," he said. "I always like to keep it simple. You know, throw some steaks and potatoes on the grill, open a cold beer, and relax in the back yard."

"I usually like to keep it simple, too," she said. "But I promised Margaret I'd make samples for the wedding. I'm thinking these could be a good appetizer. You know, put 'em all on a tray, stick a toothpick in each one? Easy eating."

"I like it," Tanner said. "What else are you making tonight? Need a sampler?"

Normally, she'd ask her mom and sisters to sample, but they were gone when she got home. Probably off doing something wedding related. Hannah sighed and kept mixing.

"Sorry," Tanner said. "I was just finishing up. I'll get out of your hair. I came in to talk to Sarah. She around?"

"It's not that," Hannah said. "I *could* use a sampler, actually. My usuals aren't here."

Now she began rolling the mixture into balls, which she put onto the cookie sheet she'd set out.

"Then why the sigh?"

"I don't know," Hannah said, even though she did know. Not that she could tell Tanner. "It's just that it already feels late, and these aren't even close to ready. And I have so many dishes to cook."

"It's only four-thirty," Tanner said. "And what else do you have to cook?"

"I was going to make some mini quesadillas, and some homemade salsa for the nacho bar. I have some meat to grill. For the tacos. It's been in the marinade since this morning. And don't forget the cakes. I wanted to make two different kinds."

"Which kinds?"

"Vanilla—I know it sounds boring, but I have this really rich recipe Margaret loves—and a lemon poppyseed."

"Why don't I help you?"

Hannah froze, a meatball between her palms.

"Help me? You know how to cook?"

Tanner's eyes crinkled at the corners. "Now, Hannah. Of course I know how to cook. My mama didn't raise a hooligan."

"I didn't mean that," Hannah said. Why did being around Tanner Lucas turn her into a spluttering maniac? "I only meant, you're in construction. You work with your hands."

Here, her face turned beet red again. She could feel it.

"I do," Tanner said. "And I work with them in the kitchen, too. I could start grilling the meat for you."

"Don't you have something better to do?"

Open mouth, extract foot.

Tanner laughed out loud.

"Only go home and do the same to my own meat. On my own grill. With my own beer. Got a beer?"

"Well, yes. I think I do," Hannah said. "In the fridge. Grab me one, too, if you don't mind."

"I don't," Tanner said.

"Are you sure you don't mind cooking my meat?"

Now there was a definite twinkle in Tanner's eye. "I don't mind at all," he said. "Not at all."

He pulled out the beers and opened them. He set one on the counter next to Hannah's workstation and she inhaled what she realized was his post-work scent: all outside and sawdust and sweat. She picked up her beer, took a good long drink. Tanner winked at her and did the same.

He went back to the fridge. "Is this it, right here? Blue glass baking dish?"

"Yeah, that's the steak," Hannah said, "and the chicken's in the orange plastic dish next to it."

He got down the dishes and set them on the counter. "I'll just fire up the grill."

Hannah nodded. "Thank you. Really. It means a lot."

Once he'd gone outside she washed her hands and popped the tray of meatballs into the preheated oven. What was he doing, here? What was *she* doing, letting him help her? She didn't even *need* help, she thought as she watched him through the window. But the truth was, she wanted help. Tanner started to make his way back inside, and Hannah jumped away from the window and picked up her beer, doing her best to look nonchalant.

"I'll just give the grill a few minutes to heat up," he said as the screen door banged shut behind him.

Everything happening in that moment—a man helping with the cooking, coming in from outside so casually, as if he were always here, walking right back into the kitchen and picking up his beer before leaning against the counter next to her—represented everything Hannah had always told herself she didn't want.

But the ease of this, the camaraderie, brought her to a realization: she *did* want this.

She wanted a partner (someone besides her mother), someone with whom to drink a beer on a Friday night, with whom to sample meatballs, maybe sit outside on the porch.

But she couldn't have it. Not now. She was approaching forty, for goodness' sake. No one would want her—especially not someone as eligible as Tanner Lucas.

Now, he took the covers off the baking dishes, and gave a long whistle. "Smells good, Hannah Bradley. Smells real good."

Unsure whether his drawl was genuine or part of an act, she gave a little laugh. "Why, thank you, Tanner Lucas. I appreciate the compliment."

She could feel the beer going to her head. At least, she hoped it was the beer. She also hoped the weird fluttery sensation in her core was unrelated to this conversation.

"What are you going to work on," Tanner said, "now that I've got the meat under control?"

"I suppose I should make the salsa, since the oven's occupied."

Tanner nodded. "I'd be happy to sample that for you, when you're done."

Was it just her imagination, or was he leaning a little closer to her than usual?

She gave her head a little shake. "Salsa's not one of my specialties, so I'll definitely need your feedback."

"Can't wait to give it," he said.

Then he grabbed the two meat dishes and headed for the door. Hannah, hoping to open it for him, rushed after him, a bit like one of the hens zigzagging toward the feeder to beat the others. She gave herself a silent reprimand for checking out the way his ass looked in his jeans as she passed him. Then, with no little amount of relief, she flung the door open and sucked in the fresh outside air. Tanner passed by, and gave her a nod of thanks, and, she thought, a knowing look.

"Want your beer?" she said before closing the door.

"That'd be nice," he said.

She retrieved it and set it on the table next to the grill as he put down the dishes and opened the grill cover. Quickly, she scuttled back inside, only to come face-to-face with Margaret.

Her seeing eye dog, Duke, gave a little start, and Margaret stopped.

"It's Hannah," Hannah blurted out.

"I could tell from your perfume," Margaret said. "And from the flirtatious sound of your voice coming through the open door. 'Why, you're welcome for the beer, Tanner Lucas, you sexy beast.'"

Hannah was grateful Margaret couldn't see her starting to sweat.

"I did *not* say that."

"Maybe not in words …" she said. "And thanks for offering. I'll take a beer, too."

Hannah snapped her mouth closed and retrieved a beer for Margaret. Realizing her own was almost empty, she grabbed another one for herself, too. "Want to sit at the counter while I work on the salsa?"

Margaret did, without answering, and Hannah pressed the cold bottle into her hand.

"That marinade smells delicious," she said. "Maybe you should quit teaching and become a chef or something."

"Nah," Hannah said, although she was pleased her sister thought so. "I love teaching too much. But cooking for your wedding is definitely exciting."

"And stressful," Margaret said. "Are you sure you don't want me to hire a caterer? When I first asked you about cooking, I didn't realize how stressful it would be."

"I wouldn't hear of you hiring a caterer," Hannah said. She'd gotten out the salsa ingredients—tomatoes, onion, jalapeños, lime juice—and started chopping. "Besides, this is good personal development for me."

Just then, the door opened, and Tanner stuck his head in. "Do you have a platter I can put this stuff on? Oh, hey, Margaret."

"He-ey," Margaret said, in a singsongy voice reminiscent of their teenage years.

"I'll bring it right out," Hannah said.

Fortunately, Margaret waited until he was gone to make her next comment: "So, I heard Tanner's your taste-tester."

Hannah rolled her eyes. "He volunteered himself. It wasn't my idea."

"I think he wants to taste stuff, you know, besides your cooking."

"Margaret!"

"What? I *do*. Think he does."

Hannah didn't answer, and Margaret said, "Hannah, are you okay?"

"Of course. What do you mean?"

"I mean," Margaret said, "about finding out you have, you know, a dad."

"I've known since I was five that I have a dad."

Margaret sighed, with emphasis, and Hannah immediately felt guilty.

"Don't take that big sister tone of voice with me," Margaret said. "You know what I'm asking. We all knew you had a father. It's biology.

But since you're forcing me to be specific, here, what I'm asking is, do you want to talk about any of it? Do you want to talk about how Mama Katherine didn't even tell your father you exist, or how she never told you who he was, and that he's probably still alive? Do you want me to help you find him? Do you want to talk about your, you know, *feelings* about all of this?"

Hannah sighed, with emphasis.

"I have so many feelings about all of this, I don't even know where to start," Hannah said. She leaned one hip up against the counter and crossed her arms. Then she remembered her new beer, and took a deep swig of it. "I'm angry. I'm angry at Mama for not telling my father that he had a child, and for not telling me that my father was out there, somewhere. When I was older, a teenager I guess, I used to imagine who my dad was, and the various scenarios that would explain his absence. Maybe he was famous, you know? In a band or something. And he and Mama met at some concert and had sex backstage and never spoke again. Or maybe he was a hero. You know, a soldier who died in a tragedy. Like a helicopter crash or an explosion. Or maybe she didn't even know who my father was. Not that I ever thought she was promiscuous. But it was an explanation."

Hannah examined the label on her beer. "I don't know. But never once, in a million years, would I have guessed that she simply kept my father and me a secret from one another. That's almost inconceivable to me."

"Me, too," Margaret said.

"So there's that," Hannah said. She set down her bottle and resumed chopping. "And then there's the humiliation. I mean, I'm so *embarrassed*. All along, I trusted her. I figured she had her reasons for not telling me who my dad was, even when I asked questions. Remember when I was in eighth grade and that mean girl, Janessa Jovial, was pestering me about it? And I wanted so badly to be able to answer her, to tell her I did have a dad. But Mama was tight-lipped. Then Sarah—my own sister— finds out before I do. I mean, it's humiliating."

"But you didn't know," Margaret said. "That would be like me being embarrassed about losing my vision. Neither of us had control in either of those situations. There's nothing to be embarrassed about."

"I see what you're saying," Hannah said. "But I went along, so naive, thinking my life was so wonderful. You know? Now I know that was an illusion. My life is a lie."

As she'd spoken, her chopping had become jerky, the knife slamming down on the cutting board with rapid, even *thunk* sounds.

"You're gonna lose a finger," Margaret said, almost under her breath.

The door creaked on its hinges as Tanner came back inside. "Platter?"

Hannah wondered how much he'd overheard. "Sorry. Coming right up."

Thinking it was probably good timing, she set down the knife, a bit too hard, and then retrieved the platter from the corner cabinet. When she brought it outside, she was surprised to see a bit of warmth in Tanner's expression.

"Thank you," he said, taking it from her.

The way he leaned in, just a little, maintaining eye contact, made it seem like he wanted to say something. But he didn't, and Hannah didn't wait for him to work up the courage. Instead, she walked right back inside and picked up her knife.

"Wow," Margaret said. "You still seem angry."

"Sure am," Hannah said. Then she set down the knife. "Sorry. Do you think Tanner heard what we were just saying?"

"Did he say so?"

"No, but when I took the platter out there, he looked all, I don't know, soft around the edges or something. Like one of those soft-focus filters they used during love scenes in old movies."

"Huh," Margaret said. "Maybe he did."

"Great." She picked up the knife again and began chopping, more gently this time.

"Why don't you talk to Mama Katherine about it?"

"I need to simmer down, first," Hannah said.

"I'll say," Margaret said. "And put that knife away before you do."

"Do you think it would be weird if I tried to find him?"

There was a beat of silence. Hannah thought maybe Margaret didn't know who she was talking about, and just as she took a breath to explain, Margaret said, "I can understand your wanting to. But if you do go down that path, I think you have to be prepared for whatever you uncover."

Hannah hadn't thought of that. She'd assumed her father would be overjoyed to learn about her existence—that he'd welcome the opportunity to meet her and get to know her. But what if he didn't? What if, like her, he was angry? But wouldn't his anger be directed at Mama? Or, what if he had a whole different family?

"You're right," she said, then. "I guess I'll have to think about it."

Tanner came back through the screen door, the platter piled high with steak and chicken.

"You know what else you've got to think about?" he said. "How to mass produce this steak. You could make millions. It's delicious."

"Fortunately, you're invited to the wedding," Margaret said, "and since you're building our marital abode, you can be first in line for the steak. After Ethan and me."

"Good logic," Tanner said.

"Thank you so much for grilling that," Hannah said. She was about to send him on his way—he'd spent way longer than usual at the house and was probably anxious to get home. But he waltzed into the kitchen, set the platter on the counter, and then grabbed a clean knife off the drying rack.

"No problem," he said. "I'll let it rest a few minutes, and then, what, just slice it up? Small pieces for tacos, right?"

Hannah felt Margaret look up at her, awaiting a response in that way sisters do. Margaret was expecting Hannah to turn him down. If Hannah accepted his help, Margaret would surely assign some sort of attraction-related feelings that acceptance. And there was no attraction, here.

"Tanner," Hannah said, and he turned toward her, his body language suggesting he was afraid of what she might say. "Why are you being so nice?"

"Why not?" he said. "I mean, weddings are special occasions, and I couldn't be happier about Margaret and Ethan tying the knot. They're both great people. I'm glad to help."

"Yeah," Hannah said, slowly. "But you despised me in college."

He looked genuinely surprised for the briefest moment. Then he turned away, picked up the knife, and began slicing the steak.

"I *despised* you?" he said.

"Sure did," Margaret said. "Hannah used to come home from class, just spittin' mad because you'd said something or other during a class discussion."

"She did?"

"Sure did," Margaret said. "She was fuming. Night after night."

Hannah could see Margaret's amusement growing. Margaret and Sarah, and even Mama, had always thought Tanner had a thing for her. They'd always told her he needled her because he found her attractive. And Hannah had always disagreed. Who'd act that way because they actually *liked* someone? Seemed to her he hated her. And when she'd told Donny as much after he hired Tanner to build the new houses, Donny had gotten a funny look on his face—like he knew the punchline to a joke and was just bursting to reveal it, but couldn't. He'd muttered something about Tanner being the best builder in town and the best man for the job, and then he'd walked away. And Tanner probably *was* the best. Hannah had heard his name come up over and over again—with her co-workers, parents of her students, people at the grocery store.

"It was that year we had philosophy together, wasn't it?" Tanner said.

So he knew exactly what they were talking about. Finally, she'd be vindicated. He was about to admit that she'd driven him crazy.

"Sure was," Hannah said. "Philosophy one-oh-one."

He chimed in, and they both said, "With professor Mort Lundenstein."

Tanner stopped slicing meat and looked at her, letting their eye contact simmer for a minute before he said, "You drove me crazy."

Hannah nodded, and a victorious feeling started to spread throughout her torso. "I knew it! You drove me so—"

"I don't think you're catching my meaning," he said. "Seeing you all wound up like that, arguing your point, turned me on. Big time."

Well. That wasn't what she expected. Judging by the triumphant, I-told-you-so look on Margaret's face, it was exactly what *she'd* expected. Hannah scooped the chopped tomatoes into a bowl and quickly started chopping the onions.

"Fortunately," Tanner said, "I've outgrown that."

"Thank goodness," Hannah said, something like relief (and a little like disappointment, too) flowing through her body. "Because that would be awkward."

"Now just being around you turns me on." Hannah dropped the knife. Margaret chuckled. Tanner shrugged, resumed slicing, his movements measured. "It does. But I've matured. I've decided to try a different tactic than I did all those years ago. Now, I'm just going to be nice. And we'll see how it goes."

"I don't think—" Hannah said, and Tanner said, "Don't worry. You'll come around."

CHAPTER FIVE

It was late afternoon Sunday when Mama finally approached Hannah. Just as she had done ever since Hannah was a little girl, she gave her a couple of days to stew. She waited until Hannah was immersed in an activity and she sauntered up, effectively cornering her. At the moment, Hannah was inside the chicken coop, collecting eggs.

John Wayne sat in the doorway, pointy ears on alert, bright eyes watchful, following every movement of the hens as they scuttled to a fro in a little pack. Now, Mama stood behind him, and stroked his head. He gave her hand a quick lick before laser-focusing on the birds again.

"Can we talk?"

"I'd rather not," Hannah said. Then, of course, she instantly felt guilty. "I'm sorry, Mama. I'm just still angry, that's all."

"I can tell," Mama said. "You've been stalking around here, mad as a wet hen, and I don't blame you."

She was almost done with the eggs, and then she'd be forced to talk to Mama. She took her time.

"Would you be willing to listen to my explanation?" Mama said.

"I guess," Hannah said, although she was thinking it didn't really matter what Mama said—she'd still kept Hannah and her father from one another for years.

"When I left your father—Philip—I was in mourning. Our son had just died, and it was my fault."

Hannah could understand why Mama felt like their son's death was her fault. She knew it wasn't, but she decided not to get into that discussion at the moment. She just didn't have the heart to try to assuage Mama's guilt.

"I didn't know I was pregnant. We hadn't been intimate in what felt like forever, so the possibility wasn't even on my mind. All I wanted was a fresh start. When I realized I was, I thought about reaching out to Philip, telling him about the baby, asking if he thought we could start over. But then I thought about moving back to California, back to the orchard, and I knew I couldn't do it. I couldn't bear to be there, in the place where our baby died."

Hannah closed the lid on the last nesting box, and turned to face Mama.

"Couldn't you have asked him to come here?"

Mama shook her head. "He'd never leave those orchards. It was in his blood."

"But you didn't even give him the option."

"No," Mama said. "I didn't."

John Wayne came toward Hannah, sniffing the egg basket like he always did.

"But, why not?"

"I don't know, Hannah. I honestly can't say. This was well before you were born. I hadn't met you yet, so I didn't have an actual human to think about. I hadn't yet seen your father in you: your dimples, the color of your eyes, the way you eat your cereal."

"But then you did."

"Yes, then I did. And then I was even more terrified to call him. By the time you were born, I'd had months to tell him about you. He'd want to know why I hadn't. And I didn't have a good explanation. Grief does crazy things to people, Hannah."

Hannah nodded. "Grief did crazy things to you. But that was *your* grief. And you let it do crazy things to *me*. And to Philip. That hardly seems fair."

"It wasn't fair," Mama said. She busied herself, uncovering the bale of straw and taking out handfuls, tossing them onto the floor of the coop as she spoke. "And I know that, now. As time passed, it became easier and easier not to reach out to him. I had myself convinced that it was the best possible situation, for all of us. It seems silly, now, but—"

"Silly's not the word I'd use," Hannah said.

"You're right," Mama said. "Anyway. It became so … big. And it felt like there was no going back."

"Just one phone call?"

Mama sighed, heavily, and again Hannah noticed how frail she looked. She'd covered the straw and was now twisting a dish towel in both hands. Her knuckles protruded. When had her skin become so papery? Hannah didn't feel like her anger was wrong or misdirected or even out of place, but she suddenly wondered if it was necessary. Maybe she should just skip the anger and go straight to forgiveness.

Maybe. But she wasn't quite ready. Not yet.

"I could have made one phone call," she said. "And I didn't. And I'm so sorry, Hannah. I really am. I wish I'd called him right away, as soon as I knew about you. I wish I'd called him the moment you were born. I wish I'd called him the night before your first day of kindergarten, or the night you got your period. My God, I wish I'd called him when you came home from college, hot as could be over Tanner Lucas. I would have said to him, then, 'Phil, he's the one. Mark my words.' I wish I could have called him when Sarah and Margaret came to live with us, or when Amelia was born. Or that time when you were in fifth grade and you got second place in the spelling bee. I wanted you to win so badly. I wish I'd called him when you asked me about that stupid father-daughter dance. But I didn't. I don't have the words to express my regret about making the decision to not call him. I made that decision over and over and over. All I can say is, I thought I was doing what was right. And now I know I wasn't. And again, I'm sorry."

Hannah could hear the truth in Mama's words, the anguish. She could also feel the ache in her own body.

At the moment, all she could do was nod and brush past her mother. She headed straight inside to wash the eggs and put them away. When she glanced out the window a few minutes later, she saw Mama standing in the same spot outside the coop, still twisting the towel in her hands.

In what she knew was some strange bond between mother and child, she felt her gut twist. She wanted, more than anything, to walk back outside and wrap her arms around Mama's shoulders, to offer forgiveness or, at the very least, comfort.

Instead, though, she dried the eggs and put them in the refrigerator. Then she walked right out the front door, down the driveway, and along the dirt road that led to the highway. She knew she'd be back in time for dinner—wasn't she always there for dinner?—but she needed time, alone, to think.

Still, no matter how far she walked, how many times she tried to distract herself by noticing the cloud formations or the way the leaves shimmered in the breeze, she couldn't stop seeing the image of Mama, standing there in the yard, twisting that towel.

———

MONDAY MORNING, Sadie Lineman showed up at Walker Elementary early again: thirty minutes before students were officially allowed on campus.

"Good morning," Hannah said when Sadie walked through the classroom door. Again, Hannah noticed the dark pouches underneath her eyes, the grease in her hair, the dirt under her fingernails.

"Morning," Sadie said.

"It's—"

"Early," Sadie said. "I know. I'm sorry. I said I wouldn't come this early any more, but I was bored at home, so…"

"So here you are," Hannah said.

Sadie shrugged. "Here I am."

She was wearing a different outfit today, too-short jeans with a too-big t-shirt. Hannah's heart did an involuntary clutch, and her throat tightened. She imagined Sadie in a dingy bedroom, sorting through this weird assortment of clothes, trying to find something the other kids wouldn't make fun of.

"Did you eat breakfast?"

Sadie shook her head.

Her chest tight, Hannah said, "You know what? I'll get you breakfast. Okay? I think the choices today are yogurt parfait or muffin and eggs."

Sadie shrugged again. "I thought it was, like, *against the rules* for teachers to get breakfasts for kids."

Her scorn indicated she'd heard that before. It was true: Hannah would be breaking the rules by getting breakfast for Sadie. But there were rules, and then there was doing the right thing. She could hardly let this girl skip breakfast every day.

"Have you ever had a yogurt parfait?" she said.

"I don't know. What's a parfait?"

In the end, they settled on the muffin and eggs, and Sadie wolfed it down within mere seconds of Hannah returning to the room.

"How's it going with the other girls?" Hannah asked. Sadie pressed her index finger against the surface of her desk to pick up stray muffin crumbs, which she scraped onto her bottom teeth. "Are you enjoying hanging out with them?"

"I mean, we don't really 'hang out,'" Sadie said. "We walk down to the playground together and go our separate ways."

Hannah certainly hadn't expected the girls to be best friends or anything, but she'd expected more than this. She'd thought Lily and Reagan would at least include Sadie in whatever they did at recess.

"Did something happen?"

"No," Sadie said.

"Then why don't you hang out?"

"I don't know. I mean, we're not exactly, like, the same kind of people, are we?"

"Aren't we all the same kind of people?" Hannah said. "Humans?"

"You know we're not. I'm old enough that you don't have to pretend, Ms. Bradley. I know we're not all the same. Girls like Lily and Reagan, they come from these perfect families with these perfect parents and perfect siblings. Their moms make their lunches and comb their hair in the morning. Their dads take them to stupid father-daughter dances and teach them how to fish. They go on vacation. Did you know Lily's family just got back from California? They went to the beach. 'It was lovely, *dahling*. Just lovely.' That's what Lily said."

Even though this conversation was making her way to cry, Hannah chuckled a little at Sadie's impression of Lily.

"You know," she said. "I grew up in what I thought was the perfect family. At first, it was just my mom and me. Then, we adopted my sisters. Sarah and Margaret. And we lived on this perfect little farm, with chickens and a huge garden and a creek and a tire swing. My mom made our lunches and combed our hair. We vacationed."

"Sounds pretty perfect. Didn't you have a dad?"

"Ah," Hannah said. "That's the thing. So I grew up thinking my life was perfect. If I ever questioned why I didn't have a dad, or, more accurately, why he wasn't in the picture, my curiosity didn't last long. After all, I had the perfect life, right? And secondly, my mom shut me down every time I asked about it. Him. Whatever."

Anger again. Hannah closed her eyes, took a deep breath, and continued. "And then I recently found out that I did have a dad. I mean, I always knew."

"Obviously," Sadie said, and Hannah felt like this little girl might be wise beyond her years.

Then, she found herself confiding in her. The words just tumbled out: "But, I mean, my mom was married to my dad, and then they split up, and she moved away before she even realized she was pregnant. And she never told him about me. Never. Not once, in forty years."

"You're forty?"

"Yeah, I'm forty. And I am just now finding out that this illusion I had of living a perfect life was a lie."

"Was it really, though?"

That was an interesting question. Was Sadie talking about Hannah's life being perfect, or that perfect life being a lie? And what was Hannah doing, having this conversation with a ten-year-old? One of her students?

"I don't know," Hannah said. Then, she surprised herself by saying exactly what Mama would: "And I guess that's a conversation for a different day. The bell's going to ring any minute."

Sadie got up and threw her breakfast tray in the trash. "Thank you for breakfast. And, well, maybe your mom just didn't know how to tell your dad, you know? I mean, think about it. That's pretty awkward. 'Hey, Mr. Bradley? I know we just split up, and I moved away, and we didn't know this, but we're expecting!'"

Again, Hannah laughed. "You might be onto something. Here, hand out this worksheet, will you?"

The second week of school wore on much like the first. Hannah's students settled into their routine, and she did, too. Every day at recess, Sadie walked down to the playground with Lily and Reagan, and came back up alone. But she slowly began to emerge from her shell: she stood up a little straighter and smiled a little more often. She didn't do anything wild and crazy, like raise her hand to answer questions or volunteer to read aloud. She mostly tried to blend in. Which, Hannah thought, must be difficult with all the weird outfits.

When Hannah talked with the school nurse, Tracy, about it, Tracy said, "Did you ever consider it's just her style? You know kids these days."

"No," Hannah said. "I honestly never did. And if it is her style, then I'm adding fashion to the curriculum this year."

"Look," Tracy said. "I don't have many clothes in those bigger sizes, but I'll keep her in mind if I get some in. And I say, if hers aren't soiled, let her wear them. Maybe she's starting a new trend."

When Hannah wasn't worrying over Sadie, she thought about her father. Philip. She wondered what he was like, which of his characteristics he's unknowingly passed on to her.

The dimples, obviously. Sarah had mentioned those when she was reading that journal. But what about the other things? What about her love of spicy foods, and the way she cocked her head to the right when she was trying to understand something complicated? What about her being left-handed?

The idea of reaching out to him, or, at the very minimum, looking him up to see whether he was still alive, sat at the back of Hannah's mind, present in the way the star of a live Broadway show is present: standing hidden behind a heavy velvet curtain just before the show begins. But every time that idea stepped into the spotlight, she experienced a kind of fear she'd never known. She was afraid he'd reject her, or, possibly worse, that he'd be indifferent. What if he was angry at her, for not seeking him out sooner? After all, he didn't even know she existed. But she, of course, knew she had a father. Why hadn't she pushed Mama harder for an answer? If Sarah hadn't found that journal, would Mama ever have told Hannah who her father was?

Not that it mattered, she reminded herself innumerable times. She knew, now. Which meant the ball was in her court.

Friday morning, Hannah heard the sounds of construction crews arriving: the rumbling of truck engines, the beeping of the back-up signal, shouted directions. She came outside to leave for work, and was surprised to see a crane parked next to the huge stack of roof trusses on Sarah and Donny's property.

Tanner came sauntering over, his travel mug in one hand and a clipboard in the other. He looked freshly shaven and, dare she say, handsome.

"Morning," he said. The lines at the corners of his eyes crinkled when he smiled.

"Morning," she said. Why hadn't she said, "Good morning"? That was weird. She never dropped the "Good" from that phrase. "Putting on the roof already, huh?"

Obviously, Hannah, she thought.

"Yeah," he said. "We're a little ahead of schedule, but let's keep that between us. You know how it is. Things always come up. We're starting three days early, but I can guarantee we won't finish three days early. I don't want your sisters getting all in a tizzy because they expect a miracle."

"It'll be our little secret," Hannah said. "My lips are sealed."

"Thanks. How's your school year going so far? My sister says Reagan says there's a new girl."

"There is. Sadie." She resisted the urge to fill him in. Men were big-picture creatures. They didn't care about details. "The school year's going well. It's a good group of kids. Including Reagan. She's got that Lucas charm."

"What? There's Lucas charm?"

She hadn't meant to say that. "You know there is." She looked at her wrist, realized she'd forgotten to put on her watch, and said anyway, "Well, I've got to get going. Have a good day."

As if she hadn't had enough on her mind, she thought as she backed the old farm truck down the driveway, now she was going to be thinking about Tanner Lucas and his cleft chin and smiling eyes. Just before she angled the truck onto the road, she glanced up at Tanner, who raised an arm to wave. She waved back.

CHAPTER SIX

THAT EVENING after Mama went to bed, Hannah sat with her sisters in the living room. An open bottle of champagne stood on the coffee table, and each sister had a full glass in her hand.

"Cheers to starting on the roofs," Margaret said, raising her glass.

"Cheers," Hannah and Sarah echoed. They clinked their glasses together and sipped their champagne.

Hannah hadn't even swallowed when Margaret spoke. "I think they're a little ahead of schedule, aren't they? Like, a couple of days, or something? Maybe they'll get done early. That would be amazing. I can't wait to get out of my childhood bedroom. I mean, it's definitely, you know, awesome to stare up at the poster of the New Kids on the Block. But really, I can't wait to live like an adult again. I hope they finish early."

Hannah took another sip of her drink, but didn't answer. It turned out she didn't need to, because Sarah chimed in: "I know, wouldn't that be amazing? I love living in the RV. You know, it's always felt like such an adventure. But there's something to be said for living in a house built on solid ground."

Now, Hannah downed her champagne, forcing herself not to laugh. She surprised herself by saying, "Don't count on it. You know how these things go. Stuff always comes up."

"But Tanner's so amazing," Margaret said.

This time, Hannah did laugh, even as images of the muscles in his shoulders paraded through her mind. Of course, her sisters wanted to know why she was laughing, and her refusal to answer—and her sudden attempt to act serious—only fanned the flames of their curiosity.

"Your lips are twitching," Sarah said. "What aren't you saying?"

The champagne was already making her lightheaded and a little loopy. Not enough that she would break the promise she'd made to Tanner, not to tell her sisters the houses were running ahead of schedule, but enough that she blurted out, "Let's change the subject. Let's talk about why Mama didn't tell me about my father. How about that?"

A stunned silence followed, and then Margaret said, so slowly Hannah knew she was treading carefully, "What do you want to talk about?"

"Well," Hannah said, leaning forward to refill her glass. "Let's talk about how Mama stole any chance I had of getting to know my own father."

"So, I totally understand your anger," Sarah said, "but what if we shifted the focus a bit, here? I mean, how can we move forward from where we are, now? We all know Mama Katherine's getting older. I would hate for you to spend the rest of her life being angry at her. So, what can we do, now? Would it help if you tried to find your dad? If you reached out to him?"

She had a point.

"Honestly, I don't know," Hannah said. "I've thought about it. Nonstop, actually. And all of my childhood fantasies are back out, in full force. Us, finally doing all those father-daughter bonding things, like fishing or playing checkers or having pancakes together."

When she said it out loud, it sounded childish. "But there's another, darker possibility, isn't there? I'm scared. What if he doesn't want to talk to me? What if he's angry at me? What if I don't like him? What if he doesn't like me?"

Margaret held up a hand. "Whoa, sister. Your mind is a runaway train. How about this? What if—well, what if you refill my champagne? And then, what if we grab my laptop and just do a little research. To find out if Philip is still alive."

Hannah felt chills blossom on the back of her neck. "I don't know."

"It's just a little research," Margaret said. "Nothing more. It doesn't mean we have to call him or email him or go riding up to his orchard in California. All it means is we type some words into a search engine, read some results."

Sarah was nodding now, in time with Margaret's words.

"Step one," Margaret said. "Refill my champagne."

She held out her glass, and Hannah stood up to follow instructions.

"Step two," Sarah said. "Refill mine."

Hannah obeyed.

"Now," Margaret said. "You're going to have to get my computer. I could do it, but it will take longer and Duke's asleep."

As if to illustrate this, Duke yipped once, in his sleep, and then started snoring.

"Where is it?" Hannah said, resigned.

She'd seen Margaret like this before—she'd get an idea in her head and she just had to follow it through. She was like a hound on the tail of a fox. Once, when Hannah was in high school—junior year?—Margaret had convinced herself Hannah liked this boy in her biology class, Neal something-or-other. More than anything, Margaret wanted Hannah to write him a note and stick it in his locker. She'd been ruthless, composing the note out loud whenever they were together, rearranging the order of the sections and rephrasing the greeting hundreds of times.

She'd even folded several different sheets of paper in several different ways—a heart, a paper crane, a little envelope—to show Hannah her options. The truth was, Hannah didn't even like Neal. Well, she liked him as a friend, but she didn't *like* him like him (didn't it say something that she couldn't even remember his last name?). But she'd finally written the note anyway, just to get Margaret to let up. What she didn't know was that Hannah had written the note in pencil, and the morning she was supposed to stick it in his locker, she went to the bathroom when they arrived at school, carefully unfolded the note, erased her own signature, and forged Margaret's before re-folding it and joining her sister in the hallway again. Margaret "supervised" Hannah as she slid the note in.

Neither of them ever heard from Neal, at least, not that Hannah knew of. And Hannah never 'fessed up and told Margaret that she'd changed the signature.

Now, though, there was no faking it. First of all, Sarah was here, which meant she'd be looking at the computer screen while Hannah researched. And secondly, Hannah did want to research. At the deepest level of her being, she wanted to know more about her father, the man who'd given her half her genes if nothing else. So she went into Margaret's bedroom and retrieved the laptop.

"Well, fire it up," Margaret said, as soon as Hannah came back and sat down.

Again, Hannah obeyed, and they all sat in silence as the computer booted up.

"What if he's filthy rich and he ends up leaving you a huge inheritance?" Margaret said. "You could finally buy your own place."

Sarah elbowed Margaret.

"What?" Margaret said. "I'm just saying."

"What if she doesn't want to buy her own place?" Sarah said. "And also, he doesn't even know about Hannah. I doubt he's planning to leave her an inheritance."

"Wow, guys," Hannah said. "Your sensitivity is amazing."

"Sorry," they said, in unison.

"So, just open up the internet browser," Margaret said. "Bottom left."

"I know what the internet browser looks like," Hannah said. "What should I search, first? Just his name?"

"Well," Sarah said, sounding a little sheepish. She cleared her throat. "I did type in his name and California, and I didn't have the best results. Obviously, his orchard had a name, but I can't remember it. Maybe type in his name, California, and orchard."

Hannah typed it in and waited for the results to appear. There would be results, right? After all, this was the twenty-first century. Wasn't everyone all over the Internet?

And there he was. Philip Carlisle, Junior. The owner of Golden Delicious Orchard, smiling at Hannah from the top of the search results page. He was Internet-famous enough to have one of those biography-synopses that listed his name, date of birth, and a couple of sentences about his achievements. If the biography-synopsis was correct, Philip was still alive. Hannah's father was a living being, flesh and blood. He was no longer simply an idea.

Hannah zoomed in on the photo. Her breath caught.

"Did you find him?"

Sarah came around to sit next to Hannah and peered over her shoulder.

"Oh my gosh, Margaret, he looks just like her!"

He did, from the dimples to the eyebrows to the cheek bones and the lines of his chin. Unexpectedly, Hannah felt like crying … not only from emotional overload, but also from sadness. He looked old: the creases around his eyes were deep, and the parentheses around his mouth, too.

It was a potent reminder that she'd missed out on most of his life. Even if she met him now—and she still wasn't sure she wanted to—she'd missed out on having a young father who could teach her to play catch, or chase her through the house, or play hide and seek with her.

"Wow," Sarah said, her voice breathy, still filled with awe. "I can't believe it. If we'd ever stumbled across this photo, we'd have known. That's crazy."

Tears made Hannah's vision blurry. Her dad was alive. This meant so many things. It meant answers to all her questions. It meant new questions, an insatiable thirst to find out *everything*.

She clicked on the first search result, a newspaper article with a headline about a new apple variety, and started reading aloud. The article itself wasn't too interesting, but the reporter had quoted orchard owner Philip Carlisle as saying, "This is the best apple I've ever tasted."

Sounded like a canned statement, Hannah thought, but still, she found herself trying to attach personality traits to it. Was it tongue-in-cheek? Did the statement mean Philip was funny? Or serious? Did it mean he liked apples? Of course he liked apples. Or maybe he didn't.

"Imagine being the owner of an orchard and not liking apples," Hannah said.

Sarah looked up at Margaret, and Margaret, as if she could sense it, shrugged. "What else is there?"

Hannah clicked back to the search results. "It doesn't look like there's much."

"Read the list," Sarah said.

Hannah did: "Drought affecting agriculture statewide, new technology keeps pests at bay, bumper crop this fall ..."

She let her voice trail off as she clicked for the next page, where something interesting caught her attention: "Philip Carlisle honored for philanthropic work."

"Ooh!" Margaret said. "Click that one."

Hannah clicked, and quickly began reading the story aloud. It explained how Philip had donated one million dollars—here, Hannah gasped—to a local children's hospital. The reporter quoted Philip as saying that ever since tragedy struck his own family when his son was a toddler, he'd had an interest in helping children. Hannah didn't even know this man, but she knew this story. She knew the anguish Mama had experienced when their first child died, and surely, Philip had experienced it, too.

Again, she tried to attach personality traits, meaning, to the information she found. Did philanthropic work mean Philip was a good person? Or did it mean he wanted a tax write-off? Did the quote about tragedy striking his family show any residual anger toward Mama, for leaving him? And one million dollars? Who had one million dollars to donate?

Not for the first time, Hannah imagined how things would be different for her if she'd grown up with both parents. Now, though, she had some inkling of how the situation might have played out. They'd be filthy rich. If Mama had stayed at the orchard with Philip Carlisle, they'd have all the finest things, certainly. Hannah wondered what his house was like, what kind of car he drove.

When Hannah finished reading, Margaret whistled. "One million dollars," she said, her voice filled with wonder.

"I know what you're thinking right now," Sarah said. "You're thinking, 'I could have grown up as the child of a millionaire.'"

Hannah nodded, and Margaret said, "And *I'm* thinking, we should all show up on Philip's doorstep and ask him to adopt us."

"We should," Sarah said. She sipped he champagne. "So, is that what you're thinking? That you could have grown up the child of a millionaire? I mean, shoot, if he has that much to give away, imagine how he lives."

"Alone," Margaret said. "Alone is how he lives."

"How do you know?" Sarah said. "It's possible he remarried."

"I suppose it is," Margaret said. "Search for that, Hannah. Philip Carlisle wedding. Or something. With that kind of cash, his wedding probably would have been in the newspaper's society pages."

Although Hannah's hands hovered over the keyboard, she didn't type. "I don't know if I really want to know that. If he remarried. I mean, if he did, then …"

"Then what?" Sarah said.

"Then it's almost certain he won't want to hear from me, or have anything to do with me."

"I doubt that's true," Margaret said. "I mean, doesn't every man feel prouder, the more offspring he produces?"

"I have no idea," Hannah said. "But I do know that I'm done researching for tonight."

"But we've just gotten started," Sarah said. "Here, give me the laptop. I'll research, and I'll tell you what I find only if I think you'll want to hear it."

That deal sounded pretty good, so Hannah handed over the computer and relaxed back into the couch cushions.

"What if you find something bad?"

"What could I find that would be bad?"

"I don't know," Hannah said, "Like—"

"Like, 'Philip Carlisle, local orchard owner, arrested for hiring a prostitute,'" Margaret said.

"Exactly," Hannah said. "Something scandalous."

Sarah was silent for a few minutes, typing and clicking, typing and clicking.

"I mean," she said, "We know the name of his orchard now. Golden Delicious. Would you want to look at some pictures? Or maybe even get an address?"

The idea of getting an address settled like snakes writhing around in Hannah's stomach. If she had an address, that meant the orchard was a real place. It meant she could enter a destination into mapping software and get driving directions. Not that she'd want to drive there. Or would she?

"I don't know …" Hannah let her voice trail off, and Sarah's focus remained on the computer screen.

Just imagining having an address and looking at pictures made an entire story unfold in Hannah's mind. Would she call ahead and meet him over the phone? No, that gave him the opportunity to say he didn't want to see her. She'd book a flight to California. And rent a car at the airport. Probably a convertible. Margaret—before she'd lost her vision— used to rent convertibles all the time, and Hannah had always been a little jealous. This was her chance. She'd rent a convertible, put the top down, and drive through California's lush agricultural area and right up to the orchard. She'd park. And then she'd freeze, unable to get out of the car.

But then someone would approach her, and, since the convertible's top was down, there would be a conversation.

"May I help you, Miss?" (The person, a butler, probably, would call her "Miss," because she still looked so young.)

She'd clear her throat and say, "I'm here to see Philip Carlisle. My father."

And then the butler would laugh, because of course Philip Carlisle didn't have a grown daughter.

The film reel stopped.

"Oh, here's something," Sarah said. "Golden Apple Orchard acquires Apple Blossom Orchard."

She clicked and waited, and then began to read to herself. Sarah had never been able to read silently, Hannah remembered now. At least she wasn't saying every word slowly and loudly like she had in first grade. Hannah had always found that annoying: she was older and wiser and had more homework, and Sarah's reading was a distraction.

"Please, read silently," she'd said, countless times.

Finally, Sarah learned to read in a whisper, but even now, her lips moved as she read the article.

"Nothing good, here," she said. "All boring business stuff."

Hannah sighed.

"What's wrong?" Margaret said.

"Let's stop for tonight," Hannah said.

"Hey, did anyone refill your champagne?"

"No," Hannah said. "I thought I should stay sober for this."

"Sarah, give the lady a refill."

"When did you get so bossy?" Sarah said to Margaret.

"I'd do it myself if I didn't think I'd spill everywhere."

Sarah filled Hannah's glass, and Hannah took a gulp.

"That's better," Margaret said. "Now. Where were we?"

Two hours later, the sisters had finished off the champagne and another bottle of wine. They'd looked up photos of Philip Carlisle's orchard, and found the address. And they'd developed a plan for storming Philip's house and demanding a meeting. Hannah, the least drunk out of all of them, didn't foresee actually carrying out that plan. In fact, she decided the best course of action now was to go to bed.

She stood up and stretched.

"I appreciate your enthusiasm," she told her sisters. "But when it comes to actually flying out to California, I'm terrified."

Still, as she brushed her teeth and changed into her pajamas, she realized part of her wanted to carry out the plan. The longing to meet her dad was so strong she could feel it in her body—an energy buzzing around, making her want to run or yell or sing or cry. And part of her didn't want anything to do with him. Her life had been perfect until she found out about him. Why mess with a good thing? Couldn't she just go back to the way it was?

The truth was, she couldn't. The fact that her father was more than an idea, that he was a living, breathing being, changed everything.

———

WHEN HANNAH LEFT the house Monday morning, she was surprised to see men on the roof of Margaret's new house, laying sheets of plywood. Tanner had the wood delivered over the weekend, and although Hannah had heard the trucks coming in and members of the crew having loud conversations as they unloaded, the massive amount of it surprised her.

Tanner was nowhere to be seen, and as Hannah drove to work, she told herself that funny feeling she felt wasn't disappointment. She didn't want to admit to anyone, not even herself, that she had looked forward to saying good morning to him today, that it would have been a nice way to start the week.

She was so immersed in this thought process as she unlocked the school building and went inside that Sadie's presence on the floor outside the classroom door made her jump.

How had she even gotten inside the building? Slipped in behind a janitor, maybe? The girl's knobby knees were pulled up under her chin, her arms were wrapped around her legs, and her head was tilted forward, like she was sleeping. When she heard Hannah approaching, her head snapped up. She looked dazed. Hannah wondered how long she'd been there.

"Well, good morning," Hannah said. "Come on in."

She unlocked the door, and Sadie stood up as if she were stiff.

"How are you today?" Hannah said.

Sadie made a kind of grunting noise, then went to her desk and put her head down.

"Are you okay?"

She made the same grunting noise, then added, in a mumble, "Just tired. I'm just going to take a nap until school starts, okay, Ms. Bradley?"

Hannah shrugged, said, "Okay," and went about setting up the classroom. Sadie's breathing was heavy and even when Hannah left to make copies in the office. When she was done, she took it upon herself to grab Sadie a breakfast before heading back. She was in the same position she'd been in, hands folded on the desk, head on her hands, sleeping like the dead. Hannah put the breakfast tray on the desk next to Sadie's.

The other fourth-grade teacher, Missy Cartwright, walked by, waved, and then backed up when she noticed Sadie. She stood in the doorway, and whisper-yelled, "Who is that?"

"Sadie Lineman," Hannah whisper-yelled back before motioning for Missy to step into the hallway. "She's been showing up early, like *very* early, and very hungry, every day. She's never eaten breakfast, and she's always wearing these weird outfits."

Missy leaned around the doorway to take a look. "Like today?"

"Yes," Hannah said. "You can't see her shorts, but they look like boxer shorts. With stripes. And that godawful yellow sweatshirt. Which not only clashes, but is about five sizes too big and has tons of holes in it."

"Huh," Missy said.

"I know," Hannah said. "I'm completely stumped. She says she lives with her aunt and uncle, but from the looks of it, she's not getting any adult supervision. I mean, her hair is so dirty. I'll bet she hasn't showered in weeks."

"How does she do with the other kids?"

"She does okay. When it's just the two of us, she's outgoing and helpful and chatty. But when the kids show up, it's a whole different story. She's withdrawn, almost antisocial."

"Huh," Missy said again.

"I know," Hannah said again.

"Maybe you should call child services. You know, have someone go to her house and do a welfare check."

"Maybe I should," Hannah said.

"Well, good luck with that," Missy said. "I'm off to make copies. Have a good day."

Back in the classroom, with Sadie snoring away, Hannah's thoughts drifted—again—to Philip and whether she wanted to go meet him. She could ask Margaret to make the call. Margaret was always so charismatic, so good at that stuff. She'd have Philip laughing and wrapped around her finger in no time, and then she'd sweet-talk him into meeting Hannah.

And Hannah could ask him all the questions she'd always wanted to ask her dad: did he like spicy food, or banana milkshakes? Did he drive fast, or tailgate, or did he take his time?

Just before the other students started to trickle in—by now, Hannah knew the first round of students showed up just before the first bell—Hannah roused Sadie with a gentle shake of the arm. When her eyes opened, she looked disoriented, and, Hannah was sad to see, scared.

"I got you breakfast," she said, keeping her voice as calm and soothing as she could.

Sadie blinked a few times, then sat up straight and wiped her mouth with the stained sleeve of her yellow sweatshirt. She didn't make eye contact, but she said, "Thanks," and slid the tray over to her desk.

"The first bell's going to ring in a few minutes," Hannah said.

Sadie, mouth full, nodded.

"Why were you here so early?" Hannah said.

Sadie shrugged and continued eating. As if that was an adequate response.

"Is everything okay?"

Another nod.

"Really?"

Another nod, less decisive this time. Something about this girl made Hannah want to make *sure* everything was okay. Maybe it was her bird-like bone structure, which made her look so vulnerable. Or maybe it was her guarded expression. Or maybe it was how it really seemed like she had nowhere else to go. Or nowhere else she wanted to be. Then inspiration struck.

"Hey, I'm going to be sending out parent-teacher conference forms soon. Do you have any idea what time might work for your aunt and uncle?"

Here, Sadie froze. Her chewing ceased, her posture became rigid, and she put down the piece of French toast she'd been holding. Then, almost as if she'd made a decision, she nodded, just once, swallowed, and said, "I'm not sure, but I'll ask." Then she went back to eating.

"Okay," Hannah said. "Then just take the form home and have them fill it out, okay?"

Sadie nodded. Hannah didn't bother telling her conferences didn't happen until after the first quarter.

At morning recess, she asked if she could stay in, and she refused to answer when Hannah asked her why. Hannah let her, and when the students filed out of the classroom on their way to the computer lab, she called Lily up to her desk.

"Any idea why Sadie doesn't want to go to recess?"

Lily's eyes met Hannah's, then darted away, and then rested on the bright green stapler Hannah kept on her desk.

"No," she said.

"Lily."

She huffed out a breath. "Fine." Her gaze met Hannah's again, and held. "Some kids are making fun of her."

"About what?"

"Want a list? Her hair. It's so dirty. And she smells. And her clothes. And the way she talks."

"How does she talk?"

"Like, one word at a time. People say she's … mental, or autistic."

"Is she nice?" Hannah said.

"I wouldn't say, 'nice,' exactly," Lily said. "She's not mean, if that's what you're asking. But she definitely isn't, you know, *friendly*. There's a word for it. My mom's used it before, about that one teller at the bank."

"The one with the blue hair," Hannah said. "Well, it's teal now, isn't it?"

"Right," Lily said. Then she remembered and held up a finger. "Standoffish. You know? My mom explained it as not unfriendly but not warm and fuzzy. It's not like it's *bad*, Ms. Bradley. It just makes it hard to, you know, talk to her."

"Right," Hannah said. "And now I have to figure out what to do about it. Thanks, Lily. You can head to the computer lab, now."

While her students were gone, Hannah placed a call to the child services hotline.

"I'm worried about one of my students," she told the woman who answered.

As she explained why, lining up all the signs that this little girl wasn't getting what she needed, Hannah wondered if maybe she'd waited too long to call. She didn't have much time to agonize over it, though. Her class was coming back down the hall. She could hear their footsteps squeaking on the vinyl flooring, along with the sounds of a bunch of rowdy kids trying (and failing) to be quiet.

CHAPTER SEVEN

WHEN HANNAH GOT HOME Wednesday and it was still light outside, she was surprised to see that the roofs on both her sisters' houses had shingles. She'd left and come home in the dark Monday and Tuesday, and this milestone was a little shocking. The houses were probably nowhere near complete, but the basic outline of each one was there, framed in with freshly cut lumber: windows and doors and rooms. Members of the crew were still working now, just before five. She could see them between the two-by-fours, hear their hammers and drills as she climbed down from the truck.

And as she shut the driver's door, she saw Tanner coming toward her. She couldn't help but notice that his expression looked like one she'd seen a million times on the faces of her students: he wanted her approval. He was proud of his project and hoping for a compliment.

As her heart beat a little faster at that realization, she thought, Who am I to disappoint him?

"Wow, Tanner," she said. "This is amazing. You and guys are moving along so quickly. You're miracle workers."

"Well, Sarah and Donny helped out. They've been swinging hammers for the past two days. And Margaret's taken over as the job boss. She's set up shop just over there."

He pointed at a camp chair Margaret had situated between the two homes.

"Yes, Margaret's always been very—"

"Bossy." Margaret, coming up to stand next to them, laughed. "You can say it. How's it looking, Hannah?"

"It's looking great, Margaret. No one could have designed it better."

"I thought so. Now, I'll leave you two to it. I've got to get ready for my date with Ethan. Pre-wedding planning."

"Is that what they're calling it these days?" Tanner said. Margaret elbowed him and walked away.

Wow," Hannah said. "It's becoming a real group effort, isn't it?"

"It is," Tanner said.

As they stood in front of the truck, surveying the week's progress, Hannah experienced a strange mix of emotions: excitement for her sisters, and, somewhere in the corner of her consciousness, a little loneliness. On one hand, it was cute that the house-building had turned into a group project. But on the other hand, she felt like she was missing out. And, on the tails of that feeling came resentment: if everyone was helping with the houses, who was helping Mama with the chores?

For the first fifteen years of her career, Hannah had practically worked two jobs. She'd gone to work at Walker Elementary, and then she'd come home and, alongside her mom, taken care of things on the Seedling Homestead. Dawn to dusk, every day. It was exhausting—especially as Mama got older and couldn't do as much—but there hadn't been another option until Donny suggested that he, Sarah, and Margaret move onto the homestead, too. As the idea developed, Sarah and Margaret had promised that Hannah would no longer have to shoulder caring for Mama and the property on her own.

Of course she knew that helping to build the houses was work. It wasn't like they were sitting in the sun, sipping margaritas and eating chips and salsa.

But still.

"Did you happen to notice if anyone weeded the garden today?" she said.

Tanner shrugged. "Didn't notice. I saw your mama outside, but I'm not sure what she was up to."

"Huh," Hannah said. "What about the fruit trees? Did you see anyone watering them?"

She saw an awareness take shape in Tanner's eyes ... he sensed she was implying the chores had been left for her.

"You know," he said. "I don't know. I'm just about done for the day, so I'm going to head out. I've got one more project to check on before I call it quits. Just across town there."

He gestured to the west, to some indistinct location. Then he hightailed it to his truck, climbed in, and backed out, giving his crew members a quick honk and a wave before turning onto the road.

Amused, Hannah felt her lips twitching. So, Tanner Lucas was perceptive. She added that to the growing list of things she liked about him, under "Great eye color," and "Looks good (okay, downright *sexy*) in jeans."

Just as she was collecting her things from the passenger seat of the old farm truck, Sarah and Margaret emerged from the house, arm in arm, chattering away like a couple of birds on a wire. Sarah said something to Margaret, and Margaret laughed as if she'd never heard anything so funny. If Hannah hadn't already been feeling a little left out, that private moment would have done it.

"Oh, hey, Hannah," Sarah said. "You're home early today. How was your day?"

"Fine, thanks," Hannah said. "It's a good thing I'm home early, because it sounds like none of the chores got done."

Her sisters froze, in stride, like they were playing freeze dance. Inwardly, Hannah cringed. Great. She hadn't meant to let her resentment show.

"Just kidding," she said. Now Sarah and Margaret swiveled back around to face her, wearing twin expressions of fear.

"Hannah," Sarah said, slowly. "Are you upset that we worked on the houses instead of doing regular chores?"

"No!" Hannah said. "Of course not. Of course you'd want to work on the houses."

"We did chores Monday and Tuesday," Margaret said, falling into the role of people-pleasing youngest sister, even now. "You just weren't here."

"You're right," Hannah said. "I was just—I've been busy at school. You know. So anyway, I thought I'd come home early tonight and we could do dinner together."

"Well," both sisters said at the same time.

"Donny and I were going to eat at that steakhouse," Sarah said, and Margaret said, "And like I said, Ethan and I were going out to dinner. Wedding planning. We wanted to work on our vows."

"So I guess it's just me and Mama," Hannah said. She infused her voice with false cheer.

Sarah looked over toward the work sites, her eyes wider than usual and her movement exaggerated. "You could ask Tanner to dinner."

"He just left," Margaret said. "Heard his truck pulling out."

"She could call him," Sarah said to Margaret.

"I appreciate both of you looking out for my best—or worst—interests," Hannah said. "But it's fine. I'll just eat with Mama. Have a lovely time, both of you."

"Suit yourself," Margaret said. Then, in unison, her sisters did an about face and walked away.

She carried her work things inside and set them on the dining room table, then washed her hands and started scrubbing potatoes. While she worked, she looked out over the farm, and was surprised to see that everything looked to be in order. From what she could see from her spot at the sink, the garden wasn't overgrown with weeds, the chickens pecked happily in their coop and drank from their waterer, and the ground was damp around each of the flower beds and tree rings. So someone had taken care of the weeds and the hens and the watering.

"Huh," Hannah said. She turned off the sink and set the scrubbed potatoes on the counter.

"Whatcha doing?"

Hannah jumped, then whirled around, hand on her heart.

"You scared me!" she said to Mama, who'd come into the kitchen and leaned a hip against the island.

"Sorry. You must have been lost in thought. I came right in, same as I always do. Figured you'd heard me but still aren't talking to me."

"I didn't hear you," Hannah said. "And I'm talking to you now, aren't I? Anyway, I'm scrubbing potatoes. I thought maybe we could grill them along with the meat."

"I already made dinner," Mama said. "Didn't know you'd be home. You've been coming in so late and the girls had plans, so I made a chicken pot pie earlier. It's in the fridge. Figured if you did come home, I'd heat it up. Otherwise I was fixin' to eat leftovers. Thought we could eat the pot pie tomorrow when everyone's home."

"We can both eat leftovers, if there's enough," Hannah said.

She didn't know why it felt easier to avoid eye contact, but it did, and she turned back around to face the sink, taking her time to dry the potatoes and put them back in the produce basket. Mama waited, not moving or speaking. When Hannah was done, she turned around again and leaned against the counter, arms folded.

"I think there are enough leftovers," Mama said. "If you don't mind a kind of smorgasbord."

"That's fine," Hannah said. Her eyes, with minds of their own, darted around the kitchen in search of something for her to do … a spot to wipe clean, a dish to scrub, a towel to fold. But there was nothing. The counter shone, the dishes were put away, and a single kitchen towel hung neatly from the oven door. This not only left Hannah without a distraction, but also proved that maybe she wasn't as necessary as she'd always thought. Things went along just fine when she wasn't here. Her eyes settled on Mama's.

"We're going to have to make up at some point," Mama said.

"Are we fighting?"

"Well, you're going to have to forgive me," Mama said.

"Am I?"

"We can't go on like this forever."

"Can't we?" At this, Hannah had to laugh, and she did see a little twinkle in her mama's eyes, too. "Okay. We can't. But I'm just so *mad*, Mama."

"I know you are, honey. And I suspect I'm as sorry as you are mad. I wish I'd done things differently. But, fact is, I didn't. So here we are."

"Here we are."

"Shall we eat?"

Just like they'd done countless times, they prepared dinner together, working like two sets of hands on the same body. Mama retrieved plates while Hannah got the leftovers out of the fridge, and they each took a dish and scooped servings onto a plate before Hannah popped the plates in the microwave while Mama got drinks. Then, they carried their food and beverages to the table, sat down at their normal spots, and began to eat. At first, Hannah thought the meal would pass in silence, but then Mama spoke:

"You know, it wasn't easy, raising you alone."

Hannah inhaled to speak, and Mama held up a hand. So Hannah took another bite and waited.

"It was a choice I made, but it wasn't easy. But I think we did okay, didn't we?" She gave Hannah only enough time to nod in response, and then she kept talking. "I taught you how to change the oil on the truck, how to drive a tractor. I taught you how to garden, how to protect the tomatoes from that early frost, the one that comes before Labor Day every year. How to milk a cow and a goat, and make cheese. How to nurture. How to take something broken and make it whole. Our life has been *good*. And that's all any of us can ask for, isn't it?"

Again, Hannah inhaled to answer, but Mama plowed on.

"I know you're angry, and I truly am sorry. But at the same time, I want you to know that I've always done what I thought was best for both of us. For all of us. Sometimes, as the decision maker, you have to do what's best for the whole, the unit. And that's what I've done, all this time. I know, in my heart, that I did the best I could with what I had. I just hope that one day, you'll come to realize that. Now. Don't get me wrong. I know I've made mistakes. If I had a second chance, I might do things differently. But I don't. And that's why I'm asking you to forgive me. I understand that it might take time. And I'm willing to wait."

Now, she lifted her glass, even though it was filled with nothing more than water, and said, "Here's to doing the best we can with what we have. And to forgiveness."

Hannah lifted her own glass and inclined her head. "Cheers."

It was more a stalemate than a truce. But bringing the conflict into the light, acknowledging it, talking it through, made life much more comfortable around the Seedling Homestead.

———

THURSDAY AFTERNOON when the bell rang, the majority of Hannah's students darted out the door, already able to taste that weekend freedom. As always, Sadie took her time, sliding her schoolwork into her backpack, straightening and re-straightening the items in and on her desk. She looked absolutely forlorn. Her cheeks sucked in between her teeth, just slightly. Her blinks were extra-long. She couldn't move any more slowly if she tried.

Another pang of empathy hit Hannah. She knew exactly what Sadie was going through: for the past few weeks, she'd been avoiding her own home. She knew the dread and the tension, that queasy feeling in the stomach. And she felt like a ten-year-old shouldn't have to experience it. That's when the idea struck. Because a lump had formed in her throat, Hannah cleared it.

"Sadie," she said.

Sadie turned toward her, revolving in slow motion, like she was a ballerina in a jewelry box whose mechanisms were wearing out.

"I'm sorry," she said. "I'm almost ready. I just wanted to clean out my desk."

"It's not that," Hannah said. "I'm not in any hurry. I still have some work to do, here."

Then she plowed ahead before she could lose her nerve. She was about to do something unconventional, something of which she wasn't sure her principal would approve. "Actually," she said, "I was wondering. How would you like to come over to my house tomorrow after school? For dinner?"

Sadie didn't respond right away. Her eyes grew rounder, maybe even distrustful. Which meant she'd probably learned kindness was a trap, not to be taken at face value. Hannah plowed on: "We usually do a big family dinner at the end of the week. And while the weather's still warm, we'll probably sit out on the deck. Maybe even roast marshmallows. I should warn you: there won't be any other kids there. My niece is in Arizona at school. Think about it. And, if you want to come, ask your aunt and uncle."

"I want to come," Sadie said.

"Tell your aunt and uncle I'll call them tomorrow to give them the details. I can bring you home afterward."

Sadie nodded once, a quick bob of her head, and then rushed out. Hannah felt herself grinning in response. Sadie's buzzing excitement and her happy energy were contagious.

The next morning when she showed up at school earlier than ever, she announced that she'd asked her aunt and uncle about coming over, and they'd said it was okay. Hannah knew better than to take her word for it, and during first recess, she called the phone number the school had on file. The woman who answered sounded like she'd been sleeping. Deeply, too.

"H'lo?"

"Is this Rita?"

"Depends who's asking." Her voice slurred.

"This is Hannah Bradley, Sadie's teacher."

"Oh." Long pause. Then, "She mentioned you might call."

"Is it all right if she comes to the family dinner at my house this evening?"

She was tempted to offer some sort of explanation: *I invite students every so often*, or, *I'm having a few kids over*, or, *Your niece seems so very sad and lonely.*

"Mmhmm. I told her you didn't have to call," Rita said.

"Well, I didn't want to just take her without giving you a heads up."

"Appreciate it. But to tell you the truth, Miz, what was it? Bard? We wouldn't have noticed, anyway. Sadie usually keeps to herself."

Hannah wasn't sure how to respond, so she said, "Um, okay. Well, thank you so much. I'll have her home by eight or so."

"Mmhmm. Thanks."

Click.

On *this* afternoon, when everyone else scampered out of the classroom before the bell finished ringing, Sadie was ready, too. Her backpack was zipped and slung over her shoulder, and she practically ran up to Hannah's desk, her eyes bright.

"Ready?" she said.

Amused, Hannah said, "Almost. You can sit for a few minutes, read, maybe? I have a couple of things to do to kind of close out the week."

"Can I help you?"

Hannah looked down at her desk. There were some packets that needed stapling, and Hannah had a vision of mismatched corners and bent staples. *Let it go*, she told herself.

"Sure. I've got two stacks of paper here. These are page ones, and these are page twos. Will you staple the pages ones to the page twos? Page ones on top. Obviously."

"Obviously," Sadie said, giving Hannah a thumbs up and a click of her tongue. "Got it."

They worked without speaking, Sadie stapling and Hannah marking papers and writing grades in her grade book. Fifteen minutes later, they walked out to the truck. Sadie stopped short, wrinkled her nose, crossed her arms.

"This is *not* the kind of car I expected you to drive."

"What did you expect me to drive?"

"I don't know, something new and shiny?"

"Well, this is it," Hannah said. "I'm afraid something new and shiny might not be appropriate for where I live. And besides, I like this old truck."

They climbed in, and for the first time in a long time, Hannah felt aware of the truck's quirks: the way the doors creaked when they opened and closed, the interior's gas-and-grease smell, the crooked angle of the sun visor, the rip in the fabric of the middle seat.

"Seat belt," she said. Sadie obeyed, Hannah started the engine, and they drove home. Now, she paid fresh attention to the details of the Seedling Homestead: the ancient sign, which Mama had just repainted, the trees lining the driveway, their leaves fluttering in the late afternoon sun, the flock of chickens roaming the yard.

"Do you live on a farm?"

"Kind of," Hannah said. "What do you think?"

"Why does it have a name?"

Hannah wanted to say, "Well that's a long story," but she remembered hating that as a child.

"My mom moved here to start over. You know, I'm sure, that a seedling is a baby plant. So she named this place the Seedling Homestead because she felt like she was a baby plant. She needed some healthy soil, some sunshine, and some water—along with some love—to really grow and thrive."

Sadie was quiet for a moment. When Hannah parked the truck, she said, "You know, Ms. Bradley, I kind of like that. The Seedling Homestead. Has a nice ring to it."

Looking at the place now, from a newcomer's perspective, Hannah felt herself falling in love with it all over again. The pre-sunset light cast a glow over the whole thing, and here and there bugs darted through the air, making it almost sparkle.

"I like it too," Hannah said. "So, just to give you the lay of the land, this here's the main house. I live here with my mama and one of my sisters, Margaret. My other sister, Sarah, lives in that RV, temporarily. And that's the garden, of course, and the chicken coop. Those two houses over there are my sisters' new houses. They're not done being built, but almost. Come on, let's go in and meet everybody."

They got out of the truck, and as they came around the side of the house, Hannah stopped short.

"Well, this wasn't part of the tour."

Apparently, Hannah wasn't the only one feeling generous. Mama must be, too, because there sat Tanner Lucas on the porch. And by the looks of him—feet on the stool and beer in hand—he wasn't going anywhere, any time soon.

"I'm a bonafide dinner guest," he said. "I can't believe I'm not part of the tour." He set his beer on the table next to him, uncrossed his legs, and stood up. "And hello, there. Who's this?"

"This is Sadie," Hannah said. "Sadie, this is Tanner. Tanner Lucas. He's the builder who's working on the new houses. He also happens to be Reagan's uncle. And, apparently, our second dinner guest."

"Nice to meet you, Sadie," Tanner said.

He put out his hand to shake, and she took it, but didn't look him in the eye.

"I was just going to take Sadie inside and introduce her to Mama."

"Go on, then," Tanner said. He gave her a very obvious once-over. "I'll just sit out here, sip my beer, and enjoy the scenery."

Had Tanner Lucas just referred to Hannah as scenery? She didn't know whether she hated that idea or absolutely loved it. Which was exactly why she didn't want him here for dinner. His presence sent all these weird feelings through her body, these weird thoughts through her mind. She'd just wondered whether he'd referred to her as scenery, for goodness' sake.

Even though she knew it was the wrong thing to do, especially in front of an impressionable ten-year-old who also happened to be her student, she marched right into the kitchen and demanded to know why Mama had invited Tanner to stay for dinner.

Mama made a show of looking at Sadie, whose eyes were about as big around as a couple of silver dollars, and then she said, "Well, why not, Hannah? He's worked hard all week and I didn't think it would hurt to show him a little appreciation. Now, who is your guest?"

As Mama spoke, Sadie had inched closer to Hannah's side.

"We *do* show him appreciation," Hannah said. "It's called, we pay him. We don't have to feed him, too, do we? And give him beer?"

Mama turned to Sadie. "Hello, dear. I hope you can excuse my oldest daughter's terrible manners. I'm Katherine. You must be Sadie. Come on into the garage. Let me show you what we have to drink."

Sadie gave Hannah a quick glance—which seemed at once to ask permission, ask what the heck was going on here, and beg Hannah not to go anywhere—and then followed Mama. Hannah stood there, frozen on the spot, while Mama rattled off a list of beverages: lemonade, orange soda, root beer, milk, water, grape juice …

It wasn't unheard of for Mama to invite people to stay for dinner. In fact, when the girls were growing up, the Bradley family hosted a constant stream of people at their kitchen table. If it wasn't friends from school, it was neighbors or the women who worked at the post office and grocery store. Mama had always loved it, and throughout the years after Margaret and Sarah moved out, she often commented on how much she missed those big, bustling dinners. It was only natural, having Margaret and Sarah back here, along with the construction crews, that Mama would take advantage of the opportunity to fill the kitchen again.

"But Tanner Lucas?"

"Are you talking to me?" Tanner said. "Because if you are, it sounds an awful lot like you're cursing me."

And there he was, right behind her. He'd come in so quietly, like a ninja. She hadn't even heard him. Flustered now, Hannah turned around and offered him what she hoped came across like a genuine smile.

"Just talking to myself," she said. "So lovely of you to stay. You know, Mama loves having dinner guests."

"She probably loves showing off her beautiful daughter," he said, and before she could comment, he added, "And anyway, it's lovely of *her* to invite me. Staying is purely selfish. A good meal with a beautiful woman? Wouldn't pass it up."

Hannah assumed he was referring to Mama, but still, she needed an escape. "I'd better go check on Sadie."

"I'm sure she's fine. Why don't you grab a beer and come sit out on the porch with me? I saved you a seat."

Why did this man, as handsome as he was, have the ability to fluster her in a way no one else could? He'd been doing it since college. She was bound to say something stupid, and she certainly didn't want to make herself a sitting duck.

"Ah, also, Mama might need help."

"She's got Sadie. I'm sure she's put her to work by now. Didn't you say once, in philosophy class, that your mother always kept you girls busy? We were talking about idle minds, weren't we?"

"To tell you the truth, I don't remember. But that does sound like something I would say."

"I brought you a beer." He held out a bottle.

Although that anti-Tanner voice in her head told her not to accept it, that doing so would somehow signal approval of his presence, she took it from him.

"Gonna sit?" Tanner inclined his head toward the door that led to the porch.

Hannah rarely just sat down and relaxed. If she had down time, she usually filled it with something she deemed important. She followed him outside and sat.

"Who's this Sadie kid?"

No small talk, she thought. He dives right in. "Just a kid from my class."

"Do you invite students over often?"

"I don't," Hannah said. "But she seems—I'm not sure how to explain it. Lonely? Although, she's also self-reliant, almost like she doesn't even know she's lonely."

"Do okay in school?"

"She does, surprisingly," Hannah said. "She finishes her work quickly, and so far, she's aced every assignment. It's easy for her. In fact, I've been working on a little box of advanced assignments she can do when she finishes her work."

"Can't let those smart ones get bored," Tanner said. He rubbed his chin.

"I take it you know from experience?"

He gave her a sideways glance. "I was a very good student, I'll have you know."

"I saw you in action, remember?"

"Ah. I meant, in elementary school. I was always finishing early, but I'd read when I was done. I was a bit of a bookworm. If you can believe it."

Hannah wasn't sure if she could. She didn't answer, and Tanner said, "How does Sadie do with the other kids?"

These questions surprised her. Grades and social acumen were two of the barometers for measuring a kid's overall chance of success, Hannah thought ... but she hadn't expected Tanner to know that.

"I'm not exactly sure." Something drove Hannah to open up, to share what she knew. "She prefers to be with adults. She's very chatty and helpful when it's just the two of us in the classroom. When the other kids come around, she's more withdrawn."

Tanner rubbed his chin. "You met her parents?"

Hannah shook her head. "Not in person. She lives with her aunt and uncle. I talked to her aunt today, on the phone."

"Did she seem, I don't know, normal? Because I'll tell you what. I wouldn't let my kid leave the house looking like that."

Hannah hummed in agreement, and Tanner went on: "I mean, don't get me wrong. I'm all for letting kids have their own style. Even I went through a phase when I wore my suit vest with everything, even my pajamas. But aren't girls her age starting to care about their appearance? Reagan is, I know that. My sister's always talking about how that girl would spend hours in the bathroom every morning. Fixing her hair, testing out different shirt and shorts combinations, fixing her hair again. In fact, Lyla has to set a kitchen timer to make sure my nephews get a chance to get in there to brush their teeth."

"I could see that," Hannah said, and she could. It was obvious that Reagan put a lot of time and thought into her coordinating outfits and fancy braided hair styles. She'd probably be mortified to show up at school with greasy hair and mismatched, poorly fitting clothes like Sadie did.

"To tell you the truth, her aunt didn't seem normal at all. She didn't seem like she could care less about Sadie's whereabouts."

"Hmm. Strange," Tanner said. "Do the other kids treat her nice?"

"I mean, I think they're a bit put off because she's so withdrawn. But they're not mean."

"They will be. Give 'em time. Maybe you should call Sadie's aunt and uncle."

"And say what? 'Your niece makes terrible fashion choices. Buy the kid some clothes'? What if they can't afford it? Then I've put them in an awkward situation."

"True."

"I did ask child services to do a welfare check. And I talked to the school nurse about giving her some clothes. She said she doesn't always get that size in, but she'll keep an eye out. Which means it could be weeks that Sadie shows up looking like she shops the garbage bin behind the thrift store. I was thinking maybe this weekend, I'd buy a few things—jeans, sweaters, shirts, shoes—and give them to the nurse to give to Sadie. Sadie would never know."

"That's real nice of you, Hannah."

Hannah blushed, quite furiously, and then blushed even harder, realizing that a compliment from Tanner made her blush.

"She's a nice kid, that's all."

Mama and Sadie emerged from the house, then, glasses of lemonade in hand.

"We mixed up a fresh batch of lemonade," Mama said. "I was just telling Sadie about that time you girls tried to poison me," Mama said.

"The infamous lemonade," Hannah said.

"Don't worry," Sadie said. "I wouldn't have known to put sugar in it, either."

Mama reached up for the beater on the triangle she'd always used as a dinner bell and handed it to Sadie. "Want to do the honors?"

Sadie looked at the beater like it was some kind of high-tech gadget, and Tanner chuckled. Then he surprised Hannah by getting up, grasping Sadie's hand, and tapping the triangle to create a lovely ringing sound.

A few minutes later, Sarah, Donny, Margaret, and Ethan had joined them, and they'd all settled around the table. Not without commentary from Margaret: "Is that the brilliant Tanner Lucas I hear?"

"The one and only," Sarah said, drilling her gaze into Hannah's in a way that compelled Hannah to say, "Mama invited him to stay for dinner."

She wanted to add, "Ain't that sweet?" but she refrained, especially because she saw Donny look at her, at Sarah, and then back at her, all the while his mouth on the rim of his glass.

"Well, it's sure nice to have another man at table," Donny said. "Ethan and I have been feeling a bit overrun."

Sarah and Margaret both rolled their eyes.

Hannah cleared her throat. "This is Sadie," she said. "My most prized student this year. Not only does she ace pretty much every single assignment, but she also helps me out in the classroom."

While the rest of the adults made small talk with Sadie, Hannah couldn't help but notice Tanner's eyes on her … and her urge to keep tucking her hair behind her ear or wiping her mouth or organizing her food on her plate. Serving platters moved around the table and people scooped up second and third helpings of mac and cheese and salad.

Hannah hated to admit, even to herself, that the mood was especially festive tonight.

Maybe it was because of the progress Tanner and his crew had made on the houses. Sarah and Margaret took turns toasting Tanner's amazing progress.

Or, maybe it was, in part, Tanner's presence at the table. Since Hannah was admitting things to herself, she had to admit he had a certain way of truly paying attention when someone spoke, making each person feel special. And, his laughter was contagious.

Or, maybe it was because there was a child in the house. Everyone seemed to be getting a kick out of sharing stories from the past. At the moment, Margaret was reliving the mud fight they'd had right before a fancy dinner Mama planned for Easter one year. The three girls were having so much fun that they lost track of time. When they heard that dinner bell, they realized dinner was on the way to the table, and they hadn't helped at all. They ran up from the creek, breathless and muddy, and slipped into their chairs hoping Mama wouldn't notice they'd been missing.

"But of course, she did notice," Sarah said.

"You should've seen them," Mama said to Sadie. "They'd never been so sneaky. They were trying so hard to be invisible, slinking into their chairs like monsters from the riverbed. But there was no way anybody'd miss them, as muddy as they were. And if they weren't covered, head to toe, they smelled to high heaven. My gosh, I thought I'd hidden rotten eggs all over the yard instead of fresh ones."

"You got all muddy, Ms. Bradley?" Sadie said.

"Oh, she was the worst of the bunch," Mama said. "She'd seen something in a magazine about a day spa where you rub mud all over yourself, so, little grown-up that she was, Hannah covered every inch of exposed skin. She was in the shower for hours, rinsing it off."

"I'm pretty sure I clogged the drain," Hannah said. "But my skin was silky smooth."

Everyone was laughing now, and Hannah felt Tanner's eyes on her. She wondered what he was thinking, and then she kicked herself for wondering.

Mama brought out a huge chocolate cake, and Tanner volunteered to slice it. By the time they'd finished eating, Hannah was stuffed, and from the looks of Sadie, who appeared ready to fall sleep on the spot, she was, too.

"Well, I guess I'd better get you home," Hannah said.

It was unlikely that anyone else noticed, with all the laughter and chatting, but Hannah did: Sadie shut down. Her entire countenance changed. Her shoulders slumped, her mouth tightened into a line, and she held herself rigid. And although she'd been boisterous all evening, she was subdued and almost impossible to hear when she said her goodbyes and thank yous.

"Everything all right?" Hannah said when they got into the car.

Sadie grunted, lifted a shoulder and let it drop back down, and then leaned against the door and looked out the window. Hannah had been teaching fourth- and fifth-graders for nearly two decades, and she'd seen this before. With a little coaxing, she could usually get kids to talk.

"How'd you like the dinner?"

"It was good."

"How'd you like the cake?"

Sadie glanced over and rewarded Hannah with a quick grin. "Liked it. A lot. Tanner sneaked me a second piece, did you see that?"

"No," Hannah said. "I guess he's pretty sly, isn't he?"

Oddly charmed and not wanting to dwell on it, Hannah to change the subject. "You're going to fall into a food coma when you get home. Better not sleep through Monday. I'd hate for you to miss school."

"Oh, I won't miss school," Sadie said. Her demeanor was still surly, but her voice was clear. Improvement, Hannah thought, and she backed off.

"Good. I've gotten accustomed to you being around."

"Yeah. I'll be there first thing Monday."

"Any plans for this weekend?"

"Besides sitting around the house? Nope."

Silence.

"Do you?" Sadie said.

"Hmm," Hannah said. "Nope. I mean, there are always things to do around the farm. But nothing special."

"No dates with Tanner?"

"Ha." Hannah was used to having the spotlight put on her—but not with a student behind it. "It's not like that. I'm his client. We're just friends."

"Yeah?" Sadie said.

"Yeah," Hannah said, then, after a beat, "Yes."

"So, your sisters don't look like you."

It was true: Margaret, with her curly black hair and bright green eyes was straight out of Ireland. And then there was Sarah, with her honey-colored skin and light brown eyes. Hannah, as blond and blue-eyed as a girl could get, didn't look a thing like either of them.

"They're adopted. My mom adopted them when I was just a little younger than you."

"You guys seem like real sisters."

"We are, aren't we? I mean, we're not related, by genetics. But we grew up together. We played and ran and fought. We sang in the car, raced for the shower, hogged the phone and the bathroom. That's true sisterhood, right?"

"That's nice."

"It is," Hannah said. "It really is."

Hannah turned the truck onto Sadie's street. "Just around that corner, right?"

Sadie nodded, and her grip tightened on the door handle. "Do I have to go?"

Something in her voice made Hannah want to stop the truck, pull over, and hug the little girl tight. She could pretend she didn't know Sadie's home life was miserable. She could pretend she didn't have some idea of how badly she wanted to avoid her aunt and uncle's place. But she couldn't. Tonight, she'd seen what Sadie had the potential to be —a witty, charming little girl with a wide smile. And right now, Hannah was seeing a transformation that must have occurred long ago. This version of Sadie was, in a word, sad. Hannah decided then that this girl deserved honesty.

"Well, yeah. You do. I know you had fun tonight, and I did, too. I promise, you can come over again, any time. As long as it's okay with your aunt and uncle."

"Really?"

"Sure. Why not?"

"I don't know. You're with students all the time. Don't you want a break?"

"Nah," Hannah said. "I'll put you to work. Slave labor."

Again, Sadie offered her a smile, this one noticeably lower-watt than the last. Hannah pulled the truck up in front of Sadie's house, a tiny shack with a shabby porch and a yard overgrown with weeds. In its heyday, it had probably been an adorable, quaint cottage with an English garden up front. But it wasn't in its heyday any more. It looked haunted at worst, deserted at best. And rat-infested, either way.

"This is it, right?" Hannah said.

Sadie groaned. "Sure is. I'll see you Monday, Ms. Bradley." She hopped down onto the asphalt, but turned around before shutting the door. "And Ms. Bradley? Thank you, for tonight. I had the best time."

"You're welcome," Hannah said. "Any time. Really."

Sadie shut the door and walked up the path, dodging the dandelions and tall grass that invaded the walkway. Hannah waited until she went inside, and found it almost impossible to shift the truck into drive and put her foot on the gas pedal. Once she did, she started to cry. Tears were running down her cheeks when she pulled into the driveway at Seedling Homestead a few minutes later. She was walking up her own path—clear and lined with cheerful marigolds—still sniffling, when she ran headlong into Tanner.

"Whoa," he said. "Everything okay?"

Hannah nodded and swiped under her eyes with the knuckles of her pointer fingers. "Everything's fine. It was just hard—leaving her there."

With her throat as tight as it was, Hannah found she couldn't say any more. But she didn't have to. Tanner drew her in and wrapped his arms around her shoulders. And although, just a few weeks before this, Hannah would have resisted, she surprised herself by laying her head on his chest and holding onto him.

CHAPTER EIGHT

Hannah had always considered herself a fairly introspective person, and she spent much of the weekend trying to figure out why Sadie's situation affected her so strongly. She thought about it as she took a long walk by the creek with John Wayne, watching him chase birds and dash in and out of the water. She thought about it while she wandered through the farmers market, absently picking up soaps and putting them down again, weighing a spaghetti squash in the palm of her hand, inhaling the scents of lavender and incense.

Hannah had seen plenty of students like Sadie come and go: students whose pants were perpetually too short, whose shoes had holes in the toes, whose parents never sent them with food or put money on their lunch accounts.

But there was something different about this one.

Yes, there was the disparity between how Sadie behaved when she was surrounded by other students and how she behaved when she was alone with Hannah. It was the stark difference between the withdrawn, almost combative version of Sadie, and the fun, exuberant, helpful Sadie.

It was more than that, though, Hannah thought.

Sadie was unusually perceptive for a ten-year-old. She was sensitive and thoughtful. She noticed things, and was smart. Really smart, judging by the scores she was getting on every assignment. She was a prime example of what people meant when they said a person was wise beyond her years.

Finally, after hours of thought, Hannah had an epiphany: Sadie was meant for more. She was meant to do something great. Hannah could just sense it. But she had none of the resources to fulfill the potential that was just under the surface.

Children might be hard-wired, in terms of personality. But Hannah had seen over and over that environment had a huge impact. Sadie was hard-wired for greatness, but was living in an environment that stifled it.

Not that it was impossible for her to succeed. Some children were resilient and ended up overcoming their adversity to build great lives, exceeding even their own expectations to go on to college and great careers and families. But some of them weren't as resilient. Hannah heard about these kids, once they reached high school. Teachers talked. These were the kids who hung out under the bleachers, smoking cigarettes and doing who knows what else.

Which category would Sadie fall into? The resilient or the kids who hung out under the bleachers? Ten years from now, where would she be?

Hannah knew the answer. Without any intervention, without action from an outside source, Sadie would fall into the second category. As she got older and entered junior high and high school, she'd fall through the cracks. If she continued getting good grades and laying low, it was unlikely that teachers would notice her.

Another thing Hannah knew was that it wasn't always possible to help, to step in, to change someone's life. Sometimes it was ... but rarely. She made a point of doing what she could in the classroom, nurturing students' interests, teaching them social skills and giving them kindness.

Her colleagues had told her, and each other, countless times, "You can't save them all."

But what if she could save just one? What if she could step in and change Sadie's life? What if their relationship could somehow serve as a turning point for Sadie?

It was more than buying her a couple of outfits or feeding her a few meals. It was more than giving Sadie small tasks in the classroom. It was help on a soul-deep level. But how could she offer that?

All weekend long, Hannah considered. She created ideas and turned them over in her mind. And by Sunday afternoon, she was still coming up empty. The situation seemed hopeless.

She was watering the mums in the oversized pots between the driveway and the house when she heard someone walking up the driveway. She had to shade her eyes to see, and was surprised when she realized it was Sadie. John Wayne, who'd been lying next to the flower pot, didn't notice Sadie until she was already standing next to Hannah, and then he lifted his head and gave a half-hearted bark.

"Hey," Hannah said, going for a neutral tone of voice even while her mind was running through a million worst-case-scenarios to explain Sadie's unexpected presence. "I was just thinking about you."

John Wayne's tail thumped against the ground.

"Hey," Sadie said, obviously doing her best to echo Hannah's relaxed attitude. Her expression was guarded, and Hannah figured she was nervous about the reception she'd get. She leaned over and scratched John Wayne's head.

"Well, this is a nice surprise," Hannah said.

Now, Sadie smiled. "I wasn't sure you'd be happy to see me."

"Of course I am. But I admit, I didn't expect you. What're you up to?"

Looking at her feet, Sadie said, "I don't know. I was just out and about, and thought I'd stop by."

"Huh. Since you're here, you might as well come inside and have a drink. I'm sure there's still some lemonade in the fridge."

Sure enough, the old ceramic pitcher was on the top shelf, and it was still half-full. Hannah poured two glasses and gestured to the porch. When they were seated, John Wayne between them, she said, as conspiratorially as she could, "Do your aunt and uncle know you're here?"

Sadie was looking out at the farm, and her gaze hardened just a bit. "I told them I was going for a walk."

"You walked all the way here?"

"I hitchhiked."

Hannah's stomach swirled. Her first instinct was to reprimand Sadie. But she knew she had to tread lightly.

"Do you think that's safe?"

"I mean, I read the news. I'm sure it's not the safest option out there. But this is Walker. It's not like we have a city bus. And I can't afford a taxi."

"You could always call me. I'd come get you."

"Don't have a phone."

"Couldn't you use your aunt or uncle's phone?"

Sadie looked at her sideways. "Yeah. If they bothered charging them. Half the time their phones are shut off because they forget to pay the bill."

"Isn't there a pay phone at that convenience store around the corner?" *Ha*, Hannah thought. *I've got her.*

"Someone pulled the handset off it, and nobody replaced it. So, no."

I guess I don't have her. "I guess we're going to have to get you a carrier pigeon."

Now, Sadie looked at her, smiled. "Do you even know how to train those things?" Sadie said.

"Nope," Hannah said. "Do you?"

"No," Sadie said. "So I guess it's hitchhiking for me."

"Promise me you won't do it again. We'll find another way for you to get in touch with people. But no more hitchhiking, okay? Horrible things happen to little girls out there alone."

"What if I need to get to the hospital? Or, what if a crazy axe murderer breaks into my house and I need to get away? Or, what if I want to go to the library? Or, what if—"

Hannah held up a hand. "I've been down this road, Sadie. No more hitchhiking. Period."

"Smoke signals?"

"That might work."

"Flares?"

"Sure. Just, no hitchhiking."

"Fine."

"Good."

When they sipped their lemonades, they did so in unison, setting the glasses down at the same time, with matching sounds. Hannah found herself thinking, what would it be like to sit here, on this porch, with a daughter? Or a son? What would it be like to share the experience of Seedling Homestead with a child?

Throughout her teaching career, Hannah had always considered her students "her kids," but she'd never experienced the satisfaction or the pressure of being the main person to mold little humans into adults. For the most part, her students loved her, but she'd never experienced that deep bond between mother and child.

"Did you like growing up here?" Sadie said.

Hannah cleared her throat. "It was the best. We used to have so much fun. I mean, there was work, of course, but what I really remember is running through the fields, picking flowers, making daisy chains, playing on that tire swing by the creek."

"There's a tire swing?"

"Oh yeah. There's a tire swing. Actually, the one we used broke. But our neighbors, the Suttons, they have a bunch of kids. We built a new one for them. There's Luke—"

But Sadie was already up and running across the field, her stringy hair flying out behind her. Hannah had never seen her so carefree. Since he was the only one around, Hannah glanced down at John Wayne, who was looking up at her. "Well," she said to the dog. "I guess we're going down to the tire swing."

He trotted alongside her as if he were four instead of fourteen, and picked up the pace when Sadie gave a loud whoop. By the time Hannah made it to the creek's edge, Sadie was emerging from the water, soaking wet, a wide smile on her face.

The image was striking. She looked like a normal little girl. Happy. Radiant. And for some reason, this made Hannah want to cry again.

"It's freezing!" Sadie said.

Hannah hooked a thumb back at the house. "Want to go in—"

"Can I do it again?" Sadie said.

"I mean, yeah," Hannah said. She tucked her hands into her pockets. "You can do it as many times as you want to, I guess. But it's not going to get any warmer."

While Sadie swung again, Hannah went inside to retrieve a towel. For the next twenty minutes, she stood in the shade of the giant tree, watching Sadie swing, jump, run, and do it all over again. Finally, teeth chattering and water droplets all over her skin, she ran up to Hannah and said, "I'm done! Can I have that towel?"

After she dried off, she spread the towel in the sun, and laid down on top of it, arms and legs stretched out, eyes closed. "There's room for you, too," she said to Hannah.

Hannah shrugged, then laid down next to Sadie, giving a little start when her back hit the wet towel.

"Brr," she said.

"I know!" Sadie said. "It's so refreshing, though."

They laid in silence for a while, and then Hannah said, "You know,

I'm thinking I should get you home. Your aunt and uncle are probably worried."

Sadie groaned. "I don't want to go home."

"Why not?"

"I don't know. We don't have a tire swing."

The truth was, Hannah didn't want Sadie to go home, either. But she couldn't just keep this kid. "Do you have a tree?"

"Ha. No."

"You can come over here any time and use our tire swing, you know that."

"I know," Sadie said. "It's not just that. My aunt and uncle are … well, I feel like they don't even know I'm there half the time."

The sky was so bright today, so blue, that Hannah's eyes watered when she opened them. "Don't all kids say that?"

"Probably," Sadie said. "But most kids don't mean it, right? My aunt and uncle, they're what other adults call deadbeats. They don't work, they don't do anything for other people. They sit around all day. You'd think that because of that, they'd actually pay attention to me, but no. When I first moved in, I used to ask them to do something for me or with me, you know? But they'd always say they were too busy. Or, 'In a minute.' But they're not busy. Well, not with anything besides watching TV or taking naps."

They did sound like deadbeats.

"Do they talk to you?"

"Yeah, like, 'Sadie, open that door, would you? It's stuffy in here.' Or, 'Sadie, you cooking hot dogs? Want to cook up some for us, too?' Or, 'Sadie, you're blocking the TV. Could you move?'"

"Really?"

"Really."

A bird flew overhead, trilling.

"Well, I really am sorry," Hannah said. "I wish I could make things better for you there."

"Me too."

"All right. That's enough sunbathing for one day. I'd better get you home."

As they neared Sadie's house, all traces of that carefree little girl disappeared, as if they were flying out the open window, one by one. When Hannah pulled up into the driveway, Sadie had withdrawn into herself again.

"Thank you, Ms. Bradley," she said.

The door creaked as she opened it. Then she hopped down, slammed the door, and walked slowly up the path. The house didn't look any more inviting in the daylight than it had in the dark. In fact, Hannah thought, it looked downright depressing. Aluminum foil covered all the windows, some of which were cracked. One of the shutters dangled by a corner. The sidewalk was cracked and uneven, with weeds growing up right in the middle of it. Hannah couldn't blame Sadie for her reluctance to come back. She was anxious to get away from here, herself.

Yes, Hannah thought as she drove away, she was angry at Mama Katherine for keeping her father's identity a secret, and even more so for not telling Hannah's father she existed. But she had to be grateful that she'd always felt loved and paid attention to, that she'd grown up in a nurturing environment. Sometimes a person couldn't walk through the house without tripping over a toy, or stepping on a crayon, or grinding play-doh into the carpet. But the Seedling Homestead always, always felt welcoming. It always felt like home.

———

THE NEXT MORNING, Sadie was waiting outside the Walker Elementary building when Hannah made her way in from the parking lot. She wore that same surly expression she had the evening before, and she responded to Hannah's greeting with nothing more than a grunt.

Taken aback, Hannah didn't try to start a conversation right away. She just unlocked the building, followed Sadie down the hall, and unlocked the classroom door.

Finally, when they were inside, she said, "Everything okay?"

She set her things down on her desk and Sadie slid into her own plastic chair.

"Same old, same old," Sadie said.

"Did you get breakfast?" Hannah had put twenty bucks on Sadie's account so she could get it on her own.

"Not open yet."

Is she mad at me? Hannah thought, and then she thought, *Maybe this is what Mama Katherine feels like.*

"Oh, I guess you're right," Hannah said. "Want to help me with something?"

"No, thanks. I'll just sit here."

"Suit yourself," Hannah said, even though she wanted to demand to know what was wrong, and why Sadie was acting this way.

Sadie put her head down on the desk, and Hannah went about erasing the white board, organizing the book case, and wiping down desk tops. When there were only fifteen minutes remaining before the first bell, Sadie was snoring. Hannah touched Sadie's shoulder to wake her up. "Hey, if you're going to eat, this is the time."

Without a word, the girl slid out of her seat and left the classroom. She returned fifteen minutes later, as the first bell rang, and spent the entire morning sulking, giving her classmates grunts instead of answers, averting her eyes from anyone who spoke to her, and tapping her pencil on her desk instead of doing her work.

At recess, for once, she was the first one out the door, and as Hannah scored her math quiz, marking a majority of the problems with a red check-mark for "incorrect," she knew Sadie was avoiding her. She was the last one to return to the classroom, and she didn't even look at her graded quiz before crumpling it up and tossing it into the wastebasket.

Hannah had planned on talking to her about what was going on, but there wasn't an opportunity until the end of the day, when Hannah blocked her from going out the doorway.

"Everything okay?" she said.

Their eyes met briefly, and then Sadie looked away. "Yeah. Why?"

"It's just that you seem, I don't know, different today."

"Different like what?" Sadie said. "My outfit?"

It was the first time that day Hannah had bothered paying attention to what Sadie was wearing, and when she looked it over, she realized it wasn't any different from usual: she wore a red sweatshirt with the sleeves cut off, and black bike shorts that were most definitely too short to meet dress code.

"No," Hannah said. "Although I think you'd be wise to choose longer shorts tomorrow. Those wouldn't pass dress code and I'm sure you don't want to wear sweats from the nurse's office. But I was talking about your attitude. You seem like something's bothering you."

Now Sadie's eyes met Hannah's, and she said, "Only the fact that I live with a couple of losers and there's nothing I can do about it. I'll spend the next eight years there. By the time I can finally move out, I'll have lived with them for more than half my life."

That gave Hannah some perspective.

"I'm so sorry, Sadie," she said.

She wanted to draw Sadie in, to hug her, to promise her everything would turn out okay. But she knew that wasn't necessarily true.

So instead, she said something she hoped *was* true: "You'll persevere. You'll get through this. I know it."

The corners of Sadie's mouth turned down, and she gave one quick nod before ducking out the classroom door.

When Hannah returned home an hour later, she wasn't surprised to see Mama Katherine sitting on the porch. But she *was* surprised to see Tanner Lucas sitting there, too. Again. His feet propped up on the ottoman, a beer in his hand. She was even more surprised when she walked up the steps and he handed her a beer, as if he'd planned to have it ready.

"Your mama said she expected you home about this time, so I had this waiting for you."

Mama watched this interaction carefully, and Hannah didn't have to wonder what she was thinking: she gave her an exaggerated wink and smile.

A mixture of gratitude and humiliation had her sinking into the seat next to Tanner's—Hannah told herself it really was the only natural option for where to sit—and taking a swig of the cold beer.

"Rough day?" Mama said. Her eyes were twinkling.

"Not really," Hannah said. "It's just that Sadie and I had such a nice day yesterday. And today, she was just so … different."

"Different how?" Mama and Tanner said at the same time.

Hannah looked from Mama to Tanner, and said, "Quiet. Withdrawn. Grumpy. Even around me. I mean, that's how she'd been at the beginning of the year, but I felt like she was coming out of her shell. And yesterday, I thought we'd had a breakthrough, you know? I was thinking that maybe she'd be more like *that* kid: fun, laughing, witty, in the classroom. But it had the opposite effect, I think."

Mama nodded, as if she were still digesting what Hannah had said. And Tanner said, "Sounds like she has a broken heart."

This was, again, unexpected, and Hannah felt tears threaten for the umpteenth time in two days.

"Your mama told me Sadie came over yesterday," he said. "And, I mean, when she was here Friday night, and again on Sunday, she got a taste of what life could be like."

"If she wasn't living with a couple of deadbeats," Hannah said.

"Exactly," Tanner said. "And so she probably feels angry. Resentful. Sad."

Mama nodded. "You're right. That's probably exactly what it is."

"Pretty thoughtful for a man who works with his hands," Hannah said, hoping her tone conveyed that she was teasing.

He looked at her, then, right into her eyes, and said, "I think you'd be surprised at how thoughtful a man who works with his hands can be."

She had no idea whether it was his intended effect, but an image flashed into Hannah's mind: Tanner's hands on her skin, his mouth on hers. She blushed—something she'd been doing a lot of lately, where Tanner was concerned.

"Well," Mama said. "I'm going to go put that casserole in the oven. I don't know why, Hannah, but having all you girls here, on Seedling Homestead land again, has really given me a lot of energy."

And she was gone.

"How would you like to have dinner with me?" Tanner said.

"Dinner?"

"Yes. The evening meal. Some people call it supper."

"The two of us?"

"Yes."

"Like a date?"

"Like, two people sharing a meal. You can call it a date, if you like. Or, if it makes you more comfortable, call it us having dinner together."

Could she actually sit down to a meal with this man? In college, he'd been her arch nemesis. He'd argued every single point she made, even if she knew he agreed with her. He'd had a comeback for everything she said. He'd even walked just behind her from class to class, and she knew it was to make her uncomfortable. But recently, she'd seen a new side of him … one she didn't hate.

Before she could verbalize a decision, he said, "Look, Hannah. I know you probably thought I had it out for you in college. I know I was an argumentative jerk. I'll attribute one-quarter of it to my immaturity at the time."

"What about the other three-quarters?" Hannah knew where this was going, but she had to ask.

"Like I said, I was crazy about you," he said, his tone implying it was obvious. "It was the only way I could get you to pay any attention to me."

"By making my life miserable? God, you made me so angry."

"And God, I loved it." His eyes took on a faraway look. "You were so incredible when you were angry."

Half of Hannah found this conversation offensive. And the other half found it arousing. She didn't want Tanner to know about the second half, so she said, "That is just offensive, Tanner Lucas."

"Then why are you smiling?"

"I'm not."

"You're smiling on the inside. I can see it."

"Can you?" Could he?

"Sure can. But we're getting off-track, here. I've just asked you to dinner. So is that a, 'Yes, I'd love to have dinner with you'?"

Now Hannah smiled, on the outside. What could it hurt? It was just a meal. With a nice man. Who was building her sisters' houses. And who, so far, had shown a surprising interest in her work. Oh, and also, who was very good-looking.

"It's a yes," she said.

CHAPTER NINE

With Margaret's wedding just around the corner, and related activities creating quite the hustle and bustle (the ordering of flowers, the setting up of chairs and tables, the buying of food), Hannah thought her non-date with Tanner would escape any scrutiny. She should have known better. With less than two days remaining before the big day, Margaret had asked Sarah, Hannah, and Mama to help assemble bouquets and centerpieces. Now, they were gathered around a long plastic table Tanner had set up just off the porch. Because she couldn't see well enough to make the floral arrangements, Margaret was forced into what she called, "supervisory mode," and now, she walked around the table, trailing her fingertips on the backs of the chairs.

"So, Hannah."

She was just passing Hannah's chair, and Hannah wondered how she'd known which was hers. The hairs stood up on the back of her neck.

"So, Margaret."

"You're going to dinner with Tanner Lucas."

Until that moment, Hannah had been studiously wrapping a white ribbon around the stems of a bunch of peonies. Now, though, her gaze snapped immediately to Mama's face, which wore an unmistakable expression of guilt.

"I don't have to ask you how you know. Mama's giddy with excitement, I'd imagine."

"She is," Sarah said, and when Hannah looked at Sarah, she realized her sister was, too.

"Seems to me, you are, too."

"We are," Margaret said, her voice gleeful.

"But, why? It's just dinner. With a friend."

"With a *man* friend," Sarah said, and Margaret added, "Who, if I recall, is a very *good-looking* man."

Hannah sighed, and Mama chuckled. "He is that," she said.

"Cradle robber," Margaret said. She'd stopped behind the other side of the table, behind Mama's chair, directly across from Hannah.

Sarah said, "Anyway. Where are you going to go?" and before Hannah could answer, Margaret held up a pointer finger and said, "More importantly, what are you going to wear?"

Hannah opened her mouth to speak, but Margaret interrupted her. "Please don't tell me you were planning to wear that pink button-up atrocity you call a *blouse*. In fact, if you still own that, or any other piece of fabric you call a *blouse*, I demand you throw them all away immediately."

Every time she said, "blouse," she sounded like she had taken a bite of rotten fruit and was spitting it out.

Sarah snickered, and when Hannah looked at her, she held a bunch of flowers up to hide her face.

"What's wrong with a blouse?" Hannah said, and Margaret said, "What's not? Listen. Maybe we need to get you a makeover. Before the date. Before you get between the sheets with Tanner Lucas."

"I most certainly am not planning to get between the sheets with Tanner Lucas," Hannah said.

"Not yet, anyway," Margaret said. "And certainly not if you wear a blouse. Also, as you know, I'd booked myself a spa day before the wedding. As soon as I heard about this date with Tanner—"

"It's dinner. Not a date."

Margaret waved her hand, dismissing Hannah. "I've since reserved spots for all three of you, as well."

"I can't afford—"

"But *I* can," Margaret said. "I have the money. And I can't think of a better way to spend it."

The next day, the four of them checked into La Fleur Day Spa. Hannah had never been to a spa, and she found the whole thing mildly awkward: the women picked up thick towels and robes and changed out of their clothes before walking (naked underneath those robes!) through a tiled hallway to separate massage rooms.

The massage was okay—actually, it was heavenly, Hannah thought as Suka, a tiny woman with very strong hands, kneaded her muscles—but then came the part where Hannah was supposed to disrobe and get into a hot tub with a bunch of other women.

When she came out of the massage room to meet her mother and sisters, Margaret said, "Don't worry, Hannah. I've reserved us a private soak tub. So you don't have to get naked with a bunch of strangers."

Hannah was relieved and perplexed. How did Margaret always seem to know what she was thinking? She sank down into the soaking tub and closed her eyes. Why had she never been to a spa before?

"So, Hannah," Sarah said, and Hannah braced herself for more talk of Tanner Lucas and their non-date that very night. She could always ask to talk about something else. But right now, as relaxed as she was, her brain was turning to mush.

"Hmm?" she said.

"Tell us more about that little girl you brought home the other night."

This wasn't what she'd expected. "Sadie," she said, leaving her eyes closed. "She lives with her aunt and uncle. I'm still trying to figure her out, to be honest."

Hannah described how Sadie was always waiting for her when she arrived at school, and how she was sweet and helpful when it was just the two of them, but standoffish, bordering on sulky, around other students. She told them what Sadie had said about her life with her aunt and uncle, and how she'd just shown up at Seedling Homestead on Sunday afternoon.

"Poor little girl," Mama Katherine said. "Sounds like she needs a lot of love."

Hannah nodded. "She does. But I'm not sure she's ready to receive it."

"We're all ready to receive love, any time," Mama said. "It's just a matter of someone giving it to us in the right way, the way we can take it."

"And that's different for everybody, I suppose," Sarah said.

"It is," Margaret said. "When I first met Ethan, I felt like he was showing an interest only out of pity. You know me. I didn't want his pity. So he had to come around, sneaky-like. A love ninja."

"He brought you that desk and the cherry tree," Sarah said, her voice dreamy.

"And he melted your little stone heart," Hannah said.

Margaret, who was sitting on the opposite side of the tub, gave Hannah's leg a gentle kick.

"And, I know you were little," Mama said, "but surely you remember how Margaret and Sarah acted when they first came to live with us."

"I was a hellion," Margaret said.

"You were," Mama said.

"Was she?" Hannah said. "I don't remember."

"She threw the biggest tantrums this side of the Mississippi," Mama said. "Whenever things didn't go her way, or whenever they went differently than she expected. Poor little thing craved structure, but didn't know how to handle it. Remember the time she broke that special birthday plate we had?"

Bits and pieces of that memory came into Hannah's mind, then. "Oh, yeah," she said. "I do. It was your birthday, and I insisted you use the 'You are special today' plate. Only, Margaret wanted to use it."

"Right," Mama said.

"It was red," Margaret said. "My favorite color."

"Before we could settle the argument," Mama said, "she'd thrown that plate right on the floor."

Hannah remembered clearly, now: it had shattered into what seemed like a million shards all over the kitchen floor. Margaret had run to her room, screaming, and Hannah, crying, had swept up the destruction, dumping it all into the trash can.

"And you told me then that children who are most in need of love ask for it in the most confounding of ways," Hannah said.

"That's right," Mama said. "So keep that in mind with Miss Sadie."

"Now," Margaret said. "Let's talk about your date with Tanner Lucas. Specifically, your outfit."

———

JUST A FEW HOURS LATER, Hannah was dressed in a Margaret-approved outfit, not coincidentally, straight from Margaret's closet: dark bootcut jeans, a green top ("not a *blouse*") and strappy sandals Hannah was positive she wouldn't be able to walk in. Sarah contributed a pair of dangly, sparkly earrings and a matching necklace. The three of them stood in front of the mirror in her bedroom, Hannah's sisters flanking her like a pair of watchful guard dogs.

"You guys, I don't even look like myself," Hannah said.

The truth was, Hannah thought she looked pretty good. And not at all like herself. She knew her typical wardrobe bordered on frumpy. But she was an elementary school teacher. A single, destined-for-spinsterhood elementary school teacher. And it wasn't like her students cared what she wore.

"You *do* look like yourself," Sarah said, insistent. "Like a super-sexy version of yourself. I love it."

"And I'm sure I'd agree with Sarah," Margaret said.

Then, she swatted Hannah's butt. "You've still got it."

Before Hannah could say she'd never had it, the doorbell rang. All the nervousness Hannah had been pushing to the back of her mind came rushing forward.

"Show time," Margaret said, moving her eyebrows up and down. "Remember, no sex on the first date."

"Margaret!" Sarah said. "I'm sure, positive actually, that Hannah is not planning on having sex with Tanner Lucas tonight."

"You never know," Margaret said. She put an arm around Hannah's waist and started herding her out of the bedroom, toward the front door.

"It's not a date. And I still haven't even decided whether I like him," Hannah said, her voice coming out in a hiss.

"Oh, you do," Margaret said, and Sarah said, "Otherwise you wouldn't have agreed to go on a date with him."

Now, the three of them were standing at the front door. Sarah reached out to open it, and Hannah whisper-yelled, "Get out of here, you guys. We can't all greet him together! This is embarrassing!"

Margaret and Sarah scuttled away, snickering, and Hannah was positive they were hiding around some corner, watching to see how this played out—just like they'd done as teenagers. She took a deep breath and opened the door. She noticed immediately that Tanner was smiling, but when he saw her, his smile faded and his eyes took on a different look. In the romance novels Mama read, Hannah was pretty sure they called that look "smoldering," but she'd never had it directed at her before.

The moment passed and Tanner smiled again. "You look great," he said, amicable, like they were just two friends going out for a bite to eat.

Which, Hannah reminded herself, they were. They were not anything like two people in one of Mama's romance novels.

"You, too," Hannah said. Then she kicked herself because that was such a cliché response. "I mean, that shirt looks really nice on you."

She kicked herself again, although the shirt did look nice on him. It showed off the muscles in his arms and shoulders, and his trim waist. What the heck was she noticing his trim waist for? Tanner walked to the passenger side of his truck and opened the door. Hannah, her stomach fluttering with nerves, thanked him and got in, noticing his trim waist again as he walked around the hood.

"I thought we could try out that new Italian place," he said. "The one around the corner from the farmers market."

Hannah cleared her throat. "Sure."

"Is that okay?" he said. "Do you like Italian?"

"I love Italian," she said. "Sounds wonderful. And I hear they have a killer vodka sauce."

"I hear they have a great house red."

He ordered a bottle when they sat down, and Hannah realized she'd never before been on a date, or non-date, as the case may be, where a man ordered a bottle of wine. An entire bottle. Was this romance, or was he just now becoming aware of the fact that he'd made a mistake, and wanted to take the edge off?

The restaurant was lavish, with high ceilings, velvet curtains, and stone pillars under a midnight blue ceiling, through which pinpricks of light shone, emulating a starry sky. Although the tables were full, the ambience was quiet.

"I have to tell you," Tanner said, leaning forward as if he were about to share a secret. "I have been waiting for this moment for a long time. Years, even."

"You have?"

"Yes. I've been waiting for the moment when I could take Hannah Bradley to dinner."

"But—then why did you never ask me before?"

"Are you kidding?" Tanner said, too loudly. His volume was lower when he said, "I was afraid you'd bite my head off. I was terrified. Me, ask Hannah Bradley to dinner? Certain humiliation. Tell me you would have accepted."

"I wouldn't have," Hannah admitted. The wine was hitting her bloodstream, making her a little bolder than usual. "I would have turned you down cold. But it's not because I hated you. It's because I would have been terrified to spend any time alone with you. You made me so—"

"Angry?"

"No. Well, yes. But also, you made me feel things I hadn't felt. Over a guy."

"Hatred?"

Hannah laughed. "Yes. But only because you were so … I don't know. So good. So good at arguing. So good at debating, at looking good. At wearing those jeans."

Tanner froze, his wine glass halfway between the table and his mouth. He looked at her over the rim of his glass, and Hannah thought he was trying to figure out how to respond, or what this revelation meant, or both.

Then he put his glass down, the wine sloshing up the sides, and laughed. Perplexed, Hannah watched him for a few seconds. "What's so funny?"

"Hannah Bradley," he said, finally. "If I'd known that's what you were thinking inside that pretty head of yours, I would have had you in my bed lickety split. But, no. I've gone all this time thinking you down-right hated me. When we reconnected, I thought that maybe, just maybe, I could persuade you to at least be friends with me. And after that, maybe you'd go on a date with me. I didn't know you thought I looked good in my jeans." He rubbed his hands together, the motion fast, and said, "So now, my pretty, I think we're getting somewhere. My work isn't going to be as hard as I thought. In fact, I've got you right where I want you."

Hannah picked up her wine glass, took a big gulp, and said, "It's been a couple of decades, Tanner. You don't look the same in your jeans as you once did."

This was like throwing water on his fire, but only for the briefest span of time. When he looked at her face and realized she was joking, he laughed again. "This is going to be fun."

Dinner, at least, *was* fun. They didn't debate as much as they had in college, but that chemistry, which allowed them to go back and forth on an issue, was still there. They talked about building and teaching and parents growing older. And at every turn, Tanner seemed thoughtful and genuine.

In what seemed like no time at all, the wine ran out, they'd finished their food and declined dessert, and the other restaurant patrons were making their way to the exit.

"Wow," Tanner said. "We closed the place down."

Again, when they got to his truck, he opened the door for her. Hannah wasn't ready to go home, yet. She wanted to ask Tanner to drive around for a while, but she didn't—it sounded too much like a come-on. When they got back to the Seedling Homestead, she felt like the evening had ended too soon, even though it was nearing eleven and way past her bedtime.

Tanner parked the truck and turned off the engine.

"I had a good time," he said. "A real good time."

"So did I." She winked at him. "Shockingly."

"Now, I'm going to walk you to the door," he said. "But don't worry. I'm not going to kiss you. I don't think a man should kiss a woman on the first date. But, if you agree to another date, which I'd like very much, that rule goes out the window."

Without waiting for her to answer, he got out and hopped down, then came around, opened her door, and offered a hand. They walked, hands linked, to the front porch. True to his word, he didn't make a move to kiss her. Instead, he wrapped his arms around her shoulders.

"Goodnight, Hannah," he said.

She said goodnight, and he was gone.

Just as she made it to her bedroom, her sisters swooped in on her.

"So?" Sarah said, and Margaret said, "Did you guys kiss?"

The situation was so reminiscent of Hannah's first real date that Hannah had to laugh. She was sixteen, and came home from dinner and a movie with Leo Marcus to find her sisters waiting in the living room. Mama had given her a midnight curfew, and she came through the front door at one minute 'til. Sarah and Margaret had ambushed her as she tried to get down the hallway without waking anyone up. At that time, she'd been so excited to share every detail of her date.

Now, she was equally excited. They sat in the living room and she told them everything. She didn't miss the way they elbowed each other when she mentioned she'd told him he looked good in his jeans, or the way Margaret tried to hold in a squeal when Hannah told them about Tanner throwing his no-kissing rule out the window on the next date.

She noticed that both sisters noticed her use of the phrase, "next date." She also noticed that they didn't say anything about the fact that it verified that tonight's dinner had, in fact, been a real date. If they weren't saying anything, she wasn't either.

"And now," she told them, "I'm spent. I'm going to bed."

She fell asleep thinking of Tanner, imagining what it would be like when he kissed her.

CHAPTER TEN

HANNAH WAS STILL THINKING about Tanner when she woke up the next morning. In fact, she thought she heard his voice, but that wasn't possible. It was only seven a.m. on a Saturday. She got out of bed and didn't bother getting dressed as she headed to the kitchen for coffee. She was still daydreaming. She must be: she could have sworn she heard Tanner's voice again, this time saying something about building a quick trellis.

This didn't make any sense.

She came around the corner, though, and realized that it was reality: a jeans-clad Tanner Lucas was standing in the kitchen, a cup of coffee in his hand, chatting with Mama, Donny, and Ethan.

And a nightgown-clad Hannah Bradley froze. But it was too late. Tanner spotted her just before she spun around and hightailed it back to her bedroom. She emerged a few minutes later, dressed, face washed, hair in a ponytail.

"Well, good morning," Mama said. "Are you ready for the big day?"

"Wait," Hannah said. "I thought tomorrow was the big day. Did we reschedule the wedding?"

"Oh, no, not at all," Mama said. "Today's the big decorating day, remember?"

"Oh, I remember," Hannah said, and she thought, *But that doesn't explain why Tanner is here, standing in our kitchen, at seven a.m.*

"I can tell you're wondering what I'm doing here," he said, handing her a cup of coffee.

"I invited him," Mama said, obviously proud of having done so. "I thought we could use an extra pair of hands today."

"Did you?" Hannah said.

"I did," Mama said. "And he's going to build us some lovely trellises to provide a backdrop for the actual ceremony. He said he could use your help."

"Did he?"

"I did," Tanner said. "So as soon as you've had your coffee and breakfast, I'll meet you outside. We've got to take some measurements and then head to the hardware store. Get some supplies. Thanks for the coffee, Katherine."

And he was gone. Hannah glared at Mama, who feigned innocence: "What? He said he could use help, and I offered your services. We're done with the flowers. And I heard you girls chattering about your date, so I assumed you wouldn't mind spending time with him."

Hannah shook her head, downed her coffee, and went outside. She and Tanner took measurements of the area behind where Margaret and Ethan would stand during the ceremony, and she couldn't help but notice that they worked well together, practically seamlessly.

"I think we're good," Tanner said after a few minutes. "Want to tag along to the hardware store?"

Hannah was impressed by Tanner's easy rapport with the employees there. He asked the guy who helped him load the wood onto a flatbed cart how his wife and new baby were doing, and he talked to the woman who rang them up at the contractor's desk about whether her fish pond was working out okay. He waved at one person after another as they walked through the store and through the parking lot, and by the time they were back in the truck, Hannah couldn't deny, even to herself, that she was impressed.

"That right there," she said, "is something I never would have imagined I'd see from Tanner Lucas."

"What?" he said, starting the truck.

"Mr. Congeniality."

He shrugged. "Just one more shiny facet of my amazing personality. Want to grab lunch?"

"Sure. I suppose it's still breakfast time. But we can eat. All that shopping made me hungry."

They stopped at the Race Track, a subway sandwich shop that specialized in "quick eats."

"Not the height of romance for our second date," Tanner said, grinning at Hannah when she shot him a look. "But it *is* fast. And we have a lot to do still, today. We're on a deadline."

"I didn't realize this was a date," Hannah said, and Tanner shrugged and said, "I know. I sneaked it in on you."

Surprised that she felt charmed, Hannah returned his shrug. "Okay. Anyway, yes, fast is good. It *would* be a bummer if we weren't done by tomorrow. I'd really like everything to be just right."

"How do you feel about your little sister getting married?"

"I'll tell you what," Hannah said. "I never thought it would happen. She's always been so independent, you know? She's dated men, but she's never been too serious about any of them. I know she's never wanted to rely on anyone. And I think Ethan gets that. He's confident enough to give her independence, and he's also reliable. So I'm happy for them."

"Good," Tanner said. "Me too. They seem like a great fit."

Hannah braced herself for the conversation that inevitably followed: the one about whether she thought she'd get married, or why she hadn't. But it didn't. They ate in silence, and when they'd both finished, Tanner said, "Well, shall we?"

They walked out to the truck, and again, Tanner opened the passenger door. But this time, instead of closing it when she sat down, he leaned in and kissed her.

Hannah was caught completely off guard, but it didn't take more than half a second for her to respond. She kissed him right back. Her body reacted in unexpected ways: it felt like her insides were turning to lava, slowly heating and on the brink of eruption. And all this just from a kiss.

She wrapped her hands around his shoulders, and before she realized what was happening, she was skimming them up the sides of his neck and burying her fingers in his hair, pulling him even closer. He leaned in, put his hands on her knees, and kept right on kissing her.

When it ended, after what seemed like a gloriously long time and no time at all, Hannah felt breathless.

"When I first said I'd tag along, I had no idea this was even a date," she said.

He winked at her. "I told you. I'm sneaky. I hope you're prepared."

He shut the door, came around to the driver's side, and headed back to the house. Hannah spent the ride in silence, her body still vibrating, wanting more.

———

MARGARET AND ETHAN couldn't have asked for a more beautiful late-summer day. The morning dawned cool and dewy, as birds chirped and flitted from tree to tree in the yard. At five a.m., Hannah put on some country music, threw open the kitchen windows, and got to work cooking.

Her schedule was tight, outlined down to the minute: she'd cook and bake from five to nine, and then she and Sarah would begin setting up chairs. Meanwhile, the men would put up the tables, including table cloths and centerpieces. They'd all work together to attach the flower arrangements to the chairs in the aisle.

By then, it would be lunchtime. Mama had ordered up a six-foot sub from the Race Track, and they'd all fuel themselves quickly before heading into final prep: Hannah and Sarah would help Margaret get dressed and style her hair, and the men would go over to Ethan's house to get dressed. If Hannah's suspicions were right, they'd have a couple of pre-wedding shots.

Just now, mixing up marinades and whipping up the icing for the cake, Hannah enjoyed her alone time. Although she'd never been one of those jealous women, who couldn't be truly happy for her sisters as they experienced big moments in their lives, she did feel an unexpected tinge of longing.

The possibility of her getting married had come and gone. She'd likely never plan her own wedding, never create and orchestrate a schedule of "day-of duties," or walk down the aisle in a wedding dress. And she'd never felt particularly disappointed about it—until now. Maybe it was because she'd never thought Margaret would get married —she'd always imagined the two of them remaining single for life, sisters galivanting off to exotic places decade after decade.

Maybe she'd never plan her own real wedding, but she could pretend. She loved the modern-yet-rustic theme Margaret had going on, but she thought she'd want brighter colors. Reds and oranges. Something passionate. And while Margaret had chosen a dress that was fitted all the way down to her knees, Hannah had always loved those gowns with cinched waists and big skirts. And a long train, she thought as she dropped meat into the baking dishes to marinate. A train so long … someone would step on it. Scratch that.

She'd seen enough weddings in real life and on TV to know that the bride always stood at the end of the aisle, clutching her bouquet, taking deep breaths before her father offered his elbow. And since this was her fantasy, wouldn't Philip Carlisle, Jr. be there to offer his elbow? The photos online didn't really give her an idea of how tall he was, so she imagined him tall and sturdy, looking into her eyes for just a second before they made their way to her groom.

"Everything okay?" Hannah jumped, a zing of pain bringing her firmly back to reality when she bumped her head on the open door of the cabinet.

"Tanner! Yes, everything's fine! Just—"

"Daydreaming, from the looks of it," he said.

She gave her head a little shake. "No, just thinking, that's all. If I get the steak in the marinade now, I'll start the smoker at ten. I'll smoke everything for a couple of hours, grill it up for thirty minutes or so. Get it in the fridge. That should be plenty of time."

As distracted as she was, she didn't notice he'd moved in on her while she spoke. And now he was standing right in front of her.

"Sounds like you've got it all figured out." His voice was quiet. "You have a little something on your face."

He used his pointer finger to wipe it off, just at the corner of her mouth, and then his demeanor changed. He licked his finger and said, "Delicious. That meat's going to be amazing. What else have you got cooking?"

She showed him: the icing, the salsa, the pinto beans, the rolls, the cake. When she was done, he whistled. "You're an amazing woman, Hannah. Cooking up a storm and still managing to look good enough to eat, yourself. Save me a dance, will you?"

Then he sauntered out—he had this mouthwatering way of sauntering—and she didn't see him again until lunchtime.

The wedding, of course, was spectacular. The Seedling Homestead shone as a wedding venue. It seemed as though all the flowers knew what a special occasion it was, and they perked up, providing a rainbow backdrop. And all the flower arrangements the sisters had worked so hard to assemble tied the scene together in a way that was at once sophisticated and quaint.

Margaret was more than spectacular. She was stunning. It was as if she were made for this role, like she'd only been waiting for just the right time to step into the spotlight and play it. Hannah could sense a tiny bit of sadness from her sister, who was unable to see the thoughtful details making up this event of a lifetime.

But overall, there was a calm joy, the feeling that Margaret realizing she was exactly where she wanted to be. Hannah wished for that. After the ceremony and a few photos, which Margaret said were mostly for Mama, since she'd never be able to see them, herself, the reception began. Hannah mingled with guests—the Suttons from the next farm over, Farmer Eddie from up the road, a few of Margaret's friends from college and her career.

Someone—was it Tanner?—pressed a cup of cold champagne into her hand, and it was so refreshing she finished it within a couple of minutes. And then someone—this time she knew it was Tanner—had his hand on her lower back and was guiding her away from the crowds, to the edge of the garden.

He twirled her to face him, put one hand on her waist and used the other to lift her hand. And they were dancing.

"I don't think you asked me to dance," Hannah said.

"Well, you haven't had hardly a moment to breathe," Tanner said, "and dancing was just an excuse to talk to you."

She was so relaxed (or tipsy?) that the words in her response slid together: "What'd you wanna talk about?"

She would have looked him in the eye, but now he'd pressed their bodies together.

"Your food. It's to-die-for. So good, Hannah. I'm tempted to ask you to marry me."

Her body froze, of its own accord, and he chuckled.

"I'm only kidding," he said. She relaxed, continued to sway with him, and he said, "Not about asking you to marry me. Just about the timing. Today is all about Margaret and Ethan. But it's only a matter of time, Hannah."

This time, when she would have frozen again, he simply kept swaying. She wondered whether it was the champagne or the ambiance or her sister in that dress that was getting to him, giving him these crazy ideas. She also wondered whether it was the champagne or the ambience or Margaret's dress getting to *her*, preventing her from doing what was reasonable and running away.

"Sorry," he said. "Just seeing you here, like this, is giving me outlandish ideas. Oh, and eating your food."

"Stop talking crazy," she said.

They danced. And, after the first song had ended, and two more had come and gone—two fast songs that warranted something other than the slow movements they were making—Hannah pulled away, with a great deal of reluctance.

"I've got to go," she said.

"You're already where you're supposed to be, aren't you?"

"Well, I mean, I've got duties to attend to. Mingling. Refilling the broiler dishes. That sort of thing."

"You're breaking my heart, Hannah Bradley."

Now, she smiled. "You're ridiculous, Tanner Lucas."

She spent the next couple of hours doing what she had said: checking to make sure the food trays weren't empty, mingling, holding up the end of Margaret's dress while she used the bathroom, dancing, sneaking bites of leftover cake, and dancing some more.

And when most of the guests had gone, and the yard was glowing under the strings of globe lights the men had hung that morning, she found herself alone with Mama, relaxing into a couple of folding chairs.

"You know," Mama said. "This reminds me of a very special evening."

"Yeah?" Hannah said.

"Your father and I had a party once."

Hannah's body remained relaxed, but her brain went on alert. This was the first time Mama had spoken about Philip without prompting.

"It was the Fourth of July," Mama said. "We hosted the party right there in our orchard. As we were setting up, you know, putting up the tables, laying out the food, all the things you do for a party, I thought, 'This is it. Our marriage is doomed.' We couldn't do anything as a team to save our lives, it seemed. I was positive our party would be a disaster, and also that our inability to work as a team signified the impending end of our marriage. We managed to get everything done just as the first guests came into the driveway."

Here, she pointed at the string of lights above them. "We were hanging lights just like those when the first car rolled in."

"And?"

"And the party was wonderful," Mama said.

Hannah could see her remembering—her eyes glistening with raw emotion that looked something like sorrow but could just as well have been happiness.

"By the time the last guests left, I realized, maybe we could make this thing work. Maybe we weren't destined for disaster after all."

But of course, Mama and Philip *were* destined for disaster, Hannah thought. She didn't speak.

"Hannah, I can tell my time is near."

Hannah gasped.

"Oh, don't be so dramatic, honey. I'm in my eighties, for goodness' sake. I've lived a good life. And I have only a few regrets. Which is more than we can say for some people, isn't it?"

"I suppose," Hannah said. "But why are you saying this to me?"

"There's something I want for you," Mama said. "I know that in my journal, I said I was completely happy raising you girls. And I was. But now that I'm older, I look back and wish I hadn't left Philip. At the time, I believed it was my only choice. But now I see that I was wrong." Her voice thickened, like she might cry, and Hannah reached over to cover her mother's hand with her own. "I was wrong," she said again. "I see that now. I deprived you of a father, and Philip of a daughter. And although we've had a lovely life together, I don't want to leave this world thinking you'll be alone."

"So you want me to saddle up and find a man?" Hannah had meant for it to come across as a joke, but it fell flat.

"Just don't convince yourself you won't," Mama said. "Do me that one favor."

A few seconds ticked by. Hannah was just thinking about getting up when she heard footsteps. And there was Tanner, again. This time, he was carrying two plates. The first was piled high with an assortment of all the dishes Hannah had cooked that morning, and the second held a delicate piece of cake.

"I noticed you were too busy to eat a single bite of food during the wedding," Tanner said. "Well, I saw you sneak a bite of cake after they served it. Anyway, I made you this plate. I know you're tired, and I'll feed it to you myself, if I have to." (Here, a shiver made its way over Hannah's skin.) "But you're dead on your feet. This will revive you."

He set the plates on the table next to Hannah, and Mama started to stand. "You're such a gentleman, Tanner," she said. Then she turned to Hannah. "Did you know he brought me a plate earlier, too? You're so good." She patted Tanner on the cheek. "I'm going to call it a night. It's been a big day."

Before leaving, she winked (quite obviously) at Hannah, who was sure Tanner noticed. When she was gone, Tanner said, "Great party. The Bradley girls really know how to throw a wedding."

"It was a fun night, for sure," Hannah said. "And thank you so much for this food. I didn't realize how hungry I was."

She felt ravenous, and a bit shy to scarf down this meal in front of Tanner.

"Want some?" she said, holding up the plate like an offering.

He shook his head and stood up. She thought he was going to call it a night, too, which she found disappointing. But then he stepped around behind her chair and began kneading her shoulders.

"You worked hard today," he said. "And I think it was worth it. Margaret and Ethan looked so happy."

"They did. I'm so happy for them."

Now his hands were on her neck, his dexterous fingers finding knots she hadn't even known were there. She took another bite of the meat, but what she really wanted to do was melt right into the chair. Exhaustion was taking over.

"Have you tried the cake? I mean, besides crumbs?" Tanner said. His fingers were massaging her scalp, and, even more relaxed now, she automatically separated a bite of cake from the slice and put it in her mouth.

"Wow," she said. "That's actually good. Really good."

"You sound surprised."

"It's just that I've never made a wedding cake before."

"I'd say it's a job well done," Tanner said. "You've earned a good night's sleep."

"If I can get myself up off this chair."

The thought of laying her head on her pillow was so tempting, she briefly considered closing her eyes and spending the night right here.

Tanner came around in front of her, then, and offered both hands. She took them, and he pulled her to standing, holding onto her hands, continuing to smile at her.

For the first time in her adult life, Hannah wished she didn't share a house with her mother. Mama may be in her eighties, but she wasn't so old as to be unaware. If Hannah invited Tanner in, and, more specifically, into her bed, Mama would know. No matter how quiet they were, she would know. And Hannah wouldn't be able to relax, thinking about Mama lying there, knowing Hannah was having sex with Tanner Lucas.

At that phrase—*having sex with Tanner Lucas*—Hannah's stomach did a little flip. Then she realized, she *wanted* to have sex with Tanner Lucas. Her body wanted to, and her mind wanted to. Now that was interesting.

"Wow," Tanner said. "There's a lot going on inside that beautiful mind of yours."

She wanted to agree, to admit that he was right, to beg him to take her, right here in the yard.

"I guess this is goodnight," she said.

"Is it?"

There was an intensity in his eyes, which Hannah knew was at once a question and an invitation. She could accept it, but not tonight.

"It is," she said.

Tanner leaned forward, slowly, giving Hannah every opportunity to stop him. Then, their fingers still linked, he kissed her. The kiss said so many things: it said he knew. He knew she wanted to take this farther. It said he was disappointed that it wasn't going to be tonight, but that he understood. And it said he cared about her. And when the kiss ended, Hannah felt like crying. She didn't know why, but she wanted nothing more than to wrap herself up in this man and his thoughtfulness and his kindness and understanding.

"Goodnight, Hannah."

He was gone. She was alone. And she felt deep regret that she hadn't invited Tanner to stay. Next time, she promised herself. Next time.

CHAPTER ELEVEN

Sunday morning dawned just as beautifully as Saturday morning had, but it carried that subdued, post-event energy. Mama and Hannah slept in, just a little, and gathered at the kitchen table to sip coffee in silence. Hands wrapped around her mug, Hannah relived the night before. Tanner's image appeared in every scene her memory offered. Hannah couldn't stop thinking about him. And Mama, who couldn't stop throwing glances at Hannah over the rim of her coffee mug, couldn't stop asking about him. Silently.

After a few minutes of this, Hannah sighed, with an exaggerated rise and fall of her chest. Then she started to laugh. Then Mama joined in.

"I can tell from the looks of you that you and Tanner didn't get down to business last night," Mama said. "You're just buzzing with the pent-up energy of an overfull balloon. I saw the way you were looking at each other, the way you were dancing. And I'm just dying to hear the story. Don't tell me you turned that man down. You want him, same as he wants you."

"There *is* no story," Hannah said.

Mama raised her eyebrows, obviously wanting an explanation.

But then the doorbell rang, and when Hannah opened the door, she found a potted plant on the stoop. Assuming it was a wedding gift for Margaret and Ethan, she lifted it up and absently noticed how pretty it was with its glossy leaves and bright red flowers. There was a little envelope tucked among the leaves. *Hannah* was written in blocky capital letters on the front.

She knew immediately that it was from Tanner, and found herself blushing like crazy (again) as she carried it to the table.

"From Tanner?" Mama said.

Maddening and funny, Hannah thought. How did Mama *know*?

"Beautiful," Mama said.

Hannah nodded and opened the card. All it said was, *Whenever you're ready*.

Her body screamed. *I'm ready now!*

"Are you going to make me ask?" Mama said.

"Nope," Hannah said.

She tucked the card into her back pocket, set the plant in the middle of the table, and went outside to get some fresh air.

After spending all day Sunday daydreaming about Tanner and what he'd do to her, whenever she was ready, it was a bit of a shock to arrive at school Monday morning and find Sadie sitting on the ground outside the school building, her arms wrapped around her legs, forehead on her knees. It was a *huge* shock to see her hair: it was shaved so close to the scalp Hannah could see the veins under the skin. If almost twenty years of teaching had taught her anything, it was that the importance of a poker face was in direct proportion to an event's shock value.

"Good morning," Hannah said, and without looking up, Sadie grunted in response.

"How was your weekend?"

Another grunt as Hannah unlocked the door, and then a reluctant, "How was yours?" as Sadie stood up, keeping her face turned toward the wall.

"It was good," Hannah said. "My sister—Margaret, the one with dark hair—got married."

"I've never been to a wedding." Sadie slouched past her and into the building. "How was it?"

How did a person describe such a thing? They walked along the hallway to Hannah's classroom. "It was beautiful and fun and tons of work and exhausting and exhilarating, all wrapped into one day."

Sadie didn't answer, but she seemed to be digesting that information.

"What did you do this weekend?" Hannah said.

In the brief span of time between her question and Sadie's response, her imagination placed Sadie into the wedding memories. She had her hair back, wore a dress, and danced with the other kids. She joined the conga line, lip syncing to "Stayin' Alive."

"Nothing much," Sadie said. She looked at the floor. "Mostly just sat around, I guess."

For the first time that morning, Sadie finally looked up at Hannah, and despite all her practice at remaining expressionless, at not reacting to students' outfits or appearances, she gasped.

A dark, purplish bruise stood out underneath Sadie's right eye, and her entire right cheek was so swollen it pushed her eye closed.

"What happened?"

It was everything Hannah could do to stop herself from grabbing Sadie's arm and demanding that she lead Hannah straight to whoever was responsible for what she was seeing, so Hannah could get her hands on him or her.

Although Sadie answered, "Nothing," she looked right into Hannah's eyes as if to ask her not to believe it was nothing, as if to say, *of course it was something*. As if to beg for help.

"That doesn't look like nothing."

Hannah waited for an excuse, something along the classic lines of the abused: "I fell," or, "I ran into an open door."

But Sadie remained silent, just staring into Hannah's eyes. Someone came through the door, and Sadie used the disruption as an opportunity to break the eye contact. She cleared her throat and sat down at her desk. She didn't speak again for the rest of the day.

Hannah watched her, though, and noticed her movements seemed stiff and tired. Almost as if she'd worked in the yard all day the day before, or done a hard workout. Or, said a voice in the back of Hannah's mind, as if she'd been beaten up.

Looking at the bruise on Sadie's face, it was impossible not to imagine all the horrible things that had happened to her over the weekend. It was impossible not to feel guilty for having so much fun, at Margaret's wedding, with Tanner, with her family.

Here she was, a responsible, caring adult, who saw a child was hurting. And yes, Wyoming state law required her to report suspected child abuse. The bruise wasn't the only thing worth checking out. So were the clothes, Sadie's behavior, her shaved head, everything. Hannah knew she had to call child services again, immediately.

But even as she asked Missy Cartwright to watch her class while she ran to the office, she wondered if there wasn't more she could do, some tangible way she could help.

The bored-sounding woman who took her call assured Hannah that someone may or may not make it to Sadie's house to investigate. She didn't say as much, but Hannah imagined her there, at a worn-out desk, popping her gum, twirling her hair, saying, "Well, you know, ma'am, we're just overrun with cases. Absolutely overrun."

That phone call was Hannah's only obligation, legally. But she had to do more. She couldn't just leave Sadie's destiny in the hands of some woman on the other end of the phone line.

For the rest of the day, as Hannah went through the motions (giving a lesson on long division, assigning a book report, going over sentence structure), she simultaneously worked on another plan. As it formulated, she weighed the risks against the benefits. Would she be breaking the law—even though it was for a good cause? Yes. Could she get arrested? Yes. But *would* she? It wasn't likely. Not only because there were just a handful of police officers in Walker—she thought now of Joey Spear, all elbows and knees and hooked nose, and knew he would be reluctant to put her in cuffs—but also because Sadie's aunt and uncle were unlikely to *want* her arrested.

Also, was it really a good idea? Would it benefit Sadie? Or was she doing it for herself? Yes, she decided: it was a good idea. It would benefit Sadie. It would get her out of that neglectful environment and into a nurturing one. And Hannah was doing it for Sadie *and* for herself.

What would Mama, Sarah, and Margaret say? What would they think? Probably that she'd lost her mind. And Tanner? Why was she even thinking about what Tanner would think? But, what *would* he think?

After an entire day of watching Sadie tiptoe around, skittish, eyes darting from one place to another, she decided it was her only option. It didn't have to be permanent. It was an immediate, temporary solution. If the people from child services came, they could decide what to do long-term. But this was the best option at the moment.

So, when the final bell rang, and Sadie was last in line to leave, as always, Hannah stopped her on her way out the door.

"Hey," she said.

"Hey," Sadie said.

"Heading home?" Hannah said.

Sadie looked away. She bit her bottom lip, and then finally said, "Yeah."

Her voice sounded thick, like her throat was tight.

"How would you like to come home with me?"

There was a pause while Sadie seemed to consider this. She looked at Hannah, then, and this time it was like she was trying to figure her out.

"Like, for dinner?"

"Or, I don't know, you could sleep over if you want."

"I'm pretty sure that's against school policy. Or the law. Or something."

Hannah shrugged. She'd worried about this. Sadie was a pretty perceptive kid. She probably knew about policies and rules. So Hannah feigned ignorance.

"I don't know," she said. "So you can hang out until we find out otherwise."

This seemed to satisfy Sadie. Something shifted, as if she'd made a decision. She nodded. "Okay."

Hannah didn't know what she'd expected. A cheer, maybe? Jumping up and down? A smile, at the very least. But not this … quiet acquiescence.

"Um, so, I have a couple more things to do before we can leave." She looked at her watch. "Technically, I'm supposed to stay until four, but it's probably okay if we scoot out a little early today. You can have a seat for now."

Sadie moved back to her desk, where she sat down, her backpack still on, as if she were ready to bolt at any moment. Hannah sat down, too, and made a show of looking at her computer screen, even though in reality, she couldn't concentrate.

Was she really about to take this child home, like a stray puppy? If she did get in trouble, would it be the end of her career? Maybe she should talk to the principal, Aaron Wells. He'd know what to do. But Hannah knew he'd tell her this was a bad idea. Maybe it was. But she'd already set it in motion.

"Ms. Bradley?"

Hannah startled, as if she'd been caught doing something she shouldn't.

"Hmm?" she said.

She looked at Sadie, and again, was shocked by the dark purple staining her face.

"Do you have any food here?"

Hannah pulled out a granola bar and tossed it to Sadie.

"Thanks."

"We have food at home, too," she said. "If you're hungry, we can eat an early dinner."

Sadie didn't answer, as wrapped up as she was in eating the granola bar—as if she hadn't eaten all weekend. Maybe she hadn't. In fact, it was likely that she hadn't.

The idea of this little girl, with skinny legs and smudges on her knees, waiting all weekend for a granola bar, made Hannah's resolve even stronger.

Taking her home was the right thing to do. It was the only thing to do.

———

THE KITCHEN HUMMED with activity as all the women prepared dinner that evening. Hannah had come in and announced that Sadie was staying for dinner—and overnight. Mama, a brief look of surprise crossing her face, sent Sadie outside to pick tomatoes for the salad. Now, Hannah faced her mom and sisters.

"I mean, it's kidnapping, Hannah," Sarah said. She snapped the ends off the asparagus and tossed them into the compost bin with a little too much force. Her voice was almost a whisper, but not quite, which made Hannah feel like she was yelling.

"Technically…" Hannah said. She let her voice trail off and whisked the marinade a little faster.

"I'd be—well, 'upset' doesn't quite cover it—if one of Amelia's teachers just decided to take her home."

"I had Sadie call home, but no one answered," Hannah said. She knew it was a weak excuse for taking a child for whom someone else was responsible.

"Weak," Margaret said, echoing Hannah's thought.

She was pitting cherries, and her lips were as stained as her fingers were.

"I know, I know," Hannah said. She lifted chicken thighs out of their tray and into the baking dish, then poured the marinade over them.

"I think it's honorable, what you're doing," Mama said. "But I'm also afraid it could land you in big trouble, Hannah."

"What if they call the police?" Sarah said.

"I don't think they'll even notice she's gone, honestly," Hannah said. Her voice carried a lot of conviction, but she wasn't as sure as she sounded. What if they did? They were probably the kind of people who could completely neglect a child, ignore their duty to care for her, and then turn around and act like she was the most precious thing in the world to them, just to get something out of it.

"There are proper channels," Mama said.

Hannah, who'd been wrestling with plastic wrap, covering the baking dish, put both hands on the counter.

"I know. But did you see her face?"

At this, everyone went silent. The injury to Sadie's face was evidence that something had to be done. And right away, too.

Sadie bounded noisily up the steps, and came banging through the screen door, a bowl of tomatoes in her hands.

"Got the tomatoes," she said.

For a moment, no one spoke. Mama recovered first.

"Thanks, honey," she said. "Why don't you bring them in and wash them? Then you can help me set the table."

Agreeable as could be, Sadie bounced over to the sink and began washing the tomatoes. It was obvious she'd never done it before. She ran water into the bowl, which quickly overflowed and ran straight onto the floor. When it splashed her feet, she jumped back, then looked around at all the adults, clearly afraid she was about to get in trouble.

"I heard a splash," Margaret said.

That broke the ice, and everyone—even Sadie—laughed.

"I'm sorry," Mama said. "I should have given you a colander. And instructions."

"You said, 'Wash the tomatoes,'" Sadie said. "So I washed the tomatoes."

Mama chuckled and grabbed the dish towel from where it hung on the oven door handle. She tossed it to Sadie, who immediately began blotting up the mess, the tips of her ears bright red. Hannah knelt down to help her.

"You know," she said, "you're not the first one to do something silly in this kitchen."

Sadie continued her industrious drying of the floor without answering.

So Hannah went on with her story. "Once, when I was about your age—maybe a little older—Mama asked me to bake a cake." She paused. "Actually, she didn't ask me. I begged and begged. I promised her I was old enough to do it myself. Now, you might be thinking you're old enough, too. But the truth is, I'd never baked *anything* all by myself before. We were having friends over for dinner, and Mama bought this strawberry baking mix. She was going to make a poke cake. Have you ever had one of those?"

Sadie shook her head.

"You bake the cake, and then you poke holes in it and pour a puree over it before icing it. Delicious. It's so good. In fact, maybe we'll make one, one of these days. Anyway. Mama bought the mix and she'd planned to make it, but I *so* wanted to. I swore to her that I could do it. So she gave me the recipe and walked right out of the kitchen."

They were done drying the floor. Hannah took the towel from Sadie, wrung it out, and then folded it and held it in both hands. Sadie seemed to have relaxed a little. She leaned back against the counter and folded her arms.

"The first part went okay. I mean, the directions are right there, on the box. I mixed up that cake, popped it in the oven, set the timer, the whole works. And when the timer went off, I even checked the cake with a toothpick, to make sure it was done, you know?"

Sadie nodded, although Hannah could tell she didn't know. Poor thing had probably never baked, with or without supervision. They'd have to remedy that.

"I'm not sure exactly where I went wrong," Hannah said. "Maybe I didn't let it cool long enough before I poked the holes. Or, it's possible that I mixed up the icing wrong. I may have gotten the wrong ratio of whipped topping to pudding, or water to pudding, or ... well, anyway. It was a disaster. By the time I'd poked the holes, poured the strawberry puree... come to think of it, the puree may have been too watery ... and then tried to frost it, it was a mess. A soggy, sticky mess. There were crumbs everywhere. The cake broke into itty bitty pieces as I spread the icing, and bigger chunks just materialized out of nowhere. I tried so hard to fix it. I used a butter knife, a spatula, my fingers, but I kept making matters worse. Nothing would smooth out that icing."

Hannah covered her eyes, as if doing so could erase the image from her memory.

"Did everyone eat it?"

Dropping her hands, Hannah nodded. "Believe it or not, everyone ate it. It looked like it had gone through a garbage disposal."

"Tasted good, though," Margaret said from her spot at the counter.

"Which doesn't mean much, coming from her," Sarah said. "She'll eat anything."

"I was so embarrassed," Hannah said. "I'd been so confident, so sure I could do it. And it was a disaster."

"I wouldn't call it a disaster, if everyone ate it," Margaret said.

"Do you remember what it looked like?"

Margaret shrugged. "Sure. But like I said. Tasted good."

"Yeah, but you'll eat anything," Hannah said.

Mama had remained silent during this conversation, which was unusual. Finally, she said, "Well, I, for one, think that's part of why you were so determined to become great in the kitchen. And it paid off."

The story seemed to have done its job. By the time they sat down to dinner, Sadie was relaxed, even if she wasn't particularly chatty. The fact that she wasn't boisterous, boiling over with excitement, made Hannah wonder if she'd made the right choice by bringing her home.

Hannah had expected her to be smiling, joking, happy. But there was none of that as the little girl listened to the adults talk about the change in the weather, the progress on the new houses, *Halloween* for goodness' sake. Halloween *always* made kids excited.

After dinner, Sadie helped with cleanup, carrying dishes to the sink, rinsing them, and putting them into the dishwasher. Her loading skills were a little haphazard, Hannah noticed, but the effort was there. When the dishwasher was humming away, the table had been wiped down, and the food had been put in the fridge, Mama sent Sadie outside to gather eggs.

"Hannah, I think you're making a mistake," Mama said. She stood at the window, arms crossed, watching Sadie. "There are proper channels for this sort of thing, and you didn't go through them."

"I called child services," Hannah said.

"But you didn't even wait for them to show up," Sarah said. "You just took someone's child."

"Someone had to do something," Hannah said. "Today, it's a bruise on her face. Who knows what it would be tomorrow? Who knows if she'd even show up at school next week, or how much damage is being done? I couldn't just stand by and watch it happen. She has so much potential. And if nobody takes a stand for her, well, you know potential goes both ways. She could turn out great, or she could put her smarts to use as a criminal mastermind."

"Kids are resilient," Sarah said. "She's spirited. She'll be fine. I think you should send her home."

"Now?"

"It's only going to get harder, the longer you keep her," Margaret said.

"What if I just went over there, talked to them? Her aunt and uncle. What if I just ask them, get their permission?"

"I suppose that would be something," Mama said. "But if anything came up, it would be your word against theirs. They could claim you never asked them."

"What if I recorded the conversation?" Hannah said, knowing even as the words left her mouth that she sounded ridiculous.

"Are you some kind of spy, now?" Sarah said.

"Our Hannah's changing, ladies," Margaret said. "First, she goes on an actual date with an actual man, and then, she breaks the law."

"It wasn't a—" Hannah started.

Mama Katherine interrupted her. "She's coming back. Let's talk about this later. But Hannah, I hope you'll get this straightened out. I don't want to have to come visit you in jail. Where did you plan on putting her tonight, by the way?"

Hannah set Sadie up in Sarah's old bedroom, since Sarah and Donny were still staying in their RV.

"Ms. Bradley?" Sadie said as Hannah put her hand on the light switch to turn off the light. "Do you think I can stay here? I mean, not just for tonight."

Although Hannah wanted to promise her everything—a home, a family, a lifetime of happiness—she knew better than to make vows she couldn't keep.

"I don't know," Hannah said. "But we'll start with tonight."

She shut the door and decided she needed some alone time, some time to think. So she sneaked out the side door and went for a walk. The sun hadn't set completely, and a few birds were still chirping in the trees by the creek. The sound of the water bubbling over the rocks soothed her, as it always did.

When it came to Sadie, Hannah knew there were options. She could call child services again, tomorrow, and say it was an emergency situation. But even if someone came right away to remove Sadie from her aunt and uncle's house, she'd just end up somewhere else—and who knew what kind of home that would be? She could take her right into the police station and report that someone had injured her. But Sadie hadn't actually admitted that. What if she really had done something clumsy? That happened with kids. And if that was what happened, Hannah would be starting a wild goose chase if she reported her suspicions.

As she often did when she found out about a child in circumstances like these, Hannah wondered how. How did the adult who was supposed to be responsible for a child wind up being so *irresponsible*? How did any human end up lacking basic compassion, or the skills to meet a child's needs?

Usually it was some kind of trauma, wasn't it? Something terrible had probably befallen Sadie's aunt and uncle when they were younger. And now, forced to live with them, Sadie was experiencing trauma, too. Which meant she faced a grim future.

This pattern wasn't true for everyone, though, Hannah realized.

Some people turned it around. Mama, for example. No matter how angry Hannah felt about the way Mama handled things when it came to Philip Carlisle, Jr., Hannah had to admit that even after going through the trauma of losing her son, she'd still managed to create a wonderful life for Hannah, and for Sarah and Margaret.

The light was almost gone. The birds were quiet, now, and Hannah turned around to head back to the house. Then, even though she had been avoiding the topic for days, pushing it away whenever it showed up on the fringes of her consciousness, she again considered reaching out to Philip Carlisle, Jr. He was her father. Shouldn't they get to know each other? Or, shouldn't they at least have the chance?

As she walked along the trail she and her sisters had been wearing through the tall grass since that golden childhood, Hannah made two decisions:

First, she would walk Sadie home after school tomorrow. She didn't know whether she'd ask the aunt and uncle if Sadie could stay for a while, but she'd at least meet them in person. Get a feel for what kind of people they were.

Second, she would track down Philip Carlisle, Jr. and see if he was willing to meet.

She had no idea what she would say, in either situation. But, Hannah knew, life doesn't come with a script.

CHAPTER TWELVE

FIRST THINGS MUST ALWAYS COME FIRST, Hannah thought, as the final bell rang Monday. She'd told Sadie at lunchtime that she planned to walk her home.

"I can't just keep you forever," she'd said.

Sadie had responded, eyes downcast in disappointment, "Why not."

It wasn't even a question, not really.

They walked side by side. Hannah wished Sadie was a little girl, small enough that she could take her hand, to offer reassurance.

But wasn't it a false reassurance? Wasn't Hannah planning to leave Sadie at the doorstep of her aunt and uncle, who, at best, ignored her existence, and at worst … her train of thought trailed off as they stopped in front of the tiny house. The sidewalk was so narrow they'd have to go single file, and Hannah gestured for Sadie to go first.

The image of the girl, in an oversized t-shirt and ragged shorts, making her way up to the dingy, hopeless-looking shack, made Hannah's heart ache. But, she reminded herself, she couldn't just take a child. And besides, she hadn't even met the aunt and uncle yet. Maybe they were perfectly nice people.

The front door opened as Sadie approached. Hannah expected the hinges to squeal, but they didn't, which seemed like a sign that things really weren't so bad. Then someone who Hannah assumed was the aunt, judging by the stringy blond hair that reached her shoulders, half-emerged. Sadie froze.

"There you are," the woman said. She didn't sound pleased or displeased, or surprised. "Didn't come home last night, eh?"

"I, uh, stayed at Ms. Bradley's." Here, Sadie hooked a thumb toward Hannah, who offered a wave and what she hoped was a friendly smile.

"Who's Ms. Bradley?" Now there was a definite sneer, a distaste, in the woman's tone.

"My teacher," Sadie said. So, Ms. Bradley wasn't a household name. At least, not in Sadie's household.

Still, the woman didn't come any further out of the house. Hannah couldn't see her face. "Well, get in here," she said.

"Oh!" Hannah said, as Sadie started to go inside. "I'd like to introduce myself."

Now the door opened, just slightly more. "You're Ms. Bradley, right?" the woman said.

"Right," Hannah said. "You must be Sadie's aunt."

"I must be," the woman said. "She lives here, doesn't she?"

This was probably happening because of Hannah's bad choice to invite Sadie to stay over without getting permission. Why had she been so stupid to think that would be okay? The magnitude of the situation hit Hannah.

"Look, I'm sorry. I tried calling, but—"

"Phone's disconnected."

Hannah pressed her lips together, then tried again. "I wanted to introduce myself. I hadn't gotten a chance to meet you at parent-teacher conferences, so—"

"We're not her parents, are we?"

"So I thought I'd come by and tell you Sadie's doing great in class."

"Doin' us proud, Sades." This, without any enthusiasm. Now, she moved back into the darkness of the house and shouted, "Hey, Mikey, Sadie's doing great in class."

There was no response.

"Well, aren't you coming in?" the aunt said to Sadie.

Sadie looked back at Hannah. Her expression showed that she was ashamed, but not caught off-guard by this behavior.

"I didn't catch your name," Hannah said.

"Rita."

"Well, it's nice to meet you." Hannah extended her hand to shake, and finally, with a loud, irritated sigh, the woman moved over the threshold and onto the porch. She squinted, hard, as if she hadn't seen the sun in days. And the squinting wasn't the only indication she hadn't spent time in the outside world: her hair was dark and greasy at the part, and her skin was so pale she looked sickly. She wore a white tank top, the ribbed kind men wore as undershirts. She wasn't wearing a bra. Her pants were cut-off sweats. There was a huge hole in one thigh, exposing her pale skin. The strangest part: she looked like she was a teenager. Hannah would be shocked if this kid had even celebrated her eighteenth birthday.

Rita took her hand, gave it one hearty shake, and then sank back into the house and opened the door wider, waiting for Sadie to follow her. Sadie did, ducking her head as she went in.

Hannah remained where she was when Rita started to close the door. When it was just slightly ajar, the girl opened it back up and stuck her head out. She was squinting again.

"Oh, by the way," she said. "Mikey and I don't care if Sadie comes to your house. You seem like a nice lady. You can have her whenever you want."

"Oh!" Hannah said. "Okay. Um, thanks?"

"No problem."

The door shut and Hannah stood there on the sidewalk, blinking in surprise. When nothing else happened, she turned around and walked back to work. As she went through the motions—wiping down the white board, writing tomorrow's date and bell work on it, placing the morning worksheets on desks—she found that she couldn't stop thinking about Sadie and her strange aunt.

It was possible Rita was older than she looked. Some women didn't seem to age at all, and if Rita spent all her time inside, then her skin wasn't exposed to the elements. But she was definitely younger than twenty-five. Was that old enough to be raising and caring for a ten-year-old? Hannah, having dealt with her fair share of ten-year-olds, didn't think so. But was it really any of her business?

Again, she compared the two versions of the Sadie she'd come to know: the helpful, talkative, funny Sadie she saw when it was just the two of them, and the quiet, mono-syllabic Sadie who showed up when the other kids were around. Again, she pictured Sadie's smile the other day when she'd walked out of the creek, soaking wet, teeth chattering. And then she thought of how she'd looked just now, when Hannah brought her home: shoulders slightly slumped, lips pressed together. *That* was her existence.

Hannah shuddered. Maybe she'd start inviting Sadie to spend the weekends with her. That could help. Maybe, with part-time normalcy, she'd thrive despite living in a dark house with a strange, vampiric adolescent as a mother figure.

Yes, she decided. That's what she'd do: invite Sadie to come home with her on Friday. Finished for the day, she stacked up her papers, grabbed her lunchbox, and made her way to the car.

It was time to shift gears and work on her second project: tracking down her father. The mere thought of finding him, calling him, terrified her. She could already feel herself coming up with ways to delay her research. Maybe she'd feed and water the chickens before she sat down at the computer. It would be efficient to start a load of laundry, so she could switch it over when she was done.

No, that wouldn't do: she couldn't use chores to procrastinate. As soon as she got home, she'd set down her things, grab a drink (iced tea or, even better, iced tea with bourbon), and get to work.

Tanner Lucas immediately sidetracked her when she pulled into the driveway. He was just getting out of his own truck, his worn cowboy boots hitting the ground as she shifted into park. He waved, casually, and she waved back. He waited, an elbow on the hood of his truck, while she gathered up her lunch box and purse and school folders.

"Hey," he said when she finally shut her door.

"Hey," she said, noticing, and hating, that she was going all warm and gooey at the sight of him and the sound of his voice.

"Everything okay?" he said.

"Yeah, why?"

"You just looked a little, I don't know, stressed."

"Oh, it's nothing," she said. "I was just talking myself into not procrastinating on a big project."

"Anything I can help with?"

"Not really, unfortunately. But thank you. Anyway, shouldn't you be, you know, building my sisters' houses?"

"I just stopped by to check the progress. We have some subs out today—the windows guys. So I wasn't planning on staying long. Let me know if you change your mind."

"I will," Hannah said, wishing she'd asked him to come in, have a drink with her, and join her at the desk. She didn't *need* help, but some moral support wouldn't hurt. Of its own free will, her body turned to face the direction Tanner had gone. Her chin lifted, as if she were about to call out to him, to let him know she had changed her mind. Her mouth opened.

Her brain stopped her. She closed her mouth, turned around, and went inside alone.

She set her things on the table and went into the kitchen, paying careful attention to each step: get out a glass. Set it on the counter. Open the freezer. Take out a handful of ice cubes. Close the freezer. Drop the ice cubes into the glass. Open the liquor cabinet. Get out the bourbon. Pour a shot into the glass. Add a little more. Put the bourbon away. Get it back out. Add another pour. Put it away. Open the fridge. Get out the iced tea pitcher. Close the fridge. Pour the tea. Put the pitcher back in. Open the utensil drawer. Get out a spoon. Stir the drink. Put the spoon in the sink. Pick up the glass. Walk to the desk. Sit down.

Okay. Here she was. She turned on the computer, waited for it to boot up, wondered where her mother was. Margaret and Ethan, and Sarah and Donny, for that matter, were probably off doing house-related stuff. They'd spent much of their time recently choosing furnishings and flooring and countertops and paint colors.

She could go look for Mama, check in, tell her about Sadie's weird aunt.

The computer emitted its friendly chime, letting her know it was all booted up and ready, reminding her not to procrastinate. She opened the Internet browser, and before she could chicken out, she typed in, *Philip Carlisle, Jr. California contact information.*

And there it was: *Golden Delicious Orchards, Linden, California.*

The address and phone number and website link were all right there. All she had to do was pick up her phone and dial. She picked it up, tapped the phone app, looked at the computer screen again, entered the numbers, and tapped the green button to call. She sipped—then gulped —her drink as the phone rang. Once, twice, and then an automated answering service clicked on. "You've reached Golden Delicious Orchards. If you know your party's extension, enter it at any time. Or, choose one of the following options. Press the star key to return to this menu."

There was no menu item for, "If you're looking to reconnect with the father you've never met."

There were choices for administrative offices, sales, public relations. She tapped three for public relations, sipped her drink. The system clicked over, Hannah heard a few more rings, and then another recording. She gulped, listening.

"This is Robin Reynolds, public relations specialist at Golden Delicious Orchards."

Robin's recorded voice gave the typical instructions for leaving a message, and Hannah hung up. What would she even *say*?

Hello, this is Hannah Bradley. A member of the public. Actually, my name should be Hannah Carlisle. Philip Carlisle has no idea, but he's my father.

How awkward would that be?

When Hannah and her sisters were teenagers, they'd spend their Saturdays listening to the radio. When the request lines opened, they'd call over and over and over until they got through, just to request the same song they'd requested the week before.

Now, the grown-up Hannah imagined herself calling Golden Delicious Orchards that way—over and over and over until she got through to a human, who she could ask to help her access Philip Carlisle, Jr.

"Get a life, Hannah," she said. She pushed back the desk chair and stood up.

It would do her good to get some fresh air. She grabbed her glass. Outside, evening was falling. The big trees shaded the yard, and the air held just the slightest chill. Not enough for a sweater, but a hint that fall was almost here. Tanner's truck was still parked in the driveway, and Hannah glanced over to the site of Sarah and Donny's house. Several other trucks were lined up in what would be the driveway, and a few crew members worked on the roof. Before Hannah made the conscious decision to do so, she found herself walking, in a meandering sort of way, over to the site.

The house was looking good, Hannah thought. The windows were in, and some of the walls were up. With any luck, Sarah and Donny would be all moved in before the end of fall. Hannah stepped through the front door, into the foyer. She sipped her drink. Not for the first time, Hannah marveled at Margaret's ability to design spaces that just felt good. And she'd done this one as she was going blind, which made it even more impressive.

The foyer opened up into the living area—great room, kitchen, and dining—on one side, and the bedrooms on the other. In the great room, windows overlooked the creek. Hannah imagined a pair of chairs there, or a smaller couch, where Sarah and Donny could sit and listen to the water, watch it go by, sparkling over the rocks.

Suddenly, she felt an overwhelming sense of loneliness. Would she ever have someone to sit with in a cozy living room? Mama wouldn't live forever, and what would Hannah do when she was gone? She would be completely alone. Yes, her sisters would live on the same property, just a few steps away, but when it really came down to it, she'd go to bed and wake up alone day after day, knowing Sarah and Donny and Margaret and Ethan were in their own houses, together. While Hannah sat alone during the evenings, sipping her tea or watching TV, her sisters and their husbands would be exchanging stories or sharing comfortable silence. Or making love.

How had she let her life come to this?

"Great view, isn't it?" Tanner's voice startled Hannah out of her pity party.

The ice clinked in her glass as she turned around to greet him. She felt moisture on her cheeks and dashed it away with her fingertips.

Tanner was at her side in a couple of quick strides. "Are you okay?"

She nodded, too quickly. "I'm fine."

"Really?" He looked concerned, and that made her feel even worse.

"Really," she said. "I promise."

"Want to talk about it?"

Did she?

"I don't know," she said. "It's kind of silly, really."

"Is it? It doesn't look silly. Let's take a walk."

She nodded, walked out through the unfinished wall on the opposite side of the great room, and stepped out next to the creek. Right away, she felt calmer—and even more so when Tanner joined her. He took her hand as if it were the most natural thing in the world to do, and led her away from the houses, along the creek's edge toward the big tree with the tire swing.

So many memories lived here.

There was the time Mama had put the girls in pristine white dresses for photos and Margaret had believed she could keep herself clean while playing in the creek. Hannah tried to stop her, but of course, it was Margaret and she wouldn't be stopped. She ran through the mud, kicking up splatters that landed all over her: on her skirt, her arms, her face. Hannah flitted after her, a little mother hen, scolding, and Sarah stood by, amused, until Mama's voice rang out through the meadow: "Girls! I'm ready."

Then they'd frozen, staring at each other, not moving until Mama came down to find them.

Mama had been angry for about a minute, and then she proceeded with the photo shoot. The favorite shot remained on the mantle to this day, showcasing a muddy-but-grinning Margaret, a peeved-looking Hannah, and a smiling Sarah.

Then there was the time Hannah had found a tiny kitten at the base of a tree. She'd been skipping rocks and heard mewling so loud, she expected to find a full-sized cat. But when she followed the sound, she found the orange tabby tucked up behind some tall grasses. He wasn't even old enough to eat regular cat food. And although Mama warned her he might not survive the week, they bought him a bottle and kitten milk, and Hannah fed him around the clock. He'd grasp onto her sleeves, his tiny claws almost clear, and drink from that bottle like a champ. Within a few weeks, he was eating on his own. They named him Champ. Although he spent summer nights out in the meadow (and slept all day on the porch), he spent all winter inside, curled up in various places throughout the house: next to the fireplace, on the foot of Hannah's bed, on the back of the couch. He lived a good, long life at Seedling Homestead, catching mice and rats and lizards and leaving them on the stoop as gifts.

Thinking about Champ reminded Hannah how much she'd enjoyed having a cat around, and she saw with a new clarity why women became cat ladies.

"Wow," Tanner said. "However silly that thing is, it's definitely taking up a lot of mental space, isn't it? I've never heard you go this long without speaking."

She elbowed him, shot him a smile. "Just remembering, that's all. And contemplating my future as a cat lady."

"Ah," he said. "So that's what's bothering you."

He took the glass from her hand and took a swig, exaggerating the motions, making her laugh, easing the tension. She hadn't even decided whether she would share her worries with him at all, much less jump in so quickly. But what could it hurt to talk about it?

"I've always thought my life was perfect," she said, accepting her drink from him. "And lately, I guess I've just been questioning whether 'perfect' is really what I thought it was. Not only has my mother kept a secret from me my entire life, but also, I've had kind of an epiphany about what my life will be like when she's gone."

Her voice threatened to crack, so she stopped there. Tanner didn't respond right away, and she began to question whether she'd said too much or not enough or something weird. They came to a spot where the grass came all the way up to the edge of the water, and Tanner sat down, his long legs bent, his elbows on his knees. He patted the grass next to him, and Hannah sat.

"You know your mama's still got quite a bit of zip, right?" he said.

Hannah chuckled.

"She does. But nobody's immortal. Her ending up in the hospital was a reminder of that, you know?"

"I get it," Tanner said. "My favorite aunt, Tess, was in the hospital last week. She's the aunt who always sneaked me cookies after dinner, brought me her favorite childhood books, drove up to the college campus to stay for a weekend my freshman year."

"She was in the hospital last week?" Hannah said.

"Yeah," he said. "She had a heart attack. Weirdest thing. She's as healthy as a person can be. It was scary. We thought we were going to lose her."

She hadn't even known. Hannah wanted to touch him, to offer him comfort, but she wasn't sure how, so she kept her arms wrapped around her knees. She pictured Tanner here last week, chatting with her mama, going over plans, cutting wood. He'd seemed so calm and normal. And she felt terrible for not knowing he was hurting.

"I'm so sorry," she said. "I wish I'd known. But she's on the mend?"

"She's a tough old bird," he said. "She's on the mend. She'll be fine. Just has to eat a heart-healthy diet and get exercise and all that. But in those moments when we thought we might lose her, it seemed unimaginable."

"I know exactly what you mean," Hannah said.

They sat there without speaking as the sun inched toward the horizon. Hannah watched a couple of birds play on the branches of the willow tree. They darted from branch to branch, unseating each other over and over, all the while chattering at each other. Tanner nudged her and pointed to the other side of the creek.

A family of deer—a buck, a doe, and two fawns—were walking toward the creek. Hannah had always loved deer, with their slender, graceful legs and their big eyes. And the babies! Knobby-kneed and fragile, they drank from the water while their parents stared at Hannah and Tanner. Hannah imagined they were assessing whether these humans were a threat, but apparently, they decided things were safe, because they took a drink, too.

When they'd had their fill, they moved away from the water and began nibbling on the bushes.

"Mama hates deer," Hannah whispered to Tanner. "They always eat her roses. But they sure are pretty. I've always secretly loved them."

"We used to have this doe that would bring her fawns into our yard every spring," Tanner said. "My mom hated them, too. Ate her irises. I'll never tell her this, and I know you won't, either, but I was luring them there. I'd take apples from the trees and make trails to lead them from the woods into our yard. I loved to watch them. So I'd set out the apples, and then I'd sit by the window and wait. And there I'd be, watching them so quietly, and suddenly Mom would realize they were there, and she'd start screeching. Run out the front door, let the screen door slam, and sprint into the yard, waving her arms above her head, screeching the whole time."

"That obviously amused you."

"It did." They made eye contact, and Tanner's eyes were twinkling.

"So you have a history of driving women crazy."

She hadn't intended the double entendre, but his expression changed, ever so slightly.

"Do I drive you crazy?"

There was something in the air now, some kind of intense energy that buzzed between them.

"You do," Hannah said.

What was she *doing*?

Tanner stood up and pulled Hannah up, too. He wrapped his hands around her shoulders, gently, and kissed her—not gently at all. For the briefest second, surprise had her frozen, uncertain of how to respond. Her body took over, and she leaned into him and kissed him right back. He put his arms around her, and she felt a yearning so strong she thought she might strip Tanner Lucas down right there in the grass.

She'd never had sex outdoors. She'd always thought that would be scandalous. But at the moment, she thought it would be wonderful.

Tanner must have thought so, too, because he was pressing his body against hers with an urgency that made Hannah's entire body ache. She'd never experienced this need before. Her fingers curled into the front of his shirt. He groaned, a sound that made Hannah think she might actually catch on fire.

Suddenly, he grasped her shoulders again and pulled back, just enough to break the contact everywhere except where his hands still curled around her shoulders and hers rested on his chest.

"Hannah," he said.

"Tanner."

He took a deep breath. "I want you. Badly. I have wanted you since I first set eyes on you in that ratty old Rockwood Farms sweatshirt you used to wear to that eight a.m. biology class."

Unable to speak (and simultaneously thinking, *that* sweatshirt?!), Hannah nodded. Her heart was beating so fast. She licked her lips, and then managed, "So, is that a problem?"

His laugh was humorless.

"Maybe? I mean, you've always hated me."

"'Hate' is a strong word. I've never *hated* you."

"That's a lie. I want to take you to bed, Hannah. Immediately. I want to make love to you right here in this grass." He released her shoulders then and rubbed his forehead, continuing on as if talking to himself. "I admit, in all the visions I had, I never imagined our first time would be in the grass."

Amused now, Hannah said, "You had visions?"

He froze, then looked up at her. "I have. Lots of them."

"Huh."

"You know I've always held a flame for you."

"So you say. But I'm still wrapping my mind around it. I always thought you thought I was … naive? Or, not very smart. Or something."

"Or something," Tanner said. "Definitely 'or something.'"

Suddenly, they were kissing again. The tone had evolved into something with which Hannah wasn't familiar. The idea of him tearing her clothes off right then and there seemed inevitable. She wanted him to. Which was weird. And exciting.

Whenever Margaret shared stories of her trysts, which often included the ripping off of shirts and hiking up of skirts, Hannah thought it all seemed a bit contrived. But here, now, she wanted nothing more than to hike up her skirt and let Tanner in. Only, she wasn't wearing a skirt. And that was a real pity.

His hands were under her shirt, against her skin, unhooking her bra. Her hands went to work, too, unbuttoning his shirt and pulling it off his arms.

Again, she thought, *What am I doing?* They were out in the middle of the property. Hannah knew from lots of experience that Mama couldn't see them from inside the house, but what if she came outside? Well, she'd probably spot them, smile, and turn right back around. She'd go inside and rejoice. Maybe even dance.

Hannah's hands had apparently developed a mind of their own, and they were unbuttoning Tanner's jeans, pulling the waistband down. Tanner lifted Hannah up and laid her down in the grass. He pulled off her bra and shirt and unbuttoned her pants. Her body responded, arching against him.

In a moment of clarity, Hannah realized that she—Hannah Bradley— was lying naked in the grass next to the creek. With a man. With a man she wanted to make love to. A giddy feeling rose up inside her. It took all of her self-control not to giggle.

"Are you okay with this?" Tanner said.

Hannah nodded and brought her mouth to his. The sound he made when he entered her stirred something in Hannah, and as they began to move together, she felt the giddiness turn to emotion. Making love to Tanner was all the good things in the world: the creek tumbling by and the birds singing and the sunshine on that first truly warm day every spring. It was fresh lemonade and blooming flowers and the smell of cinnamon almonds at the farmer's market.

When it was over, the two of them held each other without speaking. And while Hannah's body was satiated, melting, exhausted, and ener-gized, her mind picked up speed:

Did that really just happen?

What would happen now?

Was sex—really, really good, satisfying sex—with Tanner Lucas a good idea?

Would they talk about it?

Would they not talk about it?

"Wow," Tanner said, his voice husky and humor-filled. "I can just *feel* all the thoughts running around your head. I'm not sure all that thinking is really good for the post-coital relaxation phase."

Hannah laughed in response, and found that her voice, too, was husky.

Who *was* this Hannah?

"So, what are you thinking?" he said. "Or do I even want to know? Is regret creeping in at this very moment?"

"No, no, not at all," Hannah said, before wondering if she'd responded too quickly or too emphatically, and then realizing that second-guessing every phrase that came out of her mouth wasn't a good habit to get into.

"So?"

"It's just that I never thought I—or, *we*, rather—would be doing this. Here."

"You never thought the good-looking, intelligent Tanner Lucas would manage to seduce you?"

Hannah opened her eyes and saw that in addition to the humor in Tanner's, there was doubt. She ran her fingers through the hair at his temple, cupped his jaw with her hand.

"I'm not surprised, as sexy as you are. I was just thinking about how we'll move forward from here."

"I suspected you might worry about that," he said. "And also, I realized it's dinner time. So I propose we start with dinner."

Charmed, Hannah said, "I suppose we'd really better start with getting dressed."

"I suppose so."

CHAPTER THIRTEEN

FOR THE NEXT FEW DAYS, Hannah and Tanner spent so much time together she could barely remember what it was like when he wasn't around.

They started with a very pleasant dinner that Monday night, which wasn't at all awkward, as Hannah had feared.

Over an appetizer, calamari Tanner ordered because he was "absolutely famished," they talked about inconsequential things, like the best way to cook fish and the worst movies they'd ever seen. Over the main course, a huge platter of spaghetti and meatballs, they talked about books they'd read in college and since, and music they couldn't believe they'd enjoyed listening to. And over dessert, a thick slice of cheesecake with a raspberry glaze, the conversation turned to work. The server brought them coffee, and when Hannah glanced at her watch, she couldn't believe four hours had passed.

And although she never stayed up this late on school nights, she didn't want to go home. Being with Tanner was like being inside a capsule: time didn't seem to pass. It was as if they were in their own existence.

"Life must go on," Tanner said, echoing Hannah's thoughts. "I suppose we'd better get home so we can deal with reality tomorrow."

Hannah groaned. "I wish we could just stay here, like this—"

The word "forever" had threatened to make an appearance there, but she caught herself.

"So do I," Tanner said. "All night long."

Tuesday, Hannah came home after work to find Tanner repairing the deck railing—a job she was supposed to have done but just hadn't gotten around to. Her first reaction was to feel guilty (she should have gotten to it sooner), but gratitude rushed in to take guilt's place.

"Well, this is nice," Hannah said as she approached Tanner. "I'm going to have to keep you around if you keep doing my chores for me."

Tanner grinned at her. "Is it weird that I want to kiss you right now, instead of saying, 'Hello,'?"

Hannah's body responded before her voice did, but she pretended to think for a minute. "No, I don't think it is."

He gave her a kiss that made her entire body tingle, and she was blushing by the time he released her.

"Well," she said. "That was a nice greeting."

"I thought so, too. Anyway. I hope I'm not stepping on your toes by fixing this railing. I saw Sadie leaning against it the last time she was here, and it looked a little rickety. I figured, better safe than sorry. Poor kid would probably be traumatized if she broke it."

"And even more so if she fell off the porch."

"Right," Tanner said.

"You're a good guy, Tanner," Hannah said.

"And now *I'm* blushing," he said. "How *is* Sadie, anyway? We got to talking last night, and I forgot to ask."

"She seems okay," Hannah said. "She's been pretty quiet since I packed her up and brought her back to her aunt and uncle. But that was only yesterday."

"Why are you making that face when you say, 'aunt and uncle'?"

"Are you just about done with that railing? I think this conversation's going to require a beer."

Tanner tested his work, giving the railing a little shake. "Much better," he said. "And you know I'm not one to turn down a beer with a beautiful woman."

Shaking her head, mostly because she was unaccustomed to such flattery, Hannah went inside to put down her bag and grab two cold beers. Something was cooking in the big pot on the stove, and it smelled so good Hannah's mouth watered. They settled on the porch chairs and she told Tanner the story of meeting Sadie's aunt. The memory of that strange encounter made her shiver.

"Have you heard whether child services ever went to check things out?"

"No, I don't think they report back, you know?" Hannah sipped her beer. "But her aunt said it's okay with her if Sadie comes over. Any time, she said."

"You could invite her over every weekend."

"I thought about that," Hannah said. "Part of me worries that having her over every weekend is like teasing her. It's like showing a puppy a new toy. A really excellent new toy that squeaks. And then, just when you let him take it between his teeth, you snatch it away. And you just keep doing that, but you never let him just have the toy to play with it."

"But for those moments, when he has the toy in his teeth, he's really happy," Tanner said. "And isn't that something?"

Hannah sighed. "You have a point. And I suppose it is something. But is it enough?"

"Is it perfect?" Tanner said. "No. But does something have to be perfect in order for it to be worthy?"

"I suppose you have yet another point," Hannah said.

Tanner shot her a smile and a wink. "Then how about this one: coming home with me, for dinner, would be a really great idea. You won't have to cook or do dishes. And I can tell you all about the watch tower I'm putting in that new house over on the west end of town."

"A watch tower? Are you for real?"

"I'm pleased to say that I *am* for real. It's my first-ever watch tower."

"I'd love to go to dinner with you. But I don't want to leave Mama on her own."

"Taken care of," Tanner said. "I asked your sister if she'd feed her."

"Which sister? Because Margaret—"

"I asked Margaret," Tanner said. "Because she told me she was making soup. She'd accidentally doubled the recipe because she thought she was using the one-cup measuring cup, but it was actually the two-cup. And by the time she'd realized it, the soup was half-made. She offered to send some home with me. But I offered an alternate plan."

Here, he held up a finger.

"She and Katherine could share half the soup and freeze the second half. And I could take you to my place for dinner."

"Oh," Hannah said, taken off guard by the fact that someone else was making plans and solving problems. "That's nice."

"So—I think I've made a pretty good point that you should come home with me."

If Hannah was going to continue spending time with Tanner (and she wanted to!), she was going to have to learn to expect the unexpected. She didn't know why it was so difficult for her to accept his invitation (although it was more like a half-invitation, half-order). Probably, she realized, because it was different from what she'd always done. She rarely received invitations, and she never accepted.

But maybe doing things differently than you'd always done them was okay sometimes. By the time she finished this thought process, Tanner had led her to his truck. He opened the passenger door and gestured for her to get in.

And before he shut the door, he gave her a kiss that just about incinerated her.

A few minutes later, Tanner was turning off a side road, onto a long, tree-lined driveway. He parked and said, in a ghoulish voice, "Welcome to my lair."

"Are you sure this is safe?" Hannah said. "I never thought I'd be invited to spend the evening inside Tanner Lucas's lair."

"Of course it's safe," Tanner said. "Obviously, I know how to cook."

He rubbed his stomach, which made her laugh.

"That's just so nice of you, to cook for me," she said. "Unless you're really just planning to heat up leftovers your mom sent home with you. Or the soup my sister made."

"Geez, woman. You have no faith. Let me give you a quick tour, and then I'd like to get cleaned up before I start dinner."

They got out, and he held her hand as they walked up to the front of the house. It wasn't what she would have pictured if she'd thought of college-aged Tanner building a house. She would have imagined something ostentatious, something that screamed self-importance.

But now that she knew him a little better, the small wooden cabin nestled amongst the trees seemed absolutely fitting. The details—windows that ran the width of the house, a bright orange front door, and window boxes overflowing with flowers—said whoever lived here was thoughtful. And the setting—private, right in the middle of nature, and just off the beaten path—said a person could have sex anywhere in that house and not be seen.

Hannah jumped at her own thought, and looked around to see if anyone had noticed. What she'd really meant to think was, the setting said the home owner enjoyed nature. That was it. That errant train of thought added, *But isn't* sex *nature?*

"It's beautiful, Tanner," Hannah said. Her throat was dry.

"Thanks," he said, oblivious to her thoughts on the various ways she could make love to him on this property. "Let me show you around."

He did, explaining his design choices room by room: "I wanted to be able to see the forest from anywhere in the house. And I made everything as convenient as possible—for example, I can reach the fridge from the stove, so if I'm cooking, I don't have to take any extra steps to get myself a beer."

"Are you kidding?"

"Yes. Want a glass of wine?"

He poured her one, kissed her before handing it over, and went to shower, leaving her to wander the house. He'd been joking about the convenience of grabbing a beer while cooking, of course, but she noticed that he had paid a lot of attention to how things flowed. The house just worked, she thought.

The rooms all seemed to fit together, yet they provided separate spaces, too. The kitchen, with its fancy six-burner range and double oven and jet-black countertops, was a chef's kitchen, meant for serious cooking. Yet, it was also somehow relaxing. She could imagine coming home to this place, cooking a nice meal, eating at the counter or in the adjacent dining room or even out on the patio. Maybe she'd suggest sitting out there tonight.

"Can I put you to work?"

He was back, and when Hannah turned to face Tanner, her breath caught. He was wearing jeans and a white t-shirt, and he was barefoot. His hair was still damp, and it curled in a way she hadn't noticed before —a way that made her want to run her fingers through it.

She licked her lips. "Doing what?"

Again, Hannah surprised herself with the double entendre.

"Helping make dinner."

"Just tell me what to do."

Margaret would just die if she heard Hannah talking this way. Which made Hannah want to giggle.

"Would you mind chopping up some potatoes while I make the marinade for the steak and asparagus? I thought we'd roast the potatoes in the oven, and I could grill the rest of it. If we get them in now, we can sit on the patio while the rest of the stuff cooks on the grill."

"Sounds good," Hannah said, although she was really thinking that Tanner had read her mind about sitting on the patio. And also that they could probably have sex in one of those patio chairs. The cushions looked pretty comfortable.

They worked in silence for a few minutes. She scrubbed potatoes, and he mixed olive oil and seasonings for the marinades. The two of them chopped the potatoes, and Tanner tossed them in the same oil and seasonings he'd used in the marinade. Once those were in the oven, Tanner opened the glass door and they went outside.

Hannah was just thinking she'd have to get Margaret's advice on sex positions that were compatible with patio furniture when Tanner said, "I've been doing some research."

"Have you?"

If this didn't have anything to do with sex, Hannah was going to be disappointed. Tanner sat on one of the chairs, and Hannah sat on the love seat perpendicular to it. He cleared his throat.

"Would you be interested in going to meet your father?"

The sex kitten inside of Hannah flopped over and went to sleep, but another part of her perked up.

"I'll admit, I've thought about it," she said. "And I've done a few Google searches. But I haven't decided whether I'm more terrified than interested."

"What if I went with you?"

"You? Went with me?"

Tanner laughed, just a little, and took a sip of his wine. "Yes. As in, flew out there with you, stood in line for a rental car with you, and rode in it out to his orchard with you. And then, met your father with you."

He was nervous. She could tell. Tanner Lucas was nervous about this proposition. And although it made her nervous, too, to think about traveling with him (wasn't that a sign of something more between two people?), it also removed so much of the anxiety from the situation she found herself agreeing to the plan right then and there.

"I *think* I'd love it."

He set down his wine glass. "You would?"

"Wait. You made the offer, but you sound surprised that I said I think I would love it."

"I *am* surprised. You seem very self-sufficient, is all. I thought you'd turn me down cold for a dinner at home. A trip to California? I wasn't sure if you'd even *consider* letting me join you."

"I'll consider it."

Now he laughed outright. "Okay. You consider it and let me know. We could make a weekend trip out of it. A mini-vacation. I hear they have some wonderful wineries in California."

"What would we tell him about our, you know, situation?"

"We'd say we're seeing each other."

"Is that what we're doing?" Hannah said.

"Isn't it?"

"To tell you the truth, I hadn't thought to put a label on it."

"I'd say a good roll in the grass constitutes 'seeing each other,'" Tanner said. "And besides, I like labels. They make everything so ..."

"Neat and tidy?"

"Yes," Tanner said. He held up his wine glass, and she clinked hers against it.

"To neat and tidy," Hannah said, and then she added, "A 'roll in the grass,' huh? Is that what you're calling it?"

Chuckling, he got up to check on the steaks, and she said, "You know, my favorite gift ever was actually a label maker. Mama and my sisters went in on one for me at Christmas one year. It might have been my first year as a teacher."

"I'll bet you used the heck out of the thing."

"Sure did. In fact, I still do."

"Somehow that doesn't surprise me."

The food was ready. As the two of them dished it up, Hannah thought they could come to be a pretty good team. Sure, they stepped on each other's toes a few times, and Tanner almost knocked the wine bottle over with his elbow when he reached across Hannah to grab the salt and pepper off the counter. But even during the relatively small amount of time it took them to prep the meal, they began to find their rhythm, just as they had when they built the trellis for Margaret's wedding.

The meal was leisurely and they chatted some more, about Tanner's jobs—using the Seedling Homestead as a model, he'd taken on another "commune"—and the fall season in Hannah's classroom. When they'd scraped the grill, washed the dishes, and wiped down the table, they made love again. And although the lovemaking demanded all of Hannah's attention while it was happening, she found herself thinking afterward that she'd never had sex twice in one week.

This was really something.

———

THAT EVENING, her body still thrumming in all those certain places, Hannah laid in bed thinking about Tanner. Well, not Tanner specifically, the inner voice of her college self piped up. But the possibility of a real relationship with a man.

Could she and Tanner be an actual item? Or was there was too much history there? Could they be compatible, long-term?

And if not Tanner, could she be someone else's other half?

Could she make steaks and drink wine on the patio, have slow, lazy sex afterward, with the same person, over and over again?

For the first time in her adult life, she realized that's what she wanted. Deep down, she wanted a Tanner Lucas. It didn't have to be Tanner, himself. He'd probably never agree to it, anyway. Even though he said he enjoyed picturing her in that ratty red sweatshirt, he couldn't possibly think of her as real partner material if that was the image he had in his mind.

She pulled the flat sheet up under her chin.

But certainly, there were other men in Walker, or nearby. Certainly, she could find someone to settle down with. And what if, too, she started having Sadie over every weekend? As Sadie got older, she could stay for even longer periods. And if Hannah met her father ... well, it would be like she had everything, wouldn't it?

Guilt, always waiting in the wings recently, stepped in.

Didn't she already have everything? Her life with Mama, Sarah, and Margaret ... it had had its ups and downs, of course, but overall, her memories of childhood were like shining golden visions.

But did a person's needs change as she got older? Maybe they did.

Someone knocked on her bedroom door, and Hannah sat up quickly, as if she'd been caught. "Come in," she said.

The door swung open to reveal Mama, Sarah, and Margaret.

"Knock, knock," Mama said.

Someone turned on the light, and Hannah squinted.

"What are you guys *doing*?" she said. "It's late."

"And this, my dear sister, is what's wrong with your life," Sarah said.

"You're in bed by nine every night," Margaret said.

"We live in Walker, Wyoming," Hannah said. "Not Seattle, Washington. Things close down here."

"Why do you look so guilty?" Margaret said, and Sarah snickered.

"We happen to know you were just with Tanner Lucas," Sarah said.

"And by the looks of you, the two of you had a lovely evening," Mama said.

Now all three of them cackled.

"By the looks of me?" Hannah said. "What do I look like?"

"Like a horse that's been rode hard and put up wet," Mama said.

"*Ridden* hard," Hannah said, producing a fresh round of cackling from her sisters.

"Did you and Tanner Lucas do the deed?" Margaret said.

"Twice, as a matter of fact," Hannah said.

The three of them rushed in, then, and made themselves at home on the edge of her bed.

"Twice in one *day*?" Sarah wanted to know.

"Twice in one week," Hannah said, her voice a groan. She rubbed her forehead. "Are we really *having* this conversation?"

"Wait," Sarah said. "When was the other time?"

Mama said, "Give the girl some privacy. But really, honey. When was the other time?"

"Ohmygosh," Hannah said. She made shooing motions with her hands. "Get out of here, all of you."

They didn't budge. If anything, Hannah thought, they settled in more, burrowing down, cuddling right up to her.

"Why did he take you to his house for dinner?" Margaret said.

"Because I'm a lovely person, of course," Hannah said.

"He told me he wanted to talk to you about something," Margaret said.

Although she worried a little about Mama's reaction, Hannah explained that Tanner wanted to take a trip to California. To do some wine tasting, she said. And, as if it were just a little addition and not the main event, she added, "and maybe to see Philip Carlisle, Jr."

At that, her sisters gasped, and Mama closed her eyes.

The questions came rolling in. Sarah wanted to know if Hannah had contacted Philip Carlisle, Jr., and Margaret wanted to know if they'd already made flight reservations. Sarah wondered if Hannah knew how to get to the orchard, and Margaret asked where they'd stay. And, she added with raised eyebrows, whether they'd book one room or two.

At that, Hannah sent them out, saying she was exhausted and barely hanging on even though her body was now buzzing with excitement over the idea of traveling with Tanner. They filed out, Sarah first, and then Margaret, and before Mama could leave, Hannah called her back in.

"Is it okay? If we try to see my father?"

Mama's posture was stiff, and Hannah knew that meant she was taking care not to show any emotion. "Of course it is, honey," she said. "Of course it is. Goodnight, now."

Just as she had countless times, Mama turned off the light and shut the door. Hannah laid back down. She drifted off to sleep seeing visions of all of them gathered here at the Seedling Homestead—Mama, Sarah and Donny, Margaret and Ethan, and Tanner and herself—along with Sadie and Philip Carlisle, Jr.

Could that be the new perfect?

CHAPTER FOURTEEN

WHEN HANNAH WOKE up the following Monday, it was to an empty house. She experienced a slight moment of panic, wondering where everyone was, but then she realized she'd been distracted all weekend and was probably just forgetting plans they'd told her about.

Yes, that was right: Margaret and Mama had both scheduled appointments in Jackson Hole for today—they'd combined trips. Ethan had agreed to drive them and spend the day chauffeuring them around in exchange for them taking him out for lunch. And Sarah and Donny had decided they'd go to Jackson Hole, too, to order furniture for the new house.

So they hadn't forgotten her.

Still, rattling around in the empty house felt depressing. And, when she glanced outside and saw the construction sites were not buzzing with activity, she felt lonelier than she had in months. Which was silly, she told herself, because nothing had changed.

Except, maybe something had.

Mama had left her a pot of coffee, and she poured herself a cup, added sugar and milk, stirred, and thought.

Maybe this thing with Tanner, whatever it was, and this thing with Sadie, whatever *it* was, had changed something inside of Hannah. Maybe these two things had made her want something different. For the first time in her life, she felt vaguely dissatisfied. She's always just plodded along, content with the status quo.

But what if there was more?

She leaned against the counter, sipping her coffee, knowing she should get in the shower, but also so deep in her reflection that she didn't want to leave this moment. It seemed somehow significant. Pivotal, even.

What if her own acceptance of a *relationship* with a man—maybe even Tanner Lucas, surprisingly, Hannah thought—could empower her to shift from plodding along to actually enjoying things?

What if parenting a child—someone who needed her in a way different from how Mama needed her—could allow her to make a real, lasting impact on this world? More than she could do as a teacher?

Why had she never thought about these things before?

It's not like they hadn't crossed her mind. Of course, Sarah had always been desperate for her to find a partner and settle down, and Margaret was equally desperate for her to experience some sexual or romantic shenanigans. But any time these concepts floated into her consciousness, they floated right back out again without any real examination.

"Huh," Hannah said aloud, to herself. She pushed away from the counter and carried her coffee to the bathroom, where she turned on the hot water for her shower.

Why hadn't she ever stopped that film reel, paused it, and taken a good, hard look at the idea of partnership (or even sexual shenanigans)?

And what about parenthood? She loved kids. Obviously. She set her coffee mug on the counter and began taking off her pajamas.

Why hadn't she ever really, truly, considered parenthood? Mama had served as a wonderful example of being a single parent. Hannah could have adopted. She could have used a sperm donor. She could have used the rhythm method and gotten herself knocked up by a random date.

She got in the shower, which was way too hot, and she jumped out from under the spray, maniacally adjusting the faucet with one outstretched arm.

Okay, so getting knocked up by a random date possibly wasn't the best idea. But really. If she'd truly wanted to become a parent, she could have found a way.

Why now, she wondered as she wet her hair. What had triggered this change in her way of thinking?

Was it the discovery that Mama actually knew who her father was, and that he was just a hop, skip, and jump away, in California? Was it

Sadie—this fragile, strange, awkward student? Or was it Tanner? Not just Tanner, but his apparent evolution from pigheaded jerk to thoughtful professional. Make that *sexy* thoughtful professional.

Hannah scrubbed her hair, ran the bar of soap over her skin, rinsed her hair.

Did it matter why things were changing *now*? Or did it matter only that they were changing?

Really, she thought, she should stop wasting time figuring out the *why*, and decide—well, decide two things: first, did she actually want a different life? One with a partner and possibly children? And two, how would she make that happen?

She rinsed off and got out. She wasn't paying much attention as she got dressed, and was almost surprised to find herself ready for work when she went back into the kitchen to grab something to eat. There would be no pancakes today, she thought, but she'd make do with a couple of eggs.

If she had a child, what would she make for breakfast? Would she make pancakes, like Mama had? Or would she pour some cereal and milk and call it good?

"Huh," she said aloud, to herself, again.

Did it really matter what a mother made her kids for breakfast? Or did it matter that she made them breakfast at all?

"Where is all this *coming* from?" she said, half-expecting an answer. Of course, she didn't get one.

She scrambled some eggs, scarfed them down, and brushed her teeth before heading off to work. When she got there, she realized she was wearing two different shoes, and her pants were Navy blue instead of black.

Which, apparently, Sadie noticed, too.

"Get dressed in the dark this morning?" she said when Hannah approached the school building. "Those pants don't match at all. And are you wearing two different shoes?"

"Good morning to you," Hannah said. "How was your weekend?"

The bruise on Sadie's face had faded to yellow, and it had spread down past her cheekbone.

"Seriously," Sadie said. "Is everything okay? You never look mismatched."

For once, Sadie was looking into Hannah's eyes, as if she were searching for proof that Hannah hadn't lost her mind, or for proof that she had. Then, as Hannah laughed to ease the tension that resulted from Sadie thinking she was crazy or under duress, Sadie did something very unexpected: she took a stack of books and Hannah's lunchbox from Hannah's arms.

"Thanks," Hannah said. "Now. I appreciate your concern." Hannah unlocked the door to the building, held it open for Sadie, and went on, "I was just a bit distracted this morning, that's all. So, I've answered your question. You answer mine. How was your weekend?"

They stopped at the door to Hannah's classroom. Sadie sighed and looked down at the floor. "Same as most weekends. Boring."

"What'd you do?"

"Sat around, mostly. I went outside. I know it's weird, but sometimes I like to build forts and stuff."

"Why is that weird?" Hannah held this door open, too, and Sadie went in and set the stack of Hannah's belongings on the desk.

"Do you think most ten-year-old girls build forts?"

"I wouldn't say *most*, no," Hannah said. "But I also would say, you're not like most ten-year-old girls."

"Great," Sadie said. "Thanks. That's what every ten-year-old girl wants to hear."

"Do you really want to be like most other people? Wouldn't you rather stand out?"

"Have *you* ever stood out, Ms. Bradley? Like, not because you're so pretty and popular like Lily or Reagan, but because you're, you know … *strange*? If not, then we'll have to agree to disagree on this one. Standing out because you don't fit in is different from the kind of standing out you're talking about."

They went about the routine that had become normal over the past couple of weeks. Sadie wrote the date on the board, and Hannah wrote the bell question. Sadie used an antibacterial wipe to clean off all the desk surfaces, and Hannah came behind her, passing out that week's math packets.

"Wow," Hannah said when they finished. "I get done so much faster with your help. I guess I could start coming in later, if I wanted to."

"Please don't," Sadie said. "Then I'd have to sit outside the school for longer every morning."

They sat down at their desks and Hannah nearly laughed out loud when they both clasped their hands together in the same way: fingers laced, elbows out.

"So, believe it or not," Hannah said. "I have stood out. Not in a good, I'm-so-talented-and-smart, or I'm-so-gorgeous way. And not because I wore two different shoes, which will definitely make me stand out today. But when I was just a little older than you, I stood out because I was the tallest person in my class. Well, let me amend that. Not just the tallest, but the biggest. No girl wants to be the biggest person in the class in seventh grade, right? I'd always been so skinny. Mama called me a beanpole. And then, at the end of sixth grade and all summer before seventh, my appetite just grew. I was starving all the time. It was every-thing my mama could do to keep me filled up. She made me two of every meal, I'm pretty sure. That summer, of course, I didn't see any of my classmates. It was just the three of us—me and Sarah and Margaret. And even though Mama kept remarking that I was growing like a weed, we didn't really notice. Until the first day of seventh grade. I remember Mama had taken us school shopping that last week of summer, just before school started. She'd bought me this beautiful green dress. It was so pretty, Sadie. Of course, you'd laugh if you saw it now. It had frills around the shoulders and at the hem. Buttons up the front. A collar."

Sadie raised her eyebrows.

"Yes, a collar. Anyway, I loved that dress for all of seventy-two hours. Because after that, on the first day of school, I walked into my home-room class. All of us—me, my friends, and the kids who soon became my enemies—noticed how much I'd grown over the summer. I was towering over the other kids. Not just a couple of inches, mind you, but a foot."

"A foot?"

"Okay, that's a slight exaggeration. But that's what it felt like. I was huge. A giant. A freak. My shoulders were broad. My feet stuck out like waterskis. My hands were like dinner plates. And there was everyone else, dainty as could be."

"That's awful," Sadie said.

"It gets worse. That dress, the beautiful dress I *loved*. Did I mention it was green? And I was a giant? They started calling me—"

"The Jolly Green Giant," Sadie said.

"How'd you know?" Hannah said.

"Kids are mean," Sadie said. "But more than that, they're predictable. That's not even very clever."

"No, it's not. That was a tough year."

Sadie was sitting up straighter now. "But you seem so ... *normal* now."

"Well, I grew into myself, physically," Hannah said. "And their abuse didn't have permanent consequences. Except maybe in a positive way. I feel like after that, I was a little more aware of kids who didn't quite fit in, for whatever reason. Mama always said I collected misfits. And maybe I did. But it was because *I* was a misfit."

"And when you get a bunch of misfits together, then no one's a misfit."

"Exactly."

Talking to Sadie was almost like talking to an adult, Hannah thought.

"So, are you saying I'm a misfit? You've taken me under your wing."

How did a person answer a question like that?

"I am saying that I empathize with what you're saying, when you say you feel like you don't fit in. I've felt that way, too. I think I've outgrown it, although sometimes I think my sisters and mother view me as a misfit because I haven't sought the traditional life, you know? Husband, two-point-five kids, puppy, the whole deal."

"Why haven't you?"

Sadie wasn't so much of an adult, that Hannah could give an honest answer to that one. "That's kind of the question, isn't it? But the answer will have to wait. The first bell's about to ring, which means we'll have company soon."

After school, Sadie lingered, taking longer than necessary to pack up her homework and organize her desk. At first, Hannah thought it was because she wanted to pursue the line of questioning about why Hannah hadn't sought the traditional life. But then Sadie stopped moving, and, her body deflating, said, "I know you said you can't keep me forever. But can I come home with you today? Please?"

Hannah was surprised to see Tanner's truck in the driveway when she and Sadie pulled up. She'd locked up the house before leaving, so she knew he wasn't in there. He must be over at one of the sites.

"Ooh! Tanner's here!" Sadie said. "Can we go see him?"

Her reaction pretty much mirrored Hannah's. "Of course. I'm sure he's over at one of the houses."

They walked across the property together, and Hannah couldn't help but imagine what they looked like from behind: a woman and a child, walking side by side—a pair. It would make such a nice picture. Sure enough, they found Tanner inside of Sarah and Donny's house.

Sadie rushed up to him and hugged him, and when his eyes met Hannah's over the top of her head, his eyes were round with shock. Hannah had already become accustomed to Sadie's shaved head, but naturally, it came out of nowhere for Tanner.

During the next few seconds, a silent conversation ensued: Tanner said something like, "What the hell?" and Hannah responded, "I know, it's horrible. I'll tell you later," and Tanner said, "I can only imagine what you're going to say—poor kid."

He gave Sadie's shoulders a final squeeze, and by the time he looked at her, his expression showed delight.

"Well, this is a nice surprise," Tanner and Hannah said at the same time.

Sadie unlocked her arms from around Tanner's waist and looked back and forth between them.

"I wasn't expecting you today," Hannah said. "I thought you guys were working on that other project. With the watch tower."

"We were," Tanner said. "But the flooring guys come tomorrow, so I wanted to make sure my guys had prepped everything so the flooring guys can hit the ground running, first thing."

"Very responsible of you," Hannah said.

"Also, I admit, I was hoping that my timing would be right, and I'd be here when you got home, invite you to dinner, and—" He paused, winked at Hannah, and changed course. "But it's even better than I thought. You've brought my friend Sadie with you. So now, I would like to invite both of you to dinner. How do burgers and shakes sound?"

"Amazing!" Sadie said, and Hannah had to agree.

"I've just got to take care of the chickens and the garden, first," Hannah said. "Otherwise I'll be in a food coma when we get back and I know I won't want to. Give me a hand, Sadie?"

"I'm done here," Tanner said, "so we can both give you a hand."

The three of them moved around the property quickly: Sadie collecting eggs, yelping every time she thought a hen was going to peck her; Tanner pulling the last of the ripe tomatoes off the plants, and Hannah watering the rows of fall vegetables.

They were done within minutes and gathered in the kitchen to put away the vegetables and eggs. Tanner offered to drive, and the three of them climbed into his truck. As they drove through town, they chatted about the day, about the watch tower Tanner was building (Sadie wanted to know if there was a big telescope for stargazing—there wasn't, but they all agreed there should be), and about Halloween, which was happening in just a few weeks.

Tanner asked Sadie what she planned to be this year, and Sadie said she didn't usually dress up.

"My aunt and uncle don't really have the money for that kind of thing," Sadie said.

Hannah wanted to ask how old her aunt and uncle were, and whether they had jobs, and what they *did* all day. Fortunately, Tanner jumped in to save her.

"Well, what do you say, after dinner, we go to the store and get you a costume?" he said. "You can be whatever you want."

"Except popular and pretty," Sadie said, and Hannah didn't know whether to laugh or cry. After a brief pause, Sadie said, "I'm just kidding, you guys. Geez. Yes, I would love to get a costume. But I have no idea what I want to be."

"It's wide open," Tanner said. "You can be whatever you want."

To the other patrons at the Burger Shack, the three of them probably looked like a typical, run-of-the-mill family. And for the short time they were there, Hannah felt like they were. They talked and laughed together, and Sadie swatted Tanner on the arm when he snatched a couple of fries off her plate. They even shared their milkshakes, passing them around to taste the different flavors.

And when they were done, they walked happily down the street to the thrift store, where Tanner promised he'd find Sadie a costume unlike anything she'd ever seen before.

There were racks and racks of costumes: superheroes and vampires and puppies and ice cream cones. There were hairy masks and bloodied swords and braided wigs. Hats and eye patches and giant shoes.

"Wow," Sadie said. "I've never been here at Halloween. This is awesome."

Hannah and Tanner looked at each other over the top of her head, and Tanner winked.

"So, my girl, what do you want to be? A witch? A wizard? A—what is this?—a slice of bacon?"

An hour passed, during which Tanner entertained Sadie by handing her costume after costume to try on, right there in the aisle, over her clothes. At one point—when Sadie put on a sunny-side-up egg with a witch hat—Hannah snapped a picture. Tanner jumped in at the last minute, smiling like some kind of lunatic. Hannah sent the picture to Sarah, Margaret, and Mama.

In the end, Sadie put together a witch vampire costume ("Or is it a vampire witch?" Tanner wanted to know), with striped tights, a black dress, a collared cape, and a peaked hat. Two shops over at the drug store, Hannah splurged on some fancy prosthetic teeth and fake blood, and Tanner made a big deal of buying spiderweb jewelry.

Sadie practically skipped back down the sidewalk to the burger joint, her bag swinging from her hand, and she chattered all the way back to her house, telling them how she'd never gone trick or treating, how she'd always wanted to but never had a costume or anyone to take her, how she couldn't wait to try all the different kinds of candy.

It was almost like she didn't notice they were heading toward her house until Tanner pulled the truck to a stop along the side of the road. She went suddenly silent before leaning forward from the back seat and speaking to Hannah in an earnest voice: "Please take me to your house. *Please.* I know you said you can't keep me forever, but can you keep me for tonight? Please? You won't even know I'm there. I'll make my own breakfast in the morning. And I'll clean up after myself. If you want, I'll even help you with more chores."

Hannah looked at Tanner, and he shrugged. She didn't know whether the shrug meant, "Do whatever you like," or, "I have no idea." *She* had no idea.

Of course Hannah wanted to agree. Of course she wanted to take Sadie home, save her, at least tonight, from the peculiar situation in which she lived.

"Why don't you run in and ask?" Hannah said. "It's fine with me if it's fine with your aunt and uncle."

Hadn't she heard Sarah say the same to Amelia countless times? Sadie groaned, but she was already opening the door and hopping out of the truck.

"Thank you, Ms. Bradley," she shouted before she opened the front door and went inside.

In the sudden stillness, Hannah turned to Tanner.

"Thank you so much for tonight," she said. "It was really special for Sadie. And for me, too."

"That was really fun," Tanner said. "We should make it a tradition. Hey, maybe you and I should dress up for Halloween. I'll bet you guys don't get many trick-or-treaters, but we could give out candy at my place."

Before she could answer, Sadie came bounding back down the walkway and up to Hannah's window.

"They said it's okay."

"Great," Hannah said. "Did you grab what you need? Clothes for tomorrow, a toothbrush, whatever?"

"Oh!" She bounded back up the walkway, and Hannah said to Tanner, "I love that idea. Let's plan on it."

Sadie returned a moment later with an overstuffed plastic grocery bag. Moving fast, as if she were afraid Hannah might change her mind, she climbed back into the truck and buckled her seatbelt.

Tanner dropped them off a few minutes later, and when Sadie ran inside to see Mama Katherine, Tanner stopped Hannah, backing her up against the hood of the truck, leaning in to give her a long, deep kiss.

"Wow," she said when he pulled away and offered his hand. "I almost wish I'd turned Sadie down so we could go back to your place."

He kissed her again, then said, "Me, too. But did you see her face? That makes waiting worth it. I'll walk you in."

When they went inside, Sadie was showing her costume to Mama, Sarah, and Donny. With the witch hat on her head, she held the other pieces up in front of her, turning slightly to the side to model the whole thing.

"Tanner said I can be whatever I want to be," Sadie said, and Donny shot Tanner a man-to-man, *you're-crazy* look.

But Sarah and Mama beamed delighted smiles at Hannah and complimented Sadie's creativity when she showed them the striped tights and the prosthetic teeth.

"Sadie's staying here tonight," Hannah said, and she was filled with gratitude when no one skipped a beat.

"Oh, good," Mama said. "I think I'll whip up a batch of my cornbread pancakes in the morning."

"And I can't eat those all by myself," Sarah said.

"I could," Margaret said, "but I don't mind sharing."

Tanner said goodbye, and Hannah tucked Sadie into bed. When she came back into the dining room, Mama was sitting at the kitchen table, a mug of steaming tea between her hands. She gestured to the spot across from her, and Hannah sat.

"Tea?" Mama said. "Water's still hot."

"It's okay," Hannah said. "I couldn't possibly ingest anything else. We had burgers and shakes. I'm stuffed. I can't believe I'm still walking, actually."

"Burgers and shakes?" Mama said. "Is that right?"

"I think Tanner and I were both thinking we'd treat Sadie, you know? Neither one of us would normally do a shake after a burger, but—"

"You wanted to make it special for Sadie," Mama said.

"Exactly," Hannah said.

"Those moments," Mama said. "Those moments are what really matter. More than the big moments like graduations or proms. Those little moments are what we—kids and adults—remember. They're the moments that change our lives. You're changing that little girl's life, whether you believe it or not."

———

THE TUESDAY before Halloween (it fell on a Wednesday that year, which Hannah and Sadie agreed was a terrible day for such an important holiday), Sadie begged Hannah to take her trick-or-treating.

"My aunt and uncle hate Halloween!" she said. "They feel like adults should be able to trick or treat, too, but after people lectured them a few years in a row, for being too old, they stopped. Now, they hate that all these *greedy kids* come by asking for candy they want to eat, themselves. They still leave the lights on, and answer the door when kids knock, but they say all these things they think are funny, like, 'All outta candy, little guy,' or, 'Sorry, we're only giving out toothbrushes this year,' and then they shut the door and crack up."

Hannah couldn't help but laugh. She wasn't sure if what Sadie said was true, or an exaggeration, or some combination of both.

"I'll take you," she said, "on one condition. Tanner and I agreed to give out candy at his house. So here's the deal: if I take you trick-or-treating, then you have to come back to Tanner's with me and help us hand out candy."

"I've always wanted to do that," Sadie said, with an enthusiasm that surprised Hannah.

So, Sadie got permission from her aunt, and on Wednesday after school, Hannah took her to the grocery store to buy bags of candy before they headed home to get dressed.

"What are you going to be?" Sadie wanted to know.

When Hannah told her—a banana—Sadie looked at her like she'd completely lost her mind.

"Seriously? A banana?"

"Well, Tanner's going to be peanut butter. We thought that would be cute."

"I mean," Sadie said. She didn't finish the sentence.

"You mean, what?" Hannah said.

"I mean, it's cute," Sadie said.

"But?" Hannah said.

"But it's kind of weird," Sadie said, giggling.

"Whatever, you witch-vampire," Hannah said.

"Vampire-witch," Sadie said.

"Whatever."

Although Hannah had gone trick-or-treating with Sarah and Amelia a few times, Amelia had still been little enough that one of them had to walk her to the door, remind her to say, "trick or treat" and, "thank you," and hold her hand while walking to the next house.

Now, with Sadie, things were completely different. Rather than a slow-paced parade, it was a stampede. Sadie ran from house to house, thanking people as they dropped candy in her bucket and looking nothing short of gleeful every time she dashed away from someone's front door.

Hannah could hardly keep up. She was beyond exhausted, and relieved, when seven o'clock—the time they'd agreed to go to Tanner's —rolled around. They walked to his house, Sadie chatting the whole way as she dug through her basket taking inventory, offering Hannah some of the duplicates, and talking about her favorite houses: the one with the blow-up ghost in the front, the one with the zombie hand in a bowl near the door, and the one with the haunted house in the garage.

When they got to Tanner's, Sadie ran right up to him to gather one last handout, and then she went inside and collapsed on the couch.

"Looks like you're both exhausted," Tanner said.

He motioned to a chair he'd set up for Hannah, next to a table that held a huge bowl of candy. She sank into it, desperate to take off her shoes.

"You look really good as a banana," he said.

"Thanks. And you look really good as peanut butter."

"We make quite a pair."

A group of kids came charging up the sidewalk, shouting, "Trick or treat!" and clambering to be first in line.

Hannah picked up the bowl, and Tanner grabbed handfuls of candy and dropped them into the buckets and pillowcases and grocery bags.

The kids ran off, and Tanner glanced through the window at Sadie, who had fallen asleep on the couch.

"Halloween is very tiring, apparently," he said. "Think we can sneak in a quickie before she wakes up?"

"I'm scandalized," Hannah said. "I've got to get her home."

"Actually, I'm glad she's sleeping now," he said. "There's something I want to talk to you about."

They sat down again. Tanner offered Hannah a bottle of water, and as she opened it and drank, he started speaking.

"I got us plane tickets. To San Francisco. I thought we could fly out, grab a hotel, go see your dad."

Your dad. The words rolled off his tongue so easily, so naturally. As if she'd had a dad her whole life. She had, but …

"You got us plane tickets?"

He misread her emotions; where she was grateful, he seemed to think she was upset.

"Well, we'd talked about it, and you said you wanted to go, and I know how busy you are, with teaching and everything, and I thought I'd just take it off your plate. Your mama helped me choose the dates, so hopefully you won't be too busy with school. It's over a three-day week-end. Veteran's Day."

It was at that moment that Hannah Bradley fell in love with Tanner Lucas.

That was the most thoughtful thing anyone had ever done for her, and she told him as much. He shrugged it off, like it was no big deal; a favor for a friend. The gesture brought her such warmth she didn't want to leave his side that night. But eventually, the trick-or-treaters stopped coming, and it got so late Hannah felt like she really should get Sadie home.

"Can't I just stay with you again?" Sadie said when Hannah woke her up. "My aunt won't mind. She won't even notice."

Hannah took her home, anyway, and she trudged into the house like each of her feet weighed a million pounds. It almost made Hannah laugh, but at the same time, she felt like crying as she watched Sadie open the door, go inside, and close the door behind her.

As she drove home, though, she couldn't help but smile. It had been a really good night.

CHAPTER FIFTEEN

THE SUN HADN'T YET RISEN when Hannah woke up Friday morning. Blinking into the dark, she thought, *This is it. I'm hours from meeting my father.*

It was something she hadn't even truly thought of until just a few short weeks before, but since then, the idea occupied her mind almost completely. Hannah and Tanner were set to fly out of Jackson Hole that evening. They'd land at the San Francisco airport just before midnight. Tanner had arranged for them to spend the day in the city on Saturday. Sunday, they would drive out to the Golden Delicious Orchard.

Hannah was ready for work before six. Despite the godawful hour, Sadie was waiting outside the school building when Hannah walked up. She held up a grocery bag, stuffed full, a shoelace hanging out of the opening of one handle.

"TGIF," she said. "I was thinking I could stay with you this weekend."

Hannah froze.

Since Tanner had announced he bought plane tickets, Hannah hadn't even thought about Sadie coming over. Which meant, of course, that she didn't bother to tell her she'd be out of town this weekend.

"Oh, honey," Hannah said, and even as she uttered those two words, she could see the disappointment in Sadie's expression.

"I forgot to tell you," she said, lending a hand to help Sadie up. Sadie didn't take it. Hannah unlocked the building door, held it open. "I'm going to California this weekend. This evening, actually. We're flying out after school and we'll be back on Sunday."

"Who's 'we?'"

Hannah started walking down the hallway, and Sadie followed, her feet making shuffling noises. "Tanner and me. He organized the trip as kind of a surprise."

"Hmpf," Sadie said, and Hannah stifled a chuckle. "Couldn't I have come, too?"

"I'm almost positive I'd get in trouble for taking you to a whole different state," Hannah said. She unlocked the classroom door.

"So, why California? Why not surprise you and take you somewhere closer?"

The hidden subtext, Hannah thought: somewhere Sadie could have come, too.

"Didn't I tell you about my dad?" Hannah said. "When you first started hanging out in my classroom after school?"

"Yeah," Sadie mumbled. She went over to her desk and plopped down, her body language, slumped and slow-moving, conveying her unhappiness.

"Well, Tanner and I have been talking about him—my dad—and Tanner thought it would be nice if we went to visit him. So he planned the trip and bought the tickets. We'll be back late Sunday night, though, and I'll see you on Monday."

Sadie nodded, and Hannah could tell she was trying not to cry. She wanted to hug Sadie, to somehow make things right.

"I'll bring you a souvenir," she said, her voice a bit too sing-songy.

This earned her a half-grin.

"What do you like? We're going into the city—San Francisco. I could get you a cable car keychain. Or chocolate. There's a famous chocolate factory there, you know. Ooh! I know! I'll get you some dried sea cucumber and frogs' legs from Chinatown."

"Dried sea cucumber?" Sadie wrinkled her nose.

"Yeah," Hannah said. "From what Tanner says, the shops all smell like the ocean."

"I wouldn't know what the ocean smells like," Sadie said. "But I'm sure it's wonderful."

Hannah inhaled, and felt for a moment as if she could smell it now, as if she could hear the gulls. The imaginary birds were actually the voices of children. Students started coming in, and the first bell rang.

"I wish I could bottle up the ocean and bring it to you," Hannah said. Sadie harrumphed again and hunched over her bell work. Hannah started calling out good mornings.

The day dragged, but finally, *finally*, the kids packed their backpacks, the last bell rang, and Hannah was free. Room Five was nearly empty when Sadie shuffled up to her and, after an awkward movement, wrapped her arms around Hannah's waist. Caught off guard, Hannah stiffened for a second, but then hugged Sadie back.

"I'll be back by Monday. You won't even have time to notice I'm gone."

Although Hannah's mind had spent the entire day composing the first words she'd ever say to her father, now, it chastised her for not asking Mama Katherine or Sarah or even Margaret to look after Sadie over the weekend. Hannah could have arranged for Sadie to stay at the Seedling Homestead, or at least to come over for dinner one evening.

But it was too late.

"I will notice," Sadie said. "But I still hope you have a great time. Good luck, you know, meeting your dad and everything."

The nerves jumped in again, making Hannah's stomach swirl and her hands shake. Just a few minutes later, Tanner picked her up from school and they were on the road.

"You're quiet," Tanner said.

"I know."

"Nervous?" He reached over and squeezed her leg. She smiled at him.

"Yeah. How'd you guess?"

"Probably all the loud sighs. I can practically hear the butterflies in your stomach."

"You can? Then I must be really nervous." She sighed again.

"What did Sadie think of you leaving?"

"She said she was sad. But she'll be okay. I told her I'd bring her a souvenir."

"We should bring her something really great from Chinatown," Tanner said. "Maybe some dried frogs' legs or a whole, plucked duck or something."

Hannah smiled. "That's what I told her."

"So we're on the same wavelength, is what you're telling me."

"I guess that's what I'm telling you."

"You're not going to debate with me?"

"Nah," Hannah said.

Tanner turned on the radio and hit scan. It stopped on a country station, and he tapped his hand on his thigh in time to the music. Hannah hadn't pegged him for a country guy, but didn't say so. She didn't want to offend him. Not that he should be offended. But the fact that she'd thought he might be seemed offensive on its own. Now her mind was babbling—another sign of nerves.

And not only about meeting the mysterious man that was her dad, but also about spending an entire weekend with Tanner. There were so many intimate moments in traveling. Yes, they'd made love. But spending two-and-a-half consecutive days together? They'd have to remove their shoes at the airport. He'd see her *socks*. Most likely, they'd buy food or drinks from a stand at the airport, which meant he'd see inside her purse (she'd cleaned it out, removing stray gum wrappers and old receipts).

And what about when they got to the hotel? She'd reserved two separate rooms … at the time, she hadn't wanted to presume he would want to stay together. They hadn't officially decided on a label, and she didn't think "seeing each other" constituted a single room. But now, as the check-in approached, she wondered if she should have made an executive decision and gotten a king-sized bed. Wasn't standing with someone at hotel check-in pretty intimate?

It *was* possible she was overthinking this.

Especially after the time they'd spent together recently. They should be able to be together for two-and-a-half days as friends, or as two people seeing each other. Maybe she was feeling uncomfortable because she wanted them to have a more serious label.

She started to groan, and then attempted to cover her groan with a fake yawn.

Tanner stopped tapping his thigh and glanced over at her. "Everything okay?"

She smiled, she hoped sweetly, and said, "Of course. Everything's great. Thanks again for coming with me."

When they finally, *finally* arrived at the airport, it felt like it took forever to get their parking ticket from the machine and then find a spot in the tiny parking lot. Hannah clasped her hands together in her lap, willing herself to be patient as they wound through the full rows.

At last, Tanner found an available spot and pulled into it. Hannah guessed it was about a mile from the terminal.

Quickly, she opened the passenger door. When she stepped out, she missed her footing. In an attempt to catch herself, she grabbed onto the door, which swung open much farther than she'd expected. As a result, she landed on her knees right there in the parking lot, clinging to the door handle for dear life.

Tanner slammed his own door and was around the bed of the truck in a fraction of a second, asking if Hannah was all right. She was laughing so hard she could barely squeal out an affirmation. So hard she almost missed the delicious shiver that ran through her body when Tanner wrapped an arm around her waist and hauled her to her feet. Almost, but not quite.

"Let me have a look at you," he said, holding her at arms' length. "You're all in one piece, looks like, but I can't say the same for your pants. Or your shoes."

Hannah looked down at the knees of her jeans, which, sure enough, were torn. And her shoes were scuffed. Which only made her laugh harder.

"Well, if the clothes my students are wearing these days are any indication," she said, "I guess my jeans are now the height of fashion."

"What *happened*? I mean, *how* did that happen?" Tanner still hadn't let go of Hannah's upper arms, and there was a mixture of humor and concern in his eyes.

"I don't even know. I was just so distracted."

Unexpectedly, he pulled her in for a hug. Even more unexpectedly, he kissed her on the top of the head. "I know you are. I don't blame you. This is all going to turn out fine, I promise."

She nodded, and he released her, giving her arms one more steadying squeeze before shutting her door.

"I'll carry the bags. You concentrate on walking."

"Very funny," she said.

Still, she appreciated the gesture, and the fact that he motioned for her to walk ahead of him as they made their way through the parking lot and into the terminal. He really was a gentleman. Checking in and going through security wasn't as awkward as she'd expected, mostly because he kept angling his head at her, as if he were checking to make sure she wasn't going to topple over again—and she kept giggling.

He didn't even seem to look at her socks, or inside her purse when she treated him to a coffee before they boarded. In fact, together they seemed friendly, congenial, comfortable. During the flight, he surprised her again by pulling out a book. He must have caught her expression, because he said, "What? Didn't you think I read? Or did you think I was too barbaric for that?"

"You're just surprising me all the time, Tanner Lucas," she said.

Then she leaned her head against the window and went to sleep. She didn't wake up again until the pilot announced the plane's descent into San Francisco. She just had to get through about thirty-six more hours, and then she'd meet her father. Finally.

But first, the hotel. And an entire day with Tanner Lucas.

———

KNOWING they'd be getting into San Francisco late, Hannah, always one for practicality, had reserved their rooms in a utilitarian hotel near the airport. Despite the fact that its website didn't boast any bells or whistles, the lobby was clean and comfortable-looking, and there was even a case of freshly-baked chocolate chip cookies on the counter. Tanner helped himself to one, and then wandered around the space (which, with its couches and potted trees, was nicely furnished for an inexpensive place) while Hannah checked them in.

When she finished, he was examining a modern-looking sculpture on a table against the wall. He turned as she approached, and smiled.

"All set?"

Hannah felt weird about the fact that none of it felt weird. Maybe *she* was weird.

"We're in two hundred and two-oh-two," Hannah said. "Next-door neighbors."

Side by side, they walked to the elevator, which they rode in silence. As they approached the end of the hall where their rooms were, Hannah handed Tanner his key card.

"I can't believe it's after midnight and I'm still walking. See you in the morning?"

"I'll pick you up at nine for breakfast in the lobby."

Wait. Why wasn't he saying anything about the separate rooms? *Shut up, Hannah,* her inner voice said. Out loud, she said, "Sounds great."

"Good night," they said at the same time, before simultaneously opening their doors, entering their rooms, and letting the doors swing shut.

Hannah leaned against hers and exhaled. There. That had gone smoothly. If only she could get her body to stop buzzing. It was nerves, that's all. Nerves and exhaustion. This had been a long day. She nodded to herself, then pushed away from the door and carried her bag into the room. She set up the luggage stand and retrieved her pajamas and toiletries. Just as she let her nightgown drop over her body, there was a knock at the door.

It couldn't be anyone other than Tanner. She hadn't called for room service or anything. Her stomach swirled, again. She walked to the door and looked through the security viewer. Then she took a deep breath and opened the door.

"Is that what you always wear to bed?" Tanner wanted to know.

Fighting the impulse to cross her arms and cover the nightgown—which, she had to admit, looked a little like a men's button-down shirt—she said, "Yes, as a matter of fact. Can I help you?"

Can I help you? Who said that in a regular conversation?

"I'm hoping you can," he said. "I forgot toothpaste."

Here, he gave her a little shrug and held up his toothbrush.

"Couldn't call down to the front desk?"

"Well, I thought this would be faster," he said. "But I can go back to my room, call them up."

"No, no," she said. "It's fine. Come on in."

He did. The door shut. Now *this* was intimate. Here she was, barefoot, bare-legged, bra-less. In a hotel room. With Tanner Lucas. Since she was still holding her toiletries bag, she unzipped it and handed him the tube of toothpaste.

"Thanks," he said, as friendly as ever. How could he be so comfortable here, like this?

He put the toothpaste on his toothbrush, put the lid back on the toothpaste tube, and handed it to her. Then he grinned at her again, and started brushing his teeth. Right there in her hotel room, with her standing in front of him in her pajamas. The whole time, his eyes twinkled, and she could have sworn he was reading her mind. He knew the torture he was putting her through. He wandered into her bathroom and used her sink to finish up, even going so far as to use one of her towels.

"Thanks again," he said, then.

Hannah could only nod—until he used one hand to tuck her hair behind her ear, and then cup the back of her head. Her traitorous mind told her that her body was up for a whole lot more than nodding. And then Tanner kissed her, long and deep. Of course, she kissed him back. Out of reflex. Her body melted against his. Unconsciously.

He ended the kiss, and said, quietly, "Goodnight, Hannah."

Disappointment crept in. Involuntarily.

And despite the fact that she was exhausted and, a few minutes ago, had wanted nothing other than to lay her head on the fluffy pillow on the hotel's crisply-made bed, she found that sleep was elusive that night.

———

HANNAH SEEING Tanner Lucas first thing in the morning had become a regular occurrence since he'd been building two houses on her property. But only once had she seen him just ten minutes out of the shower, still smelling of soap and aftershave. She'd forgotten how much of a turn-on it was.

She remembered immediately when he knocked on her door at nine a.m. sharp, holding up his toothbrush. She let him in, and after he brushed his teeth, they went down to the hotel's buffet-style breakfast.

"No pastries?" she said when they sat down. "I took you for a donut guy."

"All protein in the mornings," he said. "Food for the brain. And the muscles."

"Naturally. You've got to keep those muscles in shape."

Tanner's face—for once—colored a little, and Hannah decided to take pity on him and change the subject. "What do you want to do in the city?"

In the car and on the flight, they'd talked a little about their options, but they hadn't made final decisions.

"I'd like to take the cable car," Tanner said. "And I know you promised Sadie chocolate, so I suppose we should go to Ghiradelli Square."

"Chinatown?" Hannah said. "We could do lunch there."

"We'd better get going." Tanner stood and offered Hannah his arm. She took it, ridiculously delighted. They walked outside into the sun.

"I hired a car to drive us in," Tanner said. "Should be here any minute. I didn't want to deal with parking. You know, you rarely get days this sunny in the city. I think you're a good-luck charm."

It was silly, Hannah thought, that she, a forty-year-old woman, felt so giddy after hearing that compliment. But she did. The car pulled up, and the two of them got in.

San Francisco never disappointed, Hannah thought—and neither did Tanner's company. The two of them walked and walked, arm in arm, laughing and chatting and pointing out fun or strange sights: a sea lion struggling to get out of the water and onto a dock, a man offering to read their palms, the fortune cookie factory.

Although they'd decided on a few destinations, the city offered them some unexpected options: a street fair where they bought fresh fruit and coffee, live music on a corner, and a group of skateboarders showing off their stunts on a wide swath of sidewalk.

Hannah found a hat for Sadie, and a necklace made of abalone shell. She even bought gifts for her sisters: colorful glass vases for their new houses. She was having so much fun, she didn't even bother thinking about how she'd get them home.

They ate all day long, snacking on churros and fortune cookies and dim sum and ice cream. Even when they'd declared themselves full, they kept eating, sampling fresh clam chowder and sourdough bread. Finally, darkness fell, and they decided to head back to the hotel.

"I know it's dinner time," Tanner said as they waited for a taxi, "but I really am too full to eat."

"Me, too," Hannah said. "Good thing we walked so much, or I'd be having a real crisis of conscience."

The taxi came, and as they moved farther and farther from the heart of the city, Hannah felt reluctant to let the day go. Tanner must have felt similarly: inside the hotel lobby, he gestured at the restaurant. "One more chance for dinner."

"Ha," Hannah said. "No dinner, but I could do with a glass of wine."

"Want to order a bottle?"

"I'm almost positive this place doesn't have room service," Hannah said, wishing then that she'd chosen a swankier spot, somewhere with all the trappings of luxury. Oh, including silk sheets. *Where did that thought come from?*

"Why don't you go on up," Tanner said, "and I'll run to that convenience store on the corner and grab a bottle."

Practical Hannah would decline, say they should call it a night. They had to get up early to make the drive to Golden Delicious Orchard. But this New, Fun Version of Hannah wanted to agree, to go freshen up and wait for Tanner to return. Practical Hannah cringed at that idea. Wasn't hotel sex with someone you weren't officially dating scandalous? The New, Fun Version of Hannah told Practical Hannah to take a hike.

"Sure," she said. "That'd be great."

She saw relief flicker across Tanner's face. He was probably afraid Practical Hannah would stifle the growing attraction between them and put an end to this day. He gave her a quick nod and nearly ran out the hotel's front door. Smiling to herself, Hannah went to her room, equal parts nervous, excited, and ... horny. Yes, the New, Fun Version of Hannah was horny. And she wasn't afraid to admit it.

She texted her sisters: *At the hotel. Tanner ran out to get a bottle of wine. A bottle! What do I do?*

Of course, Margaret was the first to text back, and Hannah pictured her at home in her childhood bedroom, lips twitching: *I'm at Ethan's. Do what I'm doing. Get undressed and wait for him naked.*

Sarah responded: *What she said. And Hannah, have fun.*

Should she really wait for him naked? Her phone dinged, and Hannah rushed to read Margaret's next message: *If you can't bring yourself to get naked, put your nightgown on. But for goodness' sake, take off your underwear.*

This was something she could get behind.

As she began to follow directions, her phone dinged again. This time, it was Sarah: *Text us after!*

Hannah giggled. Then, she put on her pajamas and removed her underwear. She folded them neatly and set them in her suitcase.

When Tanner returned, she was watching through the security viewer, and she opened the door before he knocked. She wondered if he could tell she was trying to look sexy, that she'd combed her hair to one side and reapplied her mascara.

"Wow," he said, and then she panicked, thinking he *could* tell, which probably made her seem desperate. "You must really want this wine. Were you watching through the peephole?"

"Come on in," she said. "All we have are these fancy plastic cups, but they'll do."

Chuckling, Tanner put the wine on the table. "I snagged this opener at the front desk. And I bought my own toothpaste." He opened the bottle. "Should we let it breathe?"

"Nah," Hannah said. "I don't think it matters much, since we're drinking it out of cheap plastic hotel cups."

Also, she thought, once they poured the wine, they could sit down and relax.

"All right," he said. "I'll pour. Wait. If I'm not mistaken, and if it's not some figment of my imagination, when you turned around just now and the light shone through your nightgown—are you not wearing any underwear?"

She had not expected him to call her out on it. Although she should have expected it. What would Margaret do, now? Margaret would say something clever. Something like …

"As a matter of fact, I'm not."

Okay, that wasn't that clever. But it seemed to work, because Tanner said. "Okay. Well. I'll pour the wine. As soon as I take off my shoes. That is, if that's okay with you."

"Absolutely," Hannah said, wanting to laugh at the sultry tone of her voice. She quickly added, "We must have walked ten miles today."

"At least."

He slipped off his shoes and groaned with pleasure. The airport security line hadn't felt intimate, but this certainly did.

"I'm not sure how much to pour," Tanner said, "so—"

"Just fill 'er up," Hannah said.

"Okay," Tanner said. "If you say so."

"They're small glasses," she said.

"Are we calling them glasses now?"

"Yes, because we're classy."

This small talk seemed to be a mutual attempt to draw attention away from a potentially awkward topic: where they'd sit. The table had two chairs, but they'd hardly be comfortable after such a long day. And the bed was the only other place.

"Surely we've spent enough time together now that we can sit on the bed without it being strange," Hannah said, impressing herself with her boldness.

"Surely that's true," Tanner said. "I just don't want you to feel like I'm overstepping, or making any assumptions. Especially since you're going commando under there."

She wanted to say, "So what if you *are* making assumptions?" but she wasn't feeling quite that bold. So instead, she said, "Well, those chairs do look awfully uncomfortable. So I guess sitting on the bed is our best option."

She fluffed the pillows and leaned them against the headboard, and he handed her a cup of wine.

"Cheers," he said, "to a great day."

"To a great day," she said, "and to a great friend. Thank you for coming with me."

They touched the cups together, took sips, and climbed onto the bed, where they sat side by side, leaning against the pillows, legs outstretched.

"So," he said, after they'd sat in contemplative quiet for a few minutes. "How are you feeling about tomorrow?"

Hannah sighed. "I'm not sure. I hardly gave myself time to think about it today. But I think I'm nervous. Excited. Scared. All of those things. I mean, what if this was a terrible mistake?"

"What if it was the best decision you ever made?"

"True."

"But Hannah?"

"Yeah?"

"Even if it doesn't turn out like you hope, I'm glad we had this time together."

"Me, too," she said.

He set his wine cup on the nightstand and took her hand. "Would it be all right if I kissed you?"

Practical Hannah clammed up, terrified. But the New, Fun Version of Hannah leapt up and down. "I think that would be all right."

The kiss was gentle, but not timid. It conveyed a sense of hunger, a gentle urgency. It was an offer, Hannah thought. A question. She set her wine down, too, and answered it.

———

HANNAH SHOULDN'T HAVE BEEN able to sleep, not that night. But she did. She slept hard and deep, waking only when her alarm went off. Then, though, the bliss dissolved, and was quickly replaced by an anxiety that kept her hands shaking all morning: as Tanner draped an arm over her waist and pulled her close, as she slipped out of bed to shower, and as she packed before they walked down to breakfast. She barely ate, taking a few bites of a bagel Tanner brought to the table and pushed toward her.

It was time to go.

The morning outside the hotel seemed eerily still, slow-moving. The sun was up, its golden light filtering through the leaves of the trees. But the road was nearly empty of traffic, and the sky of birds. There were no people moving along the sidewalks, and even the coffee shop drive-throughs stood unoccupied.

"Quiet this morning," Tanner said.

Hannah looked over at him and saw him studying her. She wondered what he was seeing.

"It is," she said.

"I meant you," he said.

"I'm nervous," she said.

He turned on the radio, turned it up, reached across the center console and squeezed her hand. The traffic light at which he'd stopped turned green, and he put both hands on the steering wheel.

After a few minutes, he said, "Do you want to go over your script?"

"Funny," she said. "I don't have one, but maybe I should. Too late now."

The time seemed to pass both quickly and slowly—the drive took mere moments and long years, all at once. Then, Tanner turned the rental car off the two-lane highway and onto a long dirt road, lined, of course, by apple trees.

And when Tanner said, "This is it," Hannah's heart leapt.

CHAPTER SIXTEEN

THE GOLDEN DELICIOUS Orchard looked exactly as Hannah imagined Heaven would. Rows and rows of trees offered shade, an exquisite respite from the midday sun. Apples, bright and round and cheerful, stood out against glossy green leaves. The dirt below the trees looked rich and fertile.

And although she'd always felt at home at the Seedling Homestead, she couldn't help but notice a sense of belonging here, too. It was almost as if her very soul knew this was where she'd first come into being.

"Beautiful," Tanner said.

Hannah's, "Yeah," came out in a sigh.

"I guess we'll look for the main office," Tanner said.

Unable to speak, Hannah just nodded. Then she cleared her throat and said, "Perfect."

She rolled down her window and inhaled the scents of freshly watered earth, apples (of course), and fresh, humid air. The place smelled so *alive*.

"Here we are," Tanner said. "Ready?"

She said, "Nope," and got out of the car.

Tanner grasped her hand as they started walking, and she was grateful knowing he'd hold her up if she happened to keel over from nerves. Together, they approached the office door, and she made a conscious effort to take in all the details: the pot of bright orange mums next to the entrance, the way the windows sparkled. When she did, she felt a stirring of pride. This haven, with its simple, celestial beauty, belonged to her family. She belonged to it.

They walked in.

"Good morning! Actually, guess it's afternoon now, isn't it?" The receptionist was perfect: plump like she loved apple pies (or maybe apple fritters), made up like this job was important to her, friendly like she actually enjoyed it. Her accent was southern hospitality.

"Hi," Hannah said. She looked at Tanner, and he smiled at her, gave her a little nod. "I was wondering if Philip Carlisle is available."

The woman's expression shifted, then. It morphed from polite engagement to surprise to interest to realization, and then, finally, to sadness. Clear as day. And Hannah wondered what all of it meant.

"May I ask your name, sweetheart?"

"It's Hannah. Hannah Bradley. And this is Tanner Lucas."

"Ma'am." Tanner nodded.

The woman stood up. "I'm Molly. It's a pleasure to meet the two of you."

She pushed back her chair and came around the side of the desk. Dread started to bloom in Hannah's stomach. Shouldn't Molly be saying something like, "He's in a meeting just now, but I'll go get him," or, "He's walking in the orchard. Let me page him," or, "I don't know where he is just now. He was here just a minute ago"?

Now, Molly took both of Hannah's hands and looked into her eyes.

"You don't know."

Hannah panicked. She didn't know what?

At her silence in response, Molly went on. "Philip's sick, honey. They're not expecting him to make it much longer. He has days, maybe hours."

The last Hannah had seen on the Internet, Philip Carlisle, Jr. had looked spry. Like the picture of health. How was this possible?

"Can I see him?"

"May I ask what your business is with him?"

Again, Hannah glanced at Tanner, hoping for help. Hoping he'd be able to say the words she couldn't say. He put a hand on her shoulder, but didn't speak. So Hannah said, "I just wanted to meet him, that's all."

"Are you—are you family?" Molly said. "He always kept to himself about his family, you know, after the tragedy that took his son. And then his wife left—well, you understand. I don't need to bore you with all the particulars. But there was always speculation that he might have family somewhere else."

Tanner squeezed Hannah's shoulder. "I'm his daughter."

Molly dropped Hannah's hands and placed her own hands on her chest. "Well, my word. He never mentioned he had a daughter. And your mother—never mind, it's none of my business, then, is it?"

"He didn't know about me," Hannah said, wanting to defend Philip. She wanted to be loyal to Mama Katherine, to say something to explain why she'd never told him, but she couldn't think of how to explain it. Then she worried Molly might think she was here to try to inherit Philip's fortune.

"And I'm not—" she wasn't sure how to put it into words. "I'm not here to try to get anything, ma'am. I just wanted to meet my father, that's all. I only just found out who he is."

Molly looked at Hannah, her eyes like lasers boring into Hannah's. She seemed to make a decision.

"You know," Molly said. She put her hands on her hips, tilted her head. "You look quite a bit like him. In the chin. And those dimples. Even as an old man, those dimples could make a lady's knees weak."

Then, she seemed to realize what all this meant. "You never met him. And now—"

"And now he's on his deathbed."

Molly's face softened.

"There may still be time, but …"

"But you don't know if meeting me, finding out about me, will upset him."

Hannah could tell Molly cared about Philip. She seemed genuinely concerned. But if this was Hannah's only chance, she was going to give it everything she could.

"Surely he'd want to know," she began. Her throat tightened and she found she couldn't go on.

"Could you check, do you think?" Tanner said. His voice was gentle, persuasive.

Molly nodded, just slightly, but she still looked uncertain.

"You know, why don't the two of you wait outside? I'll make a phone call, and then I'll be right out."

When Hannah would have frozen right there on the spot, Tanner took her upper arms and steered her back out the doors they'd come in. Outside, they sat down on a low brick wall that served as the edge of the patio. They didn't speak. Hannah tapped her toe, a nervous habit she'd always hated. Tanner enveloped her hand in his. After what seemed like several hours, Molly was there, gesturing for them to come back in. She cut to the chase: "I think it'd be okay. I'll walk you on up to his room."

Relief flowed through Hannah's veins, opening up everything including her tear ducts, which began overflowing.

All she could manage to croak, though, was, "He's not at the hospital?"

"No," Molly said. "There was nothing more the doctors could do. Stage four cancer. Treatments didn't work. He lived a good life, he said. So he chose to spend his final days here, at home."

Molly led them to a golf cart, and when they'd all climbed in, she drove around the office building and down a winding path. Sitting at the edge of a clearing in the orchard, Philip Carlisle, Jr.'s house was small yet grand, simple yet elegant. Hannah gasped. This had been her mother's house, once, a long time ago. It had been the place where Mama brought their baby, Benny, home, and where she and Philip had hosted that nearly-disastrous Fourth of July party.

She could almost see it now: the lights sparkling in the trees, the tables set up underneath them, people dancing and talking.

The house itself was all dark wood and glass, with big barn-style entry doors. Its windows reflected the scene before them: rows of trees bathed in sunlight. Hannah would have loved it as a child. But her father's life had happened here without her.

"Gorgeous, isn't it?" Molly said.

"It is," Hannah said.

"Come on, honey. Come meet your father."

The house was quiet, the kind of quiet that happens after a good snow: thick and muted. But it wasn't stuffy or clouded with the aura of impending death. The air felt clear and clean. The front doors opened into a parlor, where a piano sat facing a wide picture window. Framed photos of orchard life hung on the walls—single apples, people picking apples, kids drinking what Hannah thought was cider.

"Just this way, up the stairs," Molly said.

On the right side of the parlor, the stairs curved upward, guided by a sturdy banister of shining, dark wood. Hannah and Tanner followed Molly, who walked slowly, with something like reverence. Hannah noticed the carpet was thick beneath her feet. At the top of the stairs, a wide hallway opened in both directions. Molly went right, and followed a banister around to a half-open door. She did a quick double-knock, and someone answered, "Do come in."

"Wait here just a minute," Molly said. She went in and shut the door. Again, Hannah and Tanner waited. Somewhere in the house, a clock ticked, then struck eleven, the tones ringing, then echoing into the quiet.

The door opened again, and Molly came out.

"Go on in," she said, then. "When you're done, come back downstairs. I'll wait in the parlor and take you on back."

Hannah wanted to ask Molly what she should say, how she should begin, how to start a conversation with the father she'd never met when he had only hours left to live. But Molly was already gone.

"Want company?" Tanner said. Torn, Hannah froze again. "Tell you what," he said. "I'll wait out here for now, and if you need me, send me a signal."

"A signal?"

"Crow like a rooster."

"Are you kidding?" she said.

"Of course. Just come and get me."

She nodded, steeled herself.

Philip was alone in the room, sitting in a chair next to a window that overlooked the orchard. He was already looking in her direction, and Hannah saw his eyes focus on her face when she entered the room.

"You're—" he said, and she said, "Hannah."

"Hannah," he said, and, with a brief nod, she said, "Hannah Bradley."

"You look just like her."

"And you, I've heard."

"There *is* something in the chin," he said.

His blatant appraisal was terrifying and exciting at the same time. It was everything she'd always wanted, but it was nothing like she'd ever expected.

"I didn't know about you." She didn't know why she said it. She didn't owe him an explanation. Or maybe she did. She was an adult. Should she have sought him out? He had no way of knowing what her mother had told her.

"How is Hazel?"

Hannah wasn't sure how to answer. She'd wanted him to ask about her. She'd wanted to ask about him. To finally get the answers to all those questions she had—about his favorite foods and songs and color. But of course he had a right to ask about Mama, too.

"She's fine. Strong as an ox. She—we—live in Wyoming."

"Ah. She always said she'd love to live where the sky is big."

"She started a little farm. The Seedling Homestead."

Hannah tried to read his emotions as he steepled his hands, rested his elbows on the chair's arms and his chin on his fingertips. "You grew up there?"

"I did." Again, she felt like she had to issue an explanation, to tell him about the golden summer days, the musical sound of the creek, Mama's hurt being so deep that she couldn't stay in California, facing Philip day after day. He didn't look like a dying man. He looked old, yes. His skin was thin and wrinkled. He'd draped a blanket over his lap, and his knee bones protruded through it. But his eyes were sharp and clear and as blue as—hers. His eyes were the exact same color as Hannah's.

"Hannah," he said again, as if saying it this once could make up for all the times he could have said it throughout her childhood. At least, that's what she imagined. "It's a lovely name."

"Thank you."

"What's she like?" he said.

"Mama?"

"Yes. I knew her as Hazel, but I'd imagine she goes by a different name now. I never could find her, no matter how hard I tried. And I *did* try. You must know that."

"Did you?"

"Of course." He sounded tired, resigned. And suddenly, she felt guilty. For coming here. For, undoubtedly, stirring up memories and pain from years ago. Memories and pain he'd probably thought he wouldn't have to face again. Although, didn't people always spend their final days confronting the best and the worst times of their lives?

"I didn't know about you, either, Hannah."

She looked down. "I know. My sister, Sarah—she's adopted—found an old journal of Mama's. Mama was pregnant with me when she, ah, moved. She didn't know. And when she realized it, she felt like it was too late. Like she'd made an unforgivable mistake."

"Is there such a thing?" Philip said.

Again, Hannah thought that he didn't seem near death. Or, maybe he was so near death that he was experiencing that final push of mind and body, that burst of energy and clarity that preceded the final breath.

"She thought so."

"Would you give her a message for me?"

Hannah leaned toward him, her hands knit together at the waist.

"Of course."

"Would you tell her that I forgive her? That I forgave her years ago, that I looked for her, that I never stopped loving her?"

"You—"

"I never stopped loving her."

"But she—"

He lifted a hand, halting Hannah. "She did what she thought was best at the time. She's a complicated woman."

"Well, you aren't kidding about that."

This earned her a small, half-smile, a lift of the left side of his mouth.

"Why don't you sit, Hannah? I'd love the pleasure of one conversation with my daughter before I go on to the next—*phase*, shall we call it?"

She sank into a chair next to Philip's, her body finally relaxing, her hands dropping into her lap.

"Good," he said. "Now. I'll order up some snacks and we'll talk. Tell me. Tell me everything."

So she did. After Philip used the phone to order a deli tray and a pitcher of water and a bottle of wine, chilled, he placed his hands on the chair's armrests, leaned forward like Hannah had been just a moment ago, and waited. She told him about her childhood, about Mama adopting Sarah and Margaret, about growing up on the Seedling Homestead and becoming a teacher. She told him about her niece, Amelia, and Margaret losing her vision, and Sadie. Retelling the story of her life in this way was something like creating an audio journal—only, no one would have the chance to go back and listen to it.

"So, you're happy?" he said.

She nodded. Then she glanced at the door where she knew Tanner was waiting on the other side.

"But?" he said.

She'd never admitted this out loud before. But this was the only conversation she'd ever have with Philip, the only time she'd be able to confide in him, ask him to share his wisdom. Again, she told him about the soul searching she'd done recently.

"Sometimes I wonder if there's more. Sometimes I think, maybe I should find myself a good man, get hitched, have some kids."

"But you haven't."

"I haven't."

"Take it from an old man who hasn't had it," he said. "At least, not in the way I needed it. I have my orchard family, of course. But I had my one true love, and I let her go. There's nothing in this world like having someone to lie down next to at night."

Here, he gestured to his bed, which stood empty. "You need lifelong love, Hannah. Because without it, what have you got, really?"

Someone came in then, with a rolling tray piled high with cheese, crackers, and grapes. A bucket of ice chilled a bottle of wine. Philip winked at the man who rolled it in, and when the man left, Philip rolled the tray toward her. She made herself a little plate, despite the fact that she didn't feel hungry.

"I have love and companionship," she said.

"Do you? Your mother loves you. Of that, I'm sure. And your sisters. But you've told me they're married. Are you truly, truly happy, Hannah?"

This time, even though she was tempted to look at the door, at the spot where she knew Tanner was standing, she didn't.

"Of course. Now. Tell me about yourself. Tell me everything I need to know about my father."

Philip looked out the window, and Hannah studied his profile. It wasn't exactly like hers; his chin made a softer curve and his nose was a bit longer. But she could see the resemblance. If they were walking down the street, side by side, people would know. People would know he was her dad.

"There isn't too much to tell," Philip said. He sounded like his thoughts were far away. "Well. Not in the short time we have, here. I could tell you all my favorite things—I've enjoyed a deep love of lasagna ever since our cook, Betty, came on staff when I was a teenager. I abhor chocolate ice cream. But this moment, this situation, forces me to think of what I really want you to know about me. About me as a person."

He turned to look at her. His eyes were a little watery, but he didn't blink.

"I want you to know that I loved deeply. I loved Benny, your brother. And—I know we've known each other mere seconds—I love you, too."

Her eyes started to sting.

"I loved your mother. So, so much. But I don't think I loved her as hard as I could have. When Benny died, we were both broken. But instead of turning toward her, seeking comfort in her, I turned away. The truth is that I blamed her, even though we both know what happened to him wasn't her fault. I now believe that if I'd responded with love, it would have been enough."

For a brief span of time—not even a full second—Hannah wondered if it would be possible to bring Mama Katherine here before Philip took his last breath. Maybe they could talk, maybe they could reconcile. Then Philip continued speaking.

"And although I never loved anyone else in that same way, I've loved the people here at Golden Delicious. I could give you example after example, but I don't think you need them. I'd like you to spend some time here, get to know the people I knew. You'll find that I genuinely loved them. You walked through my parlor and you saw the photos, and maybe you thought I'd put up some photos of my work. Impersonal."

He lifted a hand to dismiss that thought.

"There is nothing impersonal about them, Hannah. After your mother left, I knew I couldn't remarry. So instead, I built this new family. I surrounded myself with a family of my choosing, and we all loved each other. Sure, we grow apples. We sell apples. But we also grow love. And that's really my legacy."

Emotion was taking up every cubic inch of space in Hannah's torso. She felt like it was expanding, and she was one breath away from floating right through the ceiling. Was it happiness? Longing? She couldn't tell.

"Now. I know you didn't come here asking for my advice. But I'm going to give it to you." He offered her a wry smile. "It's the only chance I've got to do some parenting, right? Build your own family, Hannah. Whatever that looks like. Find people you love, and love them as best you know how. Carry on the family legacy of love."

Everything came together, then. Because she'd grown up seeing the Seedling Homestead sign Mama made, she'd never really felt it sink in. But just below the name of the property, in smaller letters that had faded with time, there was a phrase: *Love Grows Here.*

Philip had said, "We also grow love."

And now, he was telling her to carry on the family legacy: love. It was a legacy she was getting from both of her parents.

"I think I've got to lie down, now, and get some sleep," Philip said. "I am so sorry. There's nothing I'd enjoy more than sitting here, talking with you, but death doesn't always heed what we want. Would you help me stand, get to my bed?"

She nodded, emotion once again clogging her throat, and helped him up. The fact that she could feel the bones in his arm and his rib cage made him seem frail, but he stood with such dignity. She'd thought she'd just guide him over to the bed, but Philip took a step back and opened his arms to her. Hannah stepped into his embrace, wrapped her arms around his waist. Her head came just to his shoulder, and when his arms went around hers, the tears finally fell.

"I love, you, Dad," she said. He squeezed a little tighter, then let go.

"Thank you, Hannah. Thank you for coming to see me, and giving me this opportunity. You're a wonderful woman. I'm so proud of you, and I'm so grateful that your mother raised you so well. I'm only sorry I didn't get to know you sooner."

What a cruel twist of fate, Hannah thought. They say the dying know when death is near, and it seemed Philip knew he wouldn't speak to Hannah again. So, it was hello and goodbye, all at once. It was a gift and yet, it seemed so unfair. Why would life give her a father, only to take him away?

She helped Philip into bed, where he laid back and closed his eyes. Almost immediately, the cadence of his breathing signaled sleep, and Hannah spent one long moment memorizing his features. She made her way out of the room. Tanner was waiting for her, and, just like her father had minutes ago, he opened his arms to embrace her. Without speaking, the two of them walked back down the stairs to where Molly sat in the parlor.

"Well?" she said.

Hannah simply nodded, and Molly led them back to the golf cart. "You know what you might like, honey? I could give you a tour of the orchard. Show you all of Philip's favorite places."

"That'd be nice," Hannah said.

The grounds were serene. Nothing had changed out here, Hannah thought, but everything had changed for her.

"What will happen to the orchard?" Hannah said. She realized Molly might think she wanted it, so she rushed to add, "I'm just curious. I don't want to come in and take over, or anything. I guess I'd just hate for the commercial orchards to take over the family business."

"There's a trust," Molly said. "So it'll keep running. Philip is a smart man. Good businessman. But that's not what you'll want to hear about, is it? Let me take you to his favorite spot. He spent a lot of time there. I think you'll like it."

She drove them down the main dirt path, down another one, and up to a water tower. As they approached it, Hannah glanced at Tanner, and he shrugged at her.

"Philip used to come out here at least a couple of times each week. He'd climb up the ladder and sit up there, alternating whether he faced east or west, north or south. The tower's at the very center of the property. You can see the entire orchard from here. Philip, he called it his thinking spot and if we ever had to track him down, chances were, that's where he'd be. Thinking. Working things out. He always carried this little model cable car. They say it was a gift from his wife—your mother—and he'd sort of fiddle with it while he worked things out. He'd turn it over in his hands, twirl it, run his thumb over it. When you saw him put it back in his pocket, you'd know he'd reached a conclusion, made a decision, whatever. I can't tell you how many times he took it up to the water tower."

"Can we go up?" Hannah said.

"Of course," Molly said. "I'm sure Philip would love to know you'd seen this place from his perspective."

The ladder went straight up, then fed into a set of stairs that wrapped around the lowest part of the water tank. Still in a daze, Hannah struggled to truly take in all the details, even though she wanted to. It seemed important to memorize everything, but her mind was fuzzy and numb. Their feet clanked on the metal stairs, and their hands slid along the railing. The walkway was so narrow Hannah kept her eyes down, but when they finally got to the top, she found the view breathtaking.

The sun was high in the sky now, and it shone down on rows and rows of trees, trees in every direction. And the scene buzzed with activity. People harvested apples, trimmed branches, raked the ground. Even from this perch, Hannah could hear shouts, whistles, even a song.

"It's beautiful," she said, echoing Tanner's statement from earlier. "It really is amazing."

How would her life have been different if she'd grown up here?

Would she have run between the rows of trees, barefoot, scooping up freshly-fallen apples to eat? Would she have learned early on how to make apple pies and apple tarts and apple crumb cake? Would she drink apple cider at breakfast, lunch, and dinner? Childhood here would be magical, she thought. Although, her own childhood on the Seedling Homestead had been pretty magical, too. Molly was with them now, still huffing from her own ascent up those stairs.

She pointed to the east. "That, there, belonged to your mother's father, before the merger. If you read a journal of hers, then I suppose you know they had an arranged marriage, to merge the orchards?"

"Yes, but it reads like they fell in love."

"They did," Molly said. "At least, to hear the old orchard hands tell it. The guys who were here the longest remember those days. Your father and mother would chase each other between the trees, sneak off to picnic and, you know, steal kisses, in the middle of harvest. They were very much in love."

That, at least, was good to know.

"He told me he never remarried," Hannah said.

"No, he never did. Never dated, either. Come to think of it, he never showed a speck of romantic interest in anyone after she left."

A bird flew past, landed in a tree, and twittered out a few notes. From somewhere across the way, a second bird answered.

"I could stand here forever," Hannah said.

Tanner rubbed her lower back, and she leaned into him.

"It's a really special place," Molly said. "Want to see more?"

She drove them around the entire orchard, pointing out where each variety grew, where they'd had good, mediocre, and less-than-ideal crops over the past few years. She showed them where a family of raccoons made their home, and where the big trucks loaded up the crates of fruit to take them to the supermarkets. In every spot, Hannah imagined her father directing workers or sampling apples or chuckling at the raccoons' antics. She wondered what he'd been thinking and how his voice sounded. What had people thought of him? Molly seemed to like him, but people always remembered the dying in a glowing light. What had it been like to work for him, or with him? Did he crack jokes? Did he roll up his sleeves and join in?

She would never know, not firsthand.

The tour complete, Molly drove them back to the rental car. "I'll be in touch with you tomorrow," she said. "Let you know how he's doing."

Once she was gone, Tanner suggested they grab something to eat, and he drove them into the tiny town where there were only two choices: a steakhouse and a diner. Hannah found she couldn't choose.

Tanner parked in front of the diner. "Comfort food," he said. "Can't go wrong with that."

"Okay?" he said, before they got out.

She nodded. Tanner seemed to sense Hannah wasn't up for any decision-making whatsoever, so inside, he led her to a booth by the window and ordered tuna melts, fries, and sodas for them both.

"Want to talk?" he said.

Touched by his compassion, Hannah smiled. "Not yet. But thank you. Thank you so much for being here for me, for helping make this possible."

She didn't say that she wasn't sure how she felt about meeting Philip, or what she made of his advice. Their food came, they ate, and before eight p.m., they were back at the hotel. She didn't know whether she wanted company or not, and Tanner didn't seem to want to make that particular decision for her. So he opened the door to her hotel room and said, "I'll come and check on you in a while, okay? If you need me, I'll be one room over."

Alone, she sat down on the edge of the bed. Her mind felt dazed and her body felt stiff. She was exhausted. And she was devastated. Philip had told her love was the most important thing in the world. Mama had always said the same. But the two of them had never reconnected. For them, love hadn't been enough. She dialed Tanner's room and told him she was going to bed.

In the middle of the night, the hotel room phone rang, the shrill sound jarring her out of sleep with an adrenaline spike.

She answered. It was Molly. "He's gone, honey. I'm so sorry."

Hannah opened her mouth. No sound came out. She closed it. "I—uh—he passed away? When?"

"Just a few minutes ago," Molly said. "He went in his sleep. Very peaceful. Georgia, the maid, found him in his bed. He was even half-smiling, she said, like he'd been in the middle of a beautiful dream. Actually," she said as if she were onstage and speaking to the audience, "she said he looked like he'd just looked into the eyes of God. But I'm not so sure about all that, myself."

"We'll have an informal service tomorrow. He knew this was his time, and he arranged for a little to-do. You should come. Hear what people remember about him. It's not quite the same as really getting to know him. But it's something, isn't it?"

In the dark, Hannah nodded. Cleared her throat. "It's something."

Molly gave her the details, and with a promise to call again in the morning, she hung up.

Hannah put the phone back in the receiver and laid on her back, blinking into the dark. Now, she didn't cry. Since she'd found out Tanner made the travel arrangements, she'd *so* been looking forward to this, to discovering a piece of herself she'd only just admitted was missing. Yes, she'd spoken to Philip—for all of thirty minutes. And that was it. It was too late. She questioned all the things she hadn't done, the actions she hadn't taken to find her father. As a child, she'd let Mama remain tight-lipped. She'd assumed her silence meant Hannah's father was somehow connected to something unspeakable.

What if, in college, or even as an early adult, she'd gone looking for him? Pressed Mama for details, for answers? And this summer, when Sarah found Mama's old journal … if Hannah had taken action then, she would have been able to spend more time with him. But she hadn't. She'd been scared. Of rejection, of what she'd find, of what she wouldn't find. Of everything.

In the silence of the hotel room, Hannah considered whether she should accept Molly's invitation to Philip's service. However painful it might be, perhaps attending would be healing. However hard it would be to hear from people who knew her father better than she did, perhaps it would also be enlightening. It could give her some insight into who her father was, who *she* was.

She heaved a big sigh, weighed whether she should wake Tanner and tell him Philip was gone. No, she decided. She'd let him sleep. Before she fell back to sleep, herself, she thought she'd been stupid to think she could just come here, just fly out to California and waltz up to her father's home and claim her spot as his daughter.

She should have called first. Then she would have known what she was walking into. But she hadn't. And this—this tiny glimpse of the father she'd never had, this kindness from a lovely woman who was taking pity on her, this comfort from a man she was falling for, and tomorrow's service—was what she had now.

CHAPTER SEVENTEEN

Hannah always expected funerals and memorial services to be somber affairs, but she realized immediately upon entering the big barn where Philip's service was taking place that this event would be anything but melancholy. Tons of people flowed into the barn, wearing bright colors, chatting, and laughing. Hannah and Tanner sat three-quarters of the way back from the front of the room, all the way at the end of a row. She'd thought this position would ensure they'd go unnoticed, but it had the opposite effect since everyone else was up and walking around, socializing.

"This seat taken?" A man, probably about her own age, approached them and gestured at the seat next to Hannah's. She wanted to point out that the rest of the seats were pretty much empty, but she didn't. Her eyes must have given her thoughts away as they roamed the barn, because the man said, "I know. It was a stupid line. My curiosity just got the best of me. I've never seen you around. You a friend of Philip's?"

Tanner reached out to shake hands. "I'm Tanner Lucas. This is Hannah Bradley. We're visiting from Wyoming."

"Wyoming, huh? I didn't realize Philip had people up there."

"How did you know Philip?" Tanner said.

Before he had a chance to answer, another man, suit-clad and official-looking, walked to the front of the room. He clapped his hands in rhythm, exactly like Hannah would do to get the attention of her class.

"It's about time to get started," he said, his voice commanding and friendly at the same time.

Although the group didn't quiet, people made their way to seats.

"Guess I'd better find a spot," the first guy said. "I'm Marcus, by the way."

The man in the suit started to speak.

"All of you here know that Philip wanted the Golden Delicious Orchard to be a happy place. And he wanted today to be a happy occasion. So while we all will, undoubtedly, be mourning the loss of a great friend who had nothing but compassion for everyone in this room, let's remember this is a celebration of the opportunity we all had to know him."

He gestured to Marcus, the man who'd approached Hannah and Tanner a few minutes before, and Marcus walked to the front of the room.

"I think I can speak for everyone here when I say that Philip Carlisle, Jr. was the epitome of generosity. I can't think of a nicer man. Well, except every year at Thanksgiving dinner, when he became the ultimate prankster."

This earned a few chuckles, and Hannah wondered what the inside joke was.

"I can't decide which was his best prank," Marcus said. "What do you guys say? Was it the year he said we were having a tur-ducken and he put a rubber chicken inside the duck? Or was it the time he convinced Betty to make the entire meal out of apples?"

More laughter.

"Philip had a sense of humor," he said. "But he also had a sense of what was right. When my own dad died, Philip was the first one to take me under his wing. This mogul, this larger-than-life man, found the time for a sad, hurting little boy. He found the time to teach me, to coach me, to help me with my math homework. He taught me how to fish, how to cook, and how to take a girl on a date. Once, as an adult, I thanked him. I made a very sincere show of gratitude, and you all know how hard it is for me to be serious. And do you know what he said? He told me that our relationship meant as much to him as it did to me. He thanked *me*, if you can believe it. He thanked me for giving him the chance to impart his wisdom. 'We all want to feel like we're making a difference in someone's life, Marcus,' he said. 'And I can't tell you how much fun it's been to watch you grow into such a capable young man. You're still shit at making a pie crust, but other than that, I've very much enjoyed our time together.'"

The people in the audience, Philip's friends, chuckled. Some of them laughed through tears, Hannah noticed, and even Tanner's eyes glistened. So, she thought, Philip had been kind and funny.

"Once, when I was about thirteen, I had my first real girlfriend. Daisy Mae." Marcus nodded at a woman in the second row, and she gave a little wave. "Philip told me that when you kiss girls too young, your fingernails turn black. One weekend, my mom went on a business trip, and I stayed over at Philip's. I told him I planned to take Daisy Mae out fishing that Saturday. He even let me grab a few apples to take along with the picnic he had Betty pack for us. Did we kiss that day, Daisy Mae?"

Daisy Mae grinned and blushed, and leaned up against the man she was sitting next to.

"The next morning when I woke up, my fingernails were black around the edges. Every one of them. Philip took a Sharpie to my cuticles."

He examined his fingers now, and it was as if he could still see the ink.

"Anyway," he went on. "Philip was a great man. Everything he did, he did for love. And I know I'm not the only one who will miss him."

Marcus gave a little nod and returned to his seat. The officiant gestured to someone else, a woman this time. She stood up and approached the front of the room, her hands knit together in what Hannah assumed was nervousness.

"Hi," she said. "I won't be as funny or as clever as Marcus was. But we all know he has a knack for that. I just wanted to say that Philip was a hero to me. To my family. And I'm sure we weren't the only ones. But what made him a true hero is that he never asked for acknowledgement. I don't think any of us realized how very much he did for his people. Most of you don't know that several years ago, my husband, Rocky, got real sick. At first, doctors couldn't figure out what was wrong with him. He couldn't work, and we'd already used up most of his benefits and sick leave when little Ricky got sick last year and had to stay in the hospital for months at a time. And my job at the school certainly didn't pay enough for us to cover medical bills and put food on the table for the kids. Philip came over to the house one night and met with us. He played catch with Ricky and Matthew outside, he helped me clean up after dinner, and he sat with us by the fire. We had so much fun that night. We told stories, played checkers and chess, and joked around. I thought he was just, you know, being nice. Knowing Rocky was sick and all."

The woman sniffled. "But the next day, he called Rocky into the office. We both thought Rocky was gettin' fired, you know, laid off or somethin' since he couldn't work. But no. Philip wanted Rocky to know he'd set up regular paychecks to keep on coming, even though Rocky wasn't there punching the clock every day. And you know what? When Rocky passed away last year, I expected those paychecks to stop coming. But they didn't. They get deposited in our bank account every two weeks. I approached him about it once, you know. I told him we could manage. That somehow, we *would* manage. And he just shrugged and said, 'But why *manage*, Ethel? Why not relax, and enjoy your boys and your life the best you can, without worrying about money? You've got enough to manage already. Let me manage this.' I can't tell you how much that meant to me. And I know we're not the only family he's helped out. The world lost a wonderful, wonderful man."

Person after person, friend after friend, story after story. Philip's chosen family painted a wonderful portrait of Hannah's father. As they spoke, she alternated between pride and sadness, grief and anger. It was evident that Philip had been a great person. Truly great. And he was her father. But it was also evident that he'd done so much, for so many people. He'd provided a sense of community, of belonging, of family. And he'd never been able to do that for her.

Before the service was quite over, Hannah slipped out of her seat, walked as quietly as she could down the side aisle, and escaped into the sun. Of course, Tanner was right behind her. When she got into the rental car, he did the same, and she was grateful he didn't question her.

"Home?" was all he said. She nodded. He drove to the airport, and they boarded a plane for Wyoming.

———

ON THE FLIGHT, Hannah made a decision. The epiphany had been slowly building since she'd met Philip, looked into his eyes, felt his embrace—and then said goodbye to him. And now, it was clear what she had to do. She had to cut ties with Tanner. And with Sadie.

Philip had told her love was the most important thing in the world.

He'd said she should build a family in whichever way she chose. And theoretically, that family could include Tanner and Sadie. They'd become a family of sorts in recent months, hadn't they?

But Philip was wrong. Mama was wrong.

Because what was on the other side of that coin? Hannah. Hannah was on the other side of that coin, alone and having missed out on something so important, and so wonderful, that she now had a giant void inside.

And hadn't love left both Mama and Philip alone, too?

The two of them had loved each other so deeply, and look where it had gotten them. Sure, Philip had his orchard family, and Mama had the girls, but they'd missed out on the greatest love of their lives.

They'd loved, and they'd lost.

As soon as Hannah got home, she would bid Tanner Lucas goodbye, and speak to him only in a client-builder capacity.

She'd still give Sadie the trinkets she'd bought her in San Francisco, but she couldn't carry on like she had been, pretending she was more to the little girl than she really was. They'd maintain a strict teacher-student relationship. No more playdates or meals at home.

And she'd go home to Mama, to her mother who loved her, but not enough to give her the gift of a father. For the most part, she never felt like she was missing out on anything, and maybe that was enough.

Tanner didn't seem to notice any signs of her thought process. He probably thought she was quiet only because of the events that transpired over the past few days. Wouldn't any woman be subdued and quiet mere hours after meeting her father for the first time, only to have him die almost immediately?

It would be hard to let him go. She'd miss the way he held her gaze just a minute longer than necessary when they saw each other in the mornings. She'd miss the way he asked her advice about window placement. And the way he interacted with Sadie. And, of course, the way he made love to her. But he had been in her life only for a short while, and it would take only a short while to get used to life without him again. Even if it broke her.

The plane touched down in Jackson Hole, and Tanner took Hannah's hand. Maybe it would take longer than a short while to get used to life without him. But she had to. There was no other choice.

CHAPTER EIGHTEEN

TANNER DROPPED Hannah off at home. He didn't know her kiss was a farewell, or that her hug was more than a simple thank you. And she didn't want him to. She watched his truck back down the driveway and turn onto the main road, a tightness in her throat and chest she didn't even recognize. That constricted feeling made it difficult for Hannah to make her limbs move, and she walked stiffly to the front door, where her old life welcomed her.

It was time to face Mama, who, of course, was waiting at the dining room table when she walked in.

"Well?"

Hannah wanted to run to her, to bury her face in her neck like she had hundreds of times, to tell her everything. But at some point, daughters stopped telling their mothers everything, didn't they?

"He died, Mama."

Mama gasped. Perhaps delivering the news this way, like it an announcement, was cruel. Or perhaps, in its brevity, it was kind.

"When?"

"Just yesterday."

"You got to meet him, then?" Mama's eyes bored into Hannah's, searching. Were they finding what Mama wanted to find?

"I did."

"Well?"

The air in the room seemed heavy. Hannah could barely breathe. She wished Tanner was here, and then she chastised herself for wishing that.

"Why don't you sit?" Mama said. "I'll pour you a drink."

That, at least, was a reasonable idea. Hannah dropped her suitcase at her feet and sat down. She watched Mama in the kitchen. Her movements were wooden and slow. Was she about to round the corner to death, too? Where would that leave Hannah? At least Sarah and Donny, and Margaret and Ethan, would live here, on the Seedling Homestead, with her. And John Wayne. Although, Hannah thought as she looked at him now—at his graying muzzle and rickety legs and bony hips—it was unlikely he'd be with them much longer, either.

Hannah closed her eyes. She could hear Mama removing the cork from the bottle of good bourbon, the liquid swirling into the glasses, the squeak of Mama replacing the cork. She could hear the glass bottom of the bottle settling on the counter, Mama's steps coming back her way. Mama set the glasses on the table's wood surface. She sat down with an exhale. Pushed the glass across the table to where it touched Hannah's fingertips.

Hannah opened her eyes to see her mother staring right into them. She picked up her glass and drained it in one long drink. Mama raised her eyebrows, but didn't comment. Hannah waited to speak until she felt the bourbon warming her body from the core, relaxing her limbs like some kind of magical potion.

"It—he—was wonderful, Mama," Hannah said. "We got the chance to talk, just for a short time, and I'm so grateful for that. He died that night, and there was a service this morning. We went, and it was lovely. So many people came. I mean, people loved him, Mama. Everyone who spoke had a story about how he'd changed their life."

Everyone except me, she thought. Yes, the bourbon had a warming effect, and it also was opening up a crack in the emotional barrier she'd created, letting the anger seep through.

It was mean, Hannah knew, not to tell Mama right now that Philip had never fallen in love or remarried. But she didn't want to. It was mean, but it was also satisfying in a horrible way. Just like Mama hadn't told her about Philip, she wasn't going to tell Mama, either.

"That sounds wonderful," Mama said. She sounded sincere, which made Hannah hate herself, just a little. But not enough to stop her from saying, "I'm exhausted, Mama. I'm going to bed."

———

IT SHOULDN'T HAVE SURPRISED Hannah to see Tanner at the Seedling Homestead the next morning. It was a weekday, he was building her sisters' houses, and he probably had to check their progress first thing after having been gone. But because she'd been awake all night, blinking into the dark, convincing herself she couldn't—or, wouldn't—have Tanner in her life, it was jarring, almost a surprise, to lay eyes on him when she walked out to her truck to head to work.

He was so handsome, she thought. Striking, actually. She could picture him in a catalog for men's clothing—one of those catalogs that advertise cozy fleece vests with hundred-dollar khaki pants. And lots of plaid. Maybe a Labrador Retriever. His hair would curl over the collar of a fleece-lined vest.

Tanner, not privy to Hannah's hours-long thought process and subsequent decision, started to greet her as he normally would: he approached, arms outstretched to embrace her. With the briefest possible, "Good morning," she ducked under his right arm and scampered to the driver's side of the truck. He spun around, shock evident in his features. Guilt set in, immediately. Hannah wished she could take it back —not only the duck-under, but also the decision.

But she couldn't. So she offered him her best fake smile and said, "Sorry, gotta run. I'm late."

"Hannah—"

She held up a hand, and despite the strong temptation to get in the truck and drive off without saying another word to him, she stayed. She owed him that much.

"I want to thank you for taking me to California," she said. He opened his mouth to respond, closed it when she plowed ahead. "It meant so much to me. I can't even express how much it meant. But I can't keep doing this with you, Tanner. We're going to have to keep our relationship strictly professional."

Because she could see the surprise and the hurt, she added, "I am really sorry."

Did she owe him an explanation? Probably. But she couldn't give it. It sounded childish, strange, even in her own mind. Tanner, who grew up in a large, loving, boisterous family, could never understand, anyway. So she pulled open the truck door, got in, buckled her seat belt, and turned on the engine. She resisted the urge to watch him as he watched her back out of the driveway and onto the road. She resisted the urge to glance over, just for a second, and gauge how upset he seemed. And she resisted the urge to cry as she put her foot on the gas and pressed down, hard.

Sadie was waiting when she got to school. Tamping down her irritation—because she knew it was a result of her own decision to push Sadie away—she forced another fake smile and let her into the classroom.

The little girl's eyes were alight with excitement. "So? How was it? How was the big city? Did you meet your dad?"

Hannah paused her unloading of books, her lunchbox, and her calendar and said, "It was good. And yes. But—"

"How'd it go? Was he as nice as you hoped?"

Resuming her daily organization routine, Hannah said, "He was—but then he died."

"What? He *died*? While you were *there*?" Hannah sighed. Sadie's body drooped. "I'm sorry, Hannah. I didn't know."

Hannah bit her tongue to stop herself from asking Sadie to call her Ms. Bradley from now on. She said, "I know, it's not that. Look. I need to talk to you about something. Oh! But first. I brought you some presents."

She handed Sadie the hat and necklace she'd bought her, each one wrapped in tissue paper. "Presents!"

"Presents, but—"

"Ohmygosh. I've always wanted a necklace like this. I've never had my own necklace, did you know that?"

"No, I—"

"Thank you so much!" She closed the distance between them with a couple of quick steps, and hugged Hannah, hard, around the neck. "You're the best! I can't wait to wear this. Can I wear it now?"

Before Hannah could answer, Sadie was handing her the necklace, turning around, leaning back just slightly so Hannah could fasten it. For some reason, even with the impending dissolution of their relationship weighing heavy on her mind, this excitement brought Hannah so much joy she couldn't even speak.

And then the rest of the students were coming in.

She fastened the necklace, swallowed to loosen her throat, patted Sadie's shoulders, and said, "You're welcome. I'm so glad you like it."

The announcement could wait until after school. There was no sense forcing Sadie—or herself—to endure an entire day feeling sad about it. Throughout the day, Hannah found herself watching Sadie, remembering some of the best times they'd spent together: Halloween, the quiet before-school mornings, the chatty afternoons.

Sadie really had grown during the few months she had been in Hannah's class. She smiled more, carried herself with more confidence, and actually started conversations with the other kids. She turned in her homework and participated in discussions and group assignments. Until recently. She'd skipped a few assignments, missed more than her typical number of math problems and spelling words, but they were well into the second quarter and things were getting more difficult.

Would it affect Sadie if Hannah stopped having her over, hanging out with her like they were friends?

It hurt to think of what might happen, especially if it meant Sadie would go back to the withdrawn, skinny, sickly-looking kid she had been when she first walked through the classroom doors. This image made Hannah feel sick, herself. But she couldn't subject another little girl to the pain she was experiencing now. She reminded herself of that over and over, until the final bell rang.

When it did, she went and sat at her desk, hoping Sadie would simply go home and she could avoid the conversation until tomorrow. It didn't work out that way. Sadie approached her, hands clasped in front of her, shoulders hunched, as if she knew what Hannah was going to say. Hannah looked down at a stack of math tests, uncapped her red marker, started grading.

"Hannah?" Sadie said. Her voice was a little shaky, higher-pitched than normal.

"Yeah?" Hannah looked up as if she hadn't just taken in every single detail of Sadie's nervous posture, her worried expression.

"I need to talk to you."

"I need to talk to you, too," Hannah said.

"Can I go first?"

"Oh. Um, sure." Hannah cleared her throat, capped the pen, set it down. "Of course. Let's sit at the back table."

Once they sat down, Sadie started drumming her fingers on the tabletop. Her hair was growing back, and it stuck up in a few places.

"What did you want to talk to me about?"

Sadie inhaled and exhaled, her thin chest rising and falling in an exaggerated movement. She looked at the ceiling. And then she blurted out, "I'm moving. I won't be going to this school any more. This is my last week."

Even though Hannah had already planned to break away from her relationship with Sadie, even though she spent half the day trying to think of a way to tell her so, even though she should have been relieved that the separation was coming without any assistance from her, Hannah was floored. All the air had been sucked out of the room and she couldn't breathe.

"Hannah?"

"Where are you moving to?"

"I don't know. My aunt and uncle are getting evicted, and the people from child services are putting me in a group home. Long story, but basically, my aunt and uncle haven't paid rent for like, a few months. The landlord—at least, they *think* it was the landlord, because he's never liked them, anyway—reported them to child services, and child services decided I can't live with them anymore. There aren't many foster families here, obviously, I mean, it's Walker, population five. Or whatever." She shrugged like it was no big deal, but Hannah could see the strain around her eyes. Poor thing probably hadn't slept all weekend. "So, Rita and Mike are going to be homeless. And the people from child services, they're moving me to Cheyenne. Said they have a group home lined up already."

"How long have you known about this?"

Sadie's eyes darted to the right, then down at her hands, which were fidgeting on the table, then back at Hannah. "I mean, I knew when we got the first notice that this could happen. It's been a month or so."

"Why didn't you tell me?"

No, Sadie hadn't told her, but this explained so many of the strange things Hannah had noticed recently, like the bad grades she'd been getting on assignments.

"What could you do?"

"I don't know, Sadie!" Hannah's voice was rising. "I could have helped you. But now it's too late."

A quiet, mean voice in the back of her mind told Hannah that this was exactly what she'd decided she wanted. She should be pleased.

"Anyway," Sadie said. She backed away. "Just wanted to let you know."

She started to walk toward the door, and Hannah called her name before running up to her and giving her a hug. "I am so sorry," she said. "So, so sorry."

She let Sadie leave without ever telling her they could no longer be friends. What would be the point? Then she packed up her things, left the ungraded math tests on the desk, and went home.

Tanner wasn't there, and Hannah felt a mixture of relief and disappointment. She told herself it was mostly relief.

At dinner, she told Mama Sadie's news.

"Well, that's just awful, honey. What are you going to do?"

"There's nothing I *can* do," Hannah said.

"Isn't there?" Mama said.

"It's already done," Hannah said.

"Is it?" Mama said.

Something very strange was going on, here, Hannah thought. Very strange, indeed.

"Let's talk about something else."

Dinner was very quiet, and Hannah went to bed uneasy and unhappy, thinking about how she was failing Sadie and Tanner. She found small comfort in the fact that she was saving herself ... even if it didn't quite feel that way.

CHAPTER NINETEEN

A SORE, swollen throat and a killer, pounding headache woke Hannah up Tuesday morning, forcing her to call in sick. She was certain Sadie would blame herself for Hannah's absence, but she didn't have the energy to worry much about that.

After practically crawling into the kitchen to get some ibuprofen, she called into the school district's substitute teacher line, and went back to bed, pulled the covers up to her chin, and closed her eyes. But despite feeling absolutely the worst she'd felt since she had strep throat in the fifth grade (she remembered the pain with such clarity it made her eyes water, even thirty years later!), she couldn't fall asleep. She heard Tanner's crews show up—the rumbling of truck engines, the shouted greetings, the rev of power tools and the banging of hammers. She heard the coffee pot brewing.

There was a quiet knock on her bedroom door, and she croaked in response. Mama opened it.

"You sick, honey? Or did you oversleep?"

"Sick," Hannah managed. "Already called in."

"I'm sorry," Mama said. "Can I get you anything? Tea? Ibuprofen? Food?"

"No, thank you, Mama," Hannah said, a rush of gratitude over-whelming her. "I already took ibuprofen. And there's no way I could eat. I think I'll just go back to sleep."

Mama came into the room, laid the back of her hand against Hannah's forehead. "You're burning up."

"I know," Hannah groaned. "I feel awful. I just need to sleep."

"Okay, well, you let me know," Mama said. "Just ring the bell."

"Ha," Hannah said.

After the door closed, she lay in bed listening to the sounds. More hammering, the beeping of a tractor or a truck backing up. The houses must be getting close to done, she thought, because the men were bringing in big loads of landscaping rock. The sound of it sliding out of the truck bed was almost deafening in her weakened state. She heard a bird call, but couldn't quite place which type of bird it was. Then, she heard the doorbell ring.

She didn't have to spend every day at home to know this was unusual. Most of the time if someone came by, they came right in, no knocking required. She and Mama almost always left the door unlocked and their friends and neighbors followed their strict, "Come on in," policy.

Mama's feet made quiet thumping sounds on the floor as she went to answer the door.

"Hello there," she said to whoever was on the other side.

"Good morning, ma'am," said a man's voice. "Delivery for Hannah Bradley. This the right place?"

"Sure is," Mama said. "She must have a secret admirer."

"She must," the man said. "Whoever it is sent this letter all the way from California, overnight. Must have cost a fortune. Here you go, ma'am. You have a nice day, now."

"You, too," Mama said.

Again, her footsteps came closer to Hannah's door, and she knocked quietly. Again, Hannah croaked a reply, and the door opened. Mama came in, held out the envelope. Hannah took it and let her arm drop onto the bed.

"Well, aren't you going to look at it?" Mama wanted to know.

"Ugh," Hannah said. "I couldn't possibly open it. My eyes hurt. My head hurts. Everything hurts."

"It's from your father."

Hannah said, "Hmm," as if her heart wasn't suddenly beating out a crazy rock 'n' roll rhythm. She froze as if every nerve in her body wasn't standing at alert, in fight-or-flight, deciding whether to open the envelope or toss it in some fire somewhere because she was so scared to read it.

"Would you?" she said.

Sitting down on the edge of the bed, Mama reached across and took the envelope. She removed her glasses from where they were hanging on the collar of her shirt, unfolded the arms, and put them on. Head spinning, Hannah sat up.

"It's a letter," Mama said.

"Figured as much."

"Don't use that tone with me, young lady."

"Are you gonna read it?"

"It's your mail," Mama said.

"Read it."

Mama pressed her lips together, then took a deep breath through her nose, tore open the envelope (Hannah noticed her hands were shaking), and started reading.

"Dearest Hannah,

I've just woken from a nice sleep after having met you for the first time. You truly are lovely, and I regret only that I didn't get to meet you, or know you, sooner. I can sense the end is near for me now. Nearer than it has been. I have hours, maybe. And I wanted to dedicate at least a portion of that time to you, to writing this letter.

Just a bit ago, I gave you some unsolicited advice. If you follow my request and spend some time with the people who knew me, then you'll find giving unsolicited advice is one of my specialties. You'll also find that I'm usually dead-on. I guess I shouldn't use that phrase.

Because I knew your mother so well (at least, I did a lifetime ago when we first met), and because I know myself—aren't the dying always forced into introspection?—I sense that you might find it difficult to take my advice. You might feel angry that I died practically the moment we met each other. You might feel sad that you missed out on having a dad. You might feel any number of things that prevent you from doing the one thing I recommend, which is starting a family. I can practically hear your wheels spinning now, my dear girl, just as well as I could see the pain on your expression when you were here: what if a family isn't all we expect it to be?

You feel betrayed by your mother."

(Here, Mama's voice thickened, but she kept reading.)

"You feel betrayed by me. After all, I never came to find your mother, nor

you. And you probably feel betrayed by life. I know, because I've been there. Your mother and I, we were both hurt. And I regret the way we acted, because it means we both missed out on the family we so wanted. But that doesn't mean you have to miss out, too. Isn't there a saying about paying for the sins of our parents? You don't have to pay for our mistakes. You don't have to let our wrongdoings become the family legacy. Start a family, Hannah. Your mother won't be around for long. To hear you say it, your sisters are busy with their own husbands. I'm not saying you have to run out and get married. I'm a modern man, Hannah. But I am saying that I wish you would open your heart. To love. I love you, and again, I'm sorry. Know that from wherever I end up, I'll be sending you as much love as a person (or, shall we say, a spirit) can send.

—Philip (or, if you prefer, Dad)."

By the time Mama read the last sentence and the sign-off, Hannah was in a full-on cry. Bawling. Mama, her own cheeks wet with tears, set the paper down and scooted up to the head of the bed to sit next to Hannah.

"I'm sorry, honey," she whispered.

Just as Hannah had done hundreds of times, she put her head on her mom's shoulder and cried some more. Mama rubbed her knee, made comforting *shhh* sounds. When Hannah had cried herself dry, she told Mama she was exhausted and wanted to go back to sleep. Mama simply nodded before giving Hannah the letter and leaving the room.

Alone again, Hannah didn't sleep. Although her eyes burned, her throat burned, and her head felt like it might explode, she couldn't give in to the bliss of slumber. Instead, infused with a new energy, she retrieved her phone from the nightstand and started making calls.

———

BY LUNCHTIME, thanks to the endeavor she'd taken on, Hannah was feeling much better. Her body was still screaming with whichever illness had taken residence, but she made her way to the kitchen to find some food. Coffee couldn't hurt, either, she thought. She still had so much to do, and she'd need fuel.

"Good morn—afternoon."

Tanner's voice startled her, and she crossed her arms over her night-gown-clad chest.

"Hi, there," she said.

"You look terrible," he said.

He was at the counter, eating a deli sandwich, making notes on a yellow legal pad. He put his pencil down when she came into the kitchen and started pouring coffee.

"Well, I wish I could say the same about you," she said. He, of course, looked fantastic. Before he could speak, she said, "Look. I owe you an apology. For yesterday."

"You don't," Tanner said. "I understand. I guess when I developed feelings for you, I thought those feelings were mutual. But maybe they weren't. And that's okay."

"They were," Hannah said. "They *are*. And that is terrifying to me. When I finally met my dad, and then lost him right away, I realized that maybe I'm not cut out for relationships. Losing him so quickly after finding him—it crushed me, Tanner. And it made me realize that I could lose you just as quickly. I don't think I could handle it."

He nodded. "I understand."

"So. I am really sorry. I'm sorry for giving you the cold shoulder, for thinking I couldn't make this thing between us work. I'm sorry for letting you take me all the way to California, and then telling you it was over. And you're probably thinking I'm crazy, and you're better off without a crazy person, anyway."

"Well, the thought crossed my mind." He set his sandwich on the counter. The paper wrapper crinkled. He picked up his bottle of soda and took a sip. "But to tell you the truth, I'm mostly thinking I'm disap-pointed. I'd never pressure you into being with me. But I thought—and I still think—we're a good match, Hannah. We've had so much fun together. Why not see where it takes us?"

This time, it was Tanner who held up a hand when Hannah started to respond. "Again, though, I'm not going to pressure you to be with me. So, I'll learn to be content with a—what did you call it? 'A strictly professional relationship.'"

"Actually, I have a proposal for you," Hannah said. "I wanted to run it by you. But I think I'd better get dressed first. It's serious business, not to be discussed in nightgowns."

"You're the only one wearing a nightgown."

"True."

"Which is fine with me."

She returned his smile. "Be right back."

Then, she carried her coffee into the bedroom, all the while thinking maybe she *was* crazy. Could this work? Would Tanner agree to it? What if he didn't? Well, she'd be okay. She didn't *need* him in order to carry out her plan. Would it be ideal if he agreed? Yes. But was it necessary? No.

Still, her body buzzed with nerves as she put on a bra and jeans and a t-shirt. She decided she should probably brush her teeth, too, and splash some water on her face.

"Wow, much better," he said when she came back out. "You clean up nice. What'd you want to talk about?"

"Let's sit."

"Do I need my legal pad?"

"You can bring it just in case. This idea is a little unconventional. You might want to take notes."

They sat across from each other. One eyebrow raised, Tanner turned to a fresh page in his legal pad. Hannah emitted a nervous laugh and waved her hand at it even as her heart beat wildly in her chest.

"You don't really need that," she said. "I was kidding. Although, this is serious business."

A giddiness was building. Tanner turned his pad over and slid it off to the side. Then, elbows on the table, he folded his hands and looked at her, waiting.

Hannah cleared her throat. "I'll go first. Obviously."

"Obviously."

A pause.

"Tanner, do you remember dancing with me at Margaret's wedding?"

"How could I forget?"

"It *was* pretty unforgettable, wasn't it?"

"It was," he said. "But I'm thinking that's not the serious business you're referring to."

"No," Hannah said, letting the air hang empty between them for another beat. "Do you remember what you said to me when we were dancing?"

"I said lots of things, but I'm thinking you're referring to what I said about us getting married."

She nodded, kept her eyes on his because it felt like maintaining eye contact was the only way to gauge his true reaction.

"Look," he said, his gaze breaking the connection and landing on his hands. "That was out of line. I've done some thinking, and I may have moved too fast. The feelings were there, *are* there, for me. But putting them out into the open like that, I think I spooked you. And I'm sorry for that. I understand if you need some time, some space—"

"Wait. Tanner." Hannah could hardly speak, as overcome with emotion as she felt right then. He looked back up at her, but the rest of his body remained motionless.

"The feelings are there for me, too," Hannah said. "When you said you planned to marry me, I was surprised. Not because the chemistry's not there."

She cleared her throat again, and went on. "But because I could hardly believe you'd *want* to marry me. Let's face it. I'm no spring chicken. And you're, well, *you*. You can't blame me for being caught off guard."

He opened his mouth, probably to argue, but she held up a finger to stop him.

"And then, over the past couple of weeks, you've shown me that not only are you off-the-charts good-looking, but you're also thoughtful and affectionate and patient and, well, great in bed."

He nodded and shrugged, then grinned. "So, this is a meeting wherein you demand more sex?"

"Although that is very serious business, and I'm not opposed to it, no. I have a proposal for you."

"Is it the kind of proposal I'm thinking it is?"

"It might be a little more complicated than what you're thinking," Hannah said.

Although the humor of the past couple of minutes had lessened the tension, Hannah felt her nerves taking over again, in the shaking of her hands and the blurring at the edges of her vision. This was it.

She took the plunge. She told him about all the research she'd done that day, all the phone calls she'd made and balls she'd set in motion to apply for temporary guardianship of Sadie—with plans of adopting her.

"It's just that I've fallen in love with her, Tanner. I can't imagine not having her in my life. I need to do everything I can to make sure she's happy and healthy and taken care of."

"This sounds great," he said. "It's a great idea, Hannah. She'll be so happy."

Another pause, during which Hannah imagined Tanner was

wondering what this all had to do with him, and during which she, Hannah, gathered her courage to say this last part.

"The thing is, I can do it alone. Because I'm not really alone. I have Mama and my sisters. But I don't want to. The thing is, Tanner, I've fallen in love with you, too. I can't imagine not having you in my life. I need to do everything I can to make sure you're happy. With me. And all that being said, will you marry me?"

CHAPTER TWENTY

HE'D AGREED. Tanner told Hannah he'd fallen for Sadie, too, and that he'd love nothing more than to make their family official.

Hannah's heart was soaring as she and Tanner walked through the gates of Walker Elementary School the next morning. As always, Sadie was there, waiting. When she saw Tanner, she looked puzzled for a second, and then launched herself to her feet and into his arms.

"What are *you* doing here?"

"What are *you* doing here?" he said.

"I go to school here," she said. "For one more day, anyway."

"About that," Tanner said. "There's something Hannah and I wanted to talk to you about."

They went into the classroom and before they even sat down, Sadie said, "Am I in trouble?"

"Why would you be in trouble?" Tanner said.

"I don't know," Sadie said. "Because I haven't been doing my homework? And I've been purposely misspelling words on my spelling tests?"

"Why on earth would you do that?" Hannah said. She and Tanner exchanged a look, the kind of look she figured they'd be exchanging frequently from now on.

Sadie shrugged. Her hair was starting to grow, and it stood out from her head like the tufts on a dandelion. She looked more forlorn than insolent.

"I thought that maybe if I was doing badly in school, none of the group homes in Cheyenne would take me, and I'd have to stay here."

Hannah's heart broke a little at the warped logic.

"That's what we wanted to talk to you about," Tanner said.

"About doing badly on my schoolwork?"

"No," Hannah said. "Not about that. Let's sit."

They did. Sadie folded her hands and looked from one of them to the other expectantly.

"How would you like to stay here?" Hannah said.

"At Walker Elementary?"

"Yeah," Hannah said.

"And live in Walker?" Sadie said.

"Yeah," Tanner said. "And live in Walker."

"I'd like it, but …"

"But what?" Hannah said.

Sadie leaned back in her seat, crossed her arms. "But I thought there weren't enough foster families here. Did they find a family for me?"

Tanner and Hannah looked at each other again. "You could say that," Tanner said.

"What if we…made our own family?" Hannah said.

"'We,' like who?" Sadie said.

"The three of us," Tanner said. He jerked a thumb at Hannah and himself, then pointed at Sadie.

"The three of us? Like you, you, and me?" She pointed at each of them, and then at herself, like Tanner had just done.

Hannah could see the hope springing to life.

"And maybe a dog," Tanner said. "Don't most families have a dog?"

"Wait," Sadie said. "Let me get this straight. Because it sounds too good to be true, and they always say that if it sounds too good to be true, it probably is. Are you asking me if I want to stay here in Walker, and live with the two of you? *And* I can get a dog?"

"If that's what you want," Hannah said. "Yes. That's what we're asking you."

"But what about child services? What about the group home they found for me? You can't just—*keep* me. And where will we live? I mean, you have to take care of Mama Katherine, and you have the house…"

"I've talked with child services," Hannah said.

"You *called* them?"

"I did. I explained the urgency of the situation, and they came out to the house yesterday. They're granting me temporary custody, and then they're going to do a thorough home study, to certify me for adoption."

"Adoption? You want to *adopt* me?"

Now Sadie was crying, looking every bit the little girl she was.

"We both do," Tanner said. "We want to start a family. But only if it's what you want, too."

"Where will we live?"

"At my house," Hannah said. "At least for now."

"But I'm going to keep my house, too," Tanner said. "But mostly as an investment, to help pay for your college."

"My *college*?! I never thought, in a million years, that I could go to college. I mean, I wanted to. But when you grow up like I have, at some point you realize you don't get to do the things you want to do."

"Well," Tanner said. "I'm sure you would have figured out a way. But now we'll help you. But they won't let you in if you keep writing down wrong answers and misspelled words on your schoolwork."

"I'll stop," Sadie said. "I promise."

"So," Tanner said. "You're good with our plan?"

"Good?" Sadie said. "I'm great. Fantastic. I can't believe it's real."

"It's real," Hannah said, and Tanner said, "In fact, I'm a little worried about living under the same roof with three women."

"Can we hug now?" Sadie said.

The three of them stood up and, Sadie in the middle, they hugged. And Hannah felt a tear slip out of her eye and run down her cheek.

"I love you guys," Sadie said.

"We love you, too," Tanner said.

"I'm pretty sure I'm the luckiest girl in the world," Sadie said, and Hannah said, "I think *I* am."

EPILOGUE

HANNAH HAD WORRIED a little that Margaret and Sarah might balk at her decision to adopt Sadie, to make her placement in the family official. Pre-teens and teenagers were hard enough to parent as it was, and Sadie had a troubled early childhood. But they were almost as excited as Hannah was when she made the announcement that evening.

In fact, Sarah cried ("I'm just so happy to be an aunt!"), and Margaret kept swiping at her cheeks with her fingertips but denying she was overcome with emotion. Hannah knew she was, though, because her voice was thick when she said, "I propose a celebratory dinner, tomorrow. The houses are done, we'll all be living under the same slice of sky again, and more importantly, we're welcoming two new family members."

"Make it three," Hannah said, "because we're getting a dog."

Saturday afternoon, Hannah, Tanner, and Sadie went to the shelter. They walked down the long row of adoptable dogs, the barks and yips drowning out the sound their feet must be making on the concrete floor.

"I wish we could take them all," Sadie said, echoing Hannah's thoughts, and Tanner said, "Oh, no you don't. Let's start with one."

There were several fluffy puppies and excited, jumping dogs Hannah stopped to pet through the chainlink of their kennels, some with wide grins, some with the biggest, most chocolatey eyes, and some with fur so soft she didn't want to leave their sides.

But when Sadie finally knelt down in front of a kennel, completely absorbed in the company of its occupant, who laid down to be pet, then rolled over with a groan when she scratched his neck, Hannah had to refrain from gasping.

Tanner whispered in her ear, "That very well might be the ugliest dog I've ever seen."

And it was. Brindle fur, a serious underbite and eyes that were two different colors and maybe even two different sizes, gave this dog, with his short legs and big body, a very distinct look.

"It is," Hannah said.

The dog, still on his back, groaned again, his tongue hanging out and one leg making a scratching motion.

"This one," Sadie said. "I want to take this one home."

Hannah and Tanner looked at each other and shrugged. The shelter employee opened the kennel and the dog could barely contain his excitement as she put a leash on him. She passed the leash handle to Sadie, whose smile took up her entire face.

As stocky as the dog was, and as much crazy energy as was radiating off of him, Hannah was afraid he'd pull Sadie right down the hallway and out the door, never to be seen again. But he walked on the leash like a gentleman, his tail wagging at warp speed, his muzzle bumping up against Sadie's hand every couple of seconds as if he were checking to make sure what was happening was really real.

Outside, in the meet-and-play area, Sadie took off the leash and the dog followed her everywhere. She threw toys for him, and he'd watch them arc through the air but remain standing at her side. When she gave up and went to sit down on one of the patio chairs, he went, too, and he sat down and leaned against her leg, looking up at her with his droopy eyes while she scratched him behind an ear.

"What'll we call him?" Hannah wanted to know.

"How about Murphy?" Sadie said.

They took him home to meet the rest of the family. He snagged a raw steak off the kitchen counter and barreled under the dining room table, pulling the tablecloth right off and wearing it like a cape until Donny caught up with him and removed it. Hannah was mortified—he'd seemed so well-mannered at the shelter—but Mama laughed it off.

"We've just got to teach him how to be part of a family, that's all," she said.

When dinner was ready, and they all sat at the table, Hannah was afraid Murphy would sneak food off their plates. But he didn't. He flopped down next to Sadie's chair, his chin resting on her foot, and went to sleep. Sadie beamed nonstop throughout the meal.

Looking from family member to family member—Mama, Sarah and Donny, Margaret and Ethan, Tanner and Sadie, and, of course, Murphy—Hannah felt a deep sense of contentment.

This, she thought, is perfect.

———

THE END

ABOUT THE AUTHOR

Hilary Dartt loves great adventures, whether she's writing, reading, or living them. The author of nine women's fiction novels, Hilary lives in Arizona's high desert with her husband, their three children, her Weimaraner and running partner, Leia, a failed barn cat, and a flock of chickens. She loves camping, exploring in the Jeep, and dance parties with her kids. Learn more at www.hilarydartt.com